BIRD OF PREY

Recent Titles by Vivien Armstrong from Severn House

BEYOND THE PALE
CLOSE CALL
DEAD IN THE WATER
FLY IN AMBER
FOOL'S GOLD
NO BIRDS SINGING
REWIND
SMILE NOW, DIE LATER
THE WRONG ROAD

BIRD OF PREY

Vivien Armstrong

This first world edition published in Great Britain 2003 by
SEVERN HOUSE PUBLISHERS LTD of
9–15 High Street, Sutton, Surrey SM1 1DF.
This first world edition published in the USA 2004 by
SEVERN HOUSE PUBLISHERS INC of
595 Madison Avenue, New York, N.Y. 10022.

British Library Cataloguing in Publication Data

Armstrong,   Vivien
     Bird of Prey
     1.   Women lawyers - Fiction
     2.   Serial murder investigation - Fiction
     3.   Detective and mystery stories
     I.   Title
     823.9'14 [F]

     ISBN 0-7278-6046-1

Typeset by Hewer Text Ltd.,
Edinburgh, Scotland.
Printed and bound in Great Britain by
MPG Books Ltd., Bodmin, Cornwall.

One

The heavy downpour came as a surprise. The summer was really over at last, the smell of rotting leaves dank in the dim backstreet behind the cinema. Fay Browne stood aside waiting for Frank Foster to lock up, thinking fondly of the rooms they used to have in the town hall before the empty shop became available. She wondered if the time had come to bow out gracefully, let Cheryl and her feminist cronies run the Law Centre their own way...

'You mustn't let her get to you,' he said, as if he had read her thoughts. He fussed with the double locks, obsessively checking as usual.

'Times change, Frank. I'm too feeble for this left-wing tirade each month.' She drew up her collar and, clutching the bottle of whisky in its flimsy tissue paper, wished she had remembered to bring an umbrella. He wheeled his bike along the street and walked beside her, a thoughtful man, buttoned up in a donkey jacket, his glasses glinting with drops of rain.

'At least your clients are appreciative,' he said, indicating the bottle, trying to strike a cheerful note. She smiled, a wry grin like the old days, and struggled to tie her headscarf against the whirling gusts playing incessantly around the narrow streets which backed Renham's new shopping precinct.

'Mollie MacLintock's wee giftie. I finally persuaded her landlord to see sense. Makes up for all the other lost causes.'

'You said it! Cheryl had to be rescued from an irate husband tonight. Hotfoot from the women's aid place, he was. Didn't you hear all the rumpus?'

'Could hardly miss it. I was cowering under my desk waving my white flag.' She glanced at her watch. 'I'll have to hurry,

1

Frank. I want to catch the ten-five. See you next Wednesday. We'll talk then.'

They parted at the corner and, bent against the wind, holding her briefcase and bottle to her chest, she stepped out towards the station. Fay hated these monthly committee meetings: the usual two-hour advice session followed by a takeaway curry eaten round the big table and a full turnout of all the volunteers who, since Cheryl Baker's crowd had muscled in, added political infighting to the case load.

Her steps echoed along the wet pavement. When a man sprang out in front of her she recoiled, tensing her hold on her parcels in instinctive alarm. He grunted unintelligibly, the words hoarse as if speaking was an effort.

Edging sideways, she tried to see his face which was deeply shadowed by the hood of his anorak. The rain slanted viciously in a sudden flurry, forcing them both to veer into the wall, almost colliding, his laboured breath hot in her face. The man held out a hand in mute appeal but his stance was belligerent, the beak-like nose and angled planes of his cheeks reminiscent of a bird of prey. He started to mutter incomprehensible demands in a rattle of seemingly pent-up emotion. Without pausing to listen, she raised her hand in a curt dismissive gesture, neatly sidestepped him and broke into a run. Garbled abuse rang out behind her in the empty street. She ran faster. It was only a hundred yards to the main road.

Fay reached the brightly lit railway station in a state of breathless agitation and made straight for the buffet. The encounter had unnerved her, Renham's derelicts and homeless drunks a new feature of the formerly staid country town. It was the same everywhere. The government's fault, Cheryl propounded, and Fay had to agree with her for once.

Trembling from fear or cold – she couldn't decide which – she pushed her way to the counter through a crowd of rowdy youths bent on finishing a night out, and ordered a scotch. Chilled to the bone, her feet sopping in flimsy leather pumps, and with the sour recollection of the disputes of the committee meeting now augmented by a feeling of vulnerability, a flutter-

2

ing panic gripped her as if the burning eyes of the down-and-out had followed her into the bar.

The racket in the station buffet was unendurable. Tossing down her drink, Fay grabbed her briefcase and stepped outside. The damp paper wrapping the bottle slithered under her fingers as she made her way along the platform. Two others, patiently waiting, stood beyond the station canopy in the wet. She joined them, indifferent now to the rain slashing down, only wanting a moment of quiet before joining the scramble for seats. The train was due in a few minutes.

Fay closed in behind the others, all intent on claiming a place in the front carriage. It was always packed on a Wednesday night. One person stood at the very edge of the platform, cocooned in a plastic mac, the other – a girl with shopping bags at her feet – waited a few yards away, sheltering under a flowery umbrella. A buzzer sounded. Signals clanked. The indicator confirmed the train's imminent arrival.

The buffet room crowd erupted on to the platform, pushing in behind the three women just as the lights of the train appeared round the bend. An elbow caught Fay off balance and she lurched forward behind the figure in the plastic mac as the roar of the engine exploded into the station. The bottle slid inside its paper and in a desperate effort to save it Fay buckled at the knees. In that split second as the train burst into the station she stumbled, the bottle shattered and the woman in the plastic mac tumbled on to the rails.

Fay reached out to her as the engine bore down and for a moment she felt the slithering plastic under her fingers. The woman's face swung towards her, only inches away, the eyes black with fear as she scrambled to regain her footing. Bodies seemed to press all around, screams split the air, adding to the mad cacophony of groaning brakes and a porter's frantic cry as the train came grinding to a halt. Too late.

Fay stood transfixed, her feet in a pile of broken glass, the peaty smell of whisky making her retch. Death did not come on silent wings. Death bore down like the engines of hell: the noise, the shrieks, the slamming of doors as bewildered travellers alighted, all unknowing, into the pandemonium.

The stationmaster must have seen it all before. Were suicides on the line so rare, after all? Fay found herself rooted to the edge of the platform, isolated. The youths, shocked into silence, had drawn back, standing in an awed group under the station canopy. The alighting passengers were quickly siphoned off through a side exit and those remaining seated gazed through the windows with shock and burgeoning interest. The rain continued to fall. The girl with the shopping had dropped her umbrella and stood bareheaded, sobbing like a child, her hair streaming with water, her groceries spilling on to the platform.

The stationmaster pushed all the Renham ticketholders into the waiting room while his staff cleared the station. He sent for tea and, while they waited in the cheerless valhalla, he quietly requested their names and addresses. By the time the police arrived the dreadful shunting of the train had begun. The girl started weeping afresh and Fay, pale as a ghost, roused herself sufficiently to place a hand on her arm.

She felt numb with the horror of it all. It had happened so swiftly. One moment the three women had been standing on the empty platform and the next it had been full of pushing, noisy people. The white disc of the victim's face rose again in her mind's eye, the stark terror in the eyes, the shiny wetness of the plastic mac slippery as seal's skin. Fay shivered. She knew the unknown woman's anguished scream would haunt her for ever.

The police inspector had his hands full with the mayhem on the platform. He sent his sergeant to speak to the stationmaster and they whispered in the corner of the waiting room, eyeing the dozen or so trapped witnesses with the wary consideration of zookeepers.

'We have ordered transport for all of you.' The stationmaster turned to the two women. 'Would you ladies like to telephone home, get someone here to fetch you?'

The girl nodded, blowing her nose as he escorted her to the door. Fay followed and the three crammed into the private office while they made their calls. Fay spoke to her babysitter, her words firm, making no mention of the disaster. Robert would be home tomorrow. She clung to this like the promise of sunrise.

The stationmaster, a plump, efficient young man, was kindness itself, helping the girl to restack her shopping, ordering fresh tea while they waited. Fay felt his response to her numb dignity was guarded, his slightly formal stand-off puzzling. She shrugged, discarding the thought as the door burst open and a harrassed porter admitted the inspector.

Fay guessed DCI Roger Hayes to be thirty-something. Thin almost to emaciation, his complexion sallow, a stern fortitude exaggerated the aquiline features. A man all too familiar with the grim reality of breaking bad news. She found herself staring, searching for a half-remembered association with this ascetic-looking copper. It must have been some case at the Law Centre. She pushed this aside to worry at later, forcing herself to attend to his instructions.

'. . . and so I suggest you go straight home now, Mrs Browne,' he was saying. 'It has been a horrifying experience for you. I understand you tried to heave back the suicide as she jumped.'

'She didn't jump.'

Fay wished she hadn't said that. The shock of the appalling event had stripped away an innate caution. She felt exposed. Raw.

Hayes seemed unsurprised. Interested as he listened to her version, but unsurprised. Perhaps it was a standard response of witnesses to suicide. Unbelieving. Unbelievable. That a woman waiting for a train like millions of others should decide to throw her life away, to be mangled in the grinding machinery of wheels and rails and steel cogs.

He took her arm and led her out through a storage area of some sort and into the parcels yard. A taxi stood with its engine running and Inspector Hayes bundled her inside.

'There's a lot to do here,' he said, peering at her through the window. 'I have your address, Mrs Browne. I'll call in the morning. I shall need a statement.'

The cab drew away, circling the goods yard and speeding into the placid pool of Renham after dark. Fay leaned back and drew a deep breath, finding her knees trembling as she braced herself for the journey home. There was an odd smell in the taxi. Fumes. She breathed the familiar stench and the moment of death flooded back. She lifted the hem of her coat, feeling the damp. Whisky. The broken bottle must have splashed up as it smashed on to the platform. Or, more likely, the spirit had soaked into the lining as she had knelt to grasp the woman's wet plastic mac.

Could she have dragged her up? Had she let go too easily?

Two

Next morning Fay Browne strolled in her garden. It calmed her nerves. Living in the country agreed with her, though Stamford itself had been Robert's choice. She would have preferred a fresh start, somewhere not already hung about with memories. 'My roots' as her husband expansively put it. His partner stayed in London while Robert played local squire, assuming the role with panache in the small place where he had grown up.

Scuffing through the wet grass, she savoured the moment unaware that later she would recall this as set apart, framed like an arcadian interlude or, less romantically, see herself trapped like a fly in amber. But the morning had already lost its early brightness, the sunshine, more glittering than warm, had settled for a spurious glow. The frost-blackened stalks of the dahlias leaned drunkenly together like the exhausted battalions of a retreating army.

She opened the ramshackle doors of an outhouse and an undersized grey rabbit loped from the dim interior. Lifting it on to the path, Fay swept dirty hay into one corner and emptied the water bowl. The outhouse served as a garage and the rabbit lived under the wheels of a saffron-coloured Metro, a timid domesticated creature, a poor relation to its wild family pro-liferating beyond the walled garden. It hopped back in again, nostrils twitching.

'Ottie!'

She put it inside the fruit cage where it scuttled about almost invisible in the decaying vegetation, watching with darting eyes as she pushed the rubbish into an old carrier bag before strolling back to the house. Blood-red leaves slipped from the maples as if the trees were dying from within. A sly breeze raised the soft hairs on her forearm and she shivered, the appalling accident on the railway line flooding back.

Tall and with narrow hands and feet, Fay Browne might, from a distance, have seemed a gawky adolescent instead of a woman well into her forties. Luke had been born only just in time, a gift from the gods, erasing her guilt. The illusion of suspended youth was compounded by red hair hanging straight and unpinned from a high ragged parting, but the essence of it was nothing to do with her appearance. There was an awkward charm, shyness disguised. Like someone who harboured secrets.

She wandered towards the house, brushing the bushes as she passed, snapping an overhanging spray of maple with a sudden, violent flick of the wrist. The loud crack hung in the air like a gunshot. Shredding the broken twig, she twirled the leaves against the light. A sliver of autumn already disintegrating.

The telephone rang in the house. Her eyes clouded. It was probably the police wanting to take her statement.

By the time she got inside Luke had answered it and was sitting on the stairs in the hall, yards of flex trailing. Glancing up, he grinned then continued in a whisper. Nine-year-olds were natural conspirators. Why had the CIA never tapped this potential?

Fay smiled, turning back to the kitchen to clear the plates into the dishwasher, noting with surprise 'RB Away' scrawled across ten days on the wall calendar. Starting tomorrow.

The smile faded.

The prospect of facing the boy's housemaster was no joke. Robert would have carried it off without a thought, impervious to the unspoken criticism of yet another late start of term for Luke Browne, Mr Tyrell's contempt for frail little boys was evident and asthma, especially in only children of 'mature' mothers, came under the heading of 'fussing'. She toyed with the possibility of asking Robert to delay his trip and drive Luke back to school himself as he had promised but immediately discarded the idea.

A milk bottle was filled with water for the maple twig. She

frowned, twisting it in a shaft of dusty sunlight, the leaves already dropping, dreading the misery of witnessing Luke's efforts to be a brave soldier.

He stood in the doorway peeling a banana. Still in his pyjamas, the magenta stripes accentuated the fair skin with its smattering of freckles, the inevitable inheritance of a redhead. She said, 'I thought you'd had breakfast. Isn't it about time you got dressed?'

'That was Buzz. He's been off with mumps so I won't be the only one starting late in my set.'

'Great! He can go back with you if you like.'

'I said Dad's promised to drive me back in the new Mercedes so he's going to ask his Mum. He'll ring back. Dad won't mind. He likes showing off to old Tyrell.'

Fay wondered if she should check this or just ignore it. Small boys were very astute. But before she could frame the right phrases Luke continued.

'I think Buzz is probably angling for a lift anyhow. His sister's lumpy now.' He nibbled the banana.

'Actually, I'll have to drive you back to school myself so—'

'Oh, no! Not in that old Metro!' he wailed.

She held up a warning finger. 'If Christopher wants a lift I'll pick him up about eleven on Monday. It's not much of a detour. When he rings back I'll speak to his mother.'

Fay watched him toss the banana skin across the kitchen to flop accurately in the bucket of scraps kept for the compost. He grinned, clasping his hands over his head like the successful candidate in a marginal constituency and, reaching for the portable radio, sloped off, trailing a pounding hip hop number upstairs.

She opened the fridge, investigated a few covered plates and, pushing a string bag into the pocket of her cardigan, grabbed her purse and strode out to the outhouse where the Metro eased its flaccid tyres.

Fay had decided to beard the formidable Inspector Hayes in his den – an inexplicable desire to keep the police away from home. The woman's death under the train was like an indecent wound which she had no wish to explore. Guilt festered secretly as if the accident had, in fact, somehow been her fault. Could dropping the bottle have startled the woman, thrown her off balance? Was her own claim about being jostled from behind born of an unconscious desire to excuse herself in some way? After a sleepless night she found herself wishing the wretched woman *had* committed suicide.

Backing the car she swerved neatly round the verge by the high wall that encircled Glebe House and was just easing into second gear as Rose Barton, her cleaner, emerged round the overhanging evergreens. Fay wound down the window.

'Morning, Mrs B.'

She beamed. 'See myself in, duck.'

'I'm just popping into Renham to get some things for this evening. Could you empty the fridge for me and check Luke's washing for anything he's likely to need for school on Monday? I won't be long.'

As the Metro accelerated away Fay caught a glimpse of Mrs B stumble against the kerb, recover and, with the grace of most stout people, complete a neat sidestep before passing through the gate.

Within a few minutes Fay was speeding through the new housing estate. Some of the semis were already occupied, sparkling with white paint and fresh net curtains. Builders were roofing the last two houses and heaps of clay like a ring of ribbed earthworks were being pushed to the boundary by an excavator. Several of the lawns were already seeded and a copper-green haze lay between the front doors and the continuous low brick wall which flanked the pavement. A cat flew under the wheels. She braked hard, slewing the car sideways with a sickening squeal of tyres as the cat leapt into the hedge. A near thing. It was shaping up to be one of those days.

Twenty minutes later she parked in the High Street in Renham and strolled to the market. She had no wish to park in the police station yard. It was a small town, full of eyes, there was no need to fan even more gossip about the Brownes. There was no chance of keeping her involvement in the rail accident secret, the *Renham Gazette* was sure to lap up any snippet of drama to come its way. But Thursday was publication day and the *Gazette* was hardly likely to make it a stop press item. Perhaps it was a lucky day after all? It would be old news by the time the next issue came out and Luke would be away at school. And the national press would be unimpressed. A woman falling under a train would make no more than a ripple beyond Renham. Sad really. A life cut off in that horrible way and the response probably no more than a shrug...

Fay Browne had a determination to shield her son from violence in any form. Her strict supervision of his television viewing was almost pathological. If it were possible to get the boy away before her role as witness was bandied about the village it would be worth a try. Innocence was so brief. The transformation of every tragic incident into public entertainment, feeding the vicarious excitement of strangers, was something from which she tried to shelter Luke for as long as possible.

Robert found this attitude ridiculous, taunting her that she would turn the boy into a milksop. 'Do you really think the little buggers don't lap up every bit of bloodshed when they get the chance? School's no nunnery, Fay. Boys talk, see the news on the telly. *The Simpsons* is pretty crude, and as for those historical docusoap things he's crazy about ... You can't keep him wrapped in cotton wool for ever.'

It had been at Robert's insistence that Luke was a boarder. Her friend Maeve's boys had never been sent away to prep school. It rankled. But Robert was adamant.

Fay had been inside Renham police station before. A square Victorian building in a quiet street behind the shops, with a modern annexe tacked on like a shamefaced acknowledgement of current crime figures. Fay had occasionally been called in to interview a client for the Law Centre. But Inspector Roger Hayes was a new face. She guessed he would not stay long. His shrewd eyes were targeted on higher things than petty larceny and traffic offences, which were about the limit of criminality in this town. She hoped he would be out on a case. She could make her statement to one of the officers she was familiar with and get back home.

Sergeant Mollis was on duty. He greeted her from behind the counter with genuine pleasure. Fay's role at the Law Centre was piggy in the middle between the police and the legal aid crew. Strictly advisory. The sergeant liked Mrs Brown. A real lady. He liked her quiet efficiency. None of that flag waving like the other lot from the centre who made no bones about their attitude to the force. She smoothed the way between the interested parties, helping the wives and parents of the accused, the innocent bystanders, often more damaged by the judicial system than 'the villains', as he called them.

'I have to make a statement about the Renham Junction accident, Sergeant Mollis. I haven't much time. Could one of your people deal with it straight away? There's not much I can say really.'

'The chief inspector particularly wants a word with you, Mrs Browne. Just details,' he assured her.

'I can't wait, I'm afraid. There's little enough I can add to clarify things. It all happened in a flash and—'

A door opened and the appearance of Roger Hayes put paid to any excuses. The sergeant stiffened, taking a formal stance.

Hayes stood to one side, holding open the door for her. 'Come through to my office, Mrs Browne. I was coming out to Stamford later this morning. There was no need for you to drive in specially. I took the young lady's statement first. A student nurse. She had to be on duty.'

'I had some shopping in Renham,' she lied, her disquiet in his presence flooding back. She could almost feel the icy squelch in her rain-sodden shoes. The man had a piercing concentration which Fay guessed must be hard to live with. Hardly a natural when it came to PR, Hayes seemed to have a thin sense of humour to boot. Not that his job was any laughing matter. Like her own struggles at the centre he must be continually at odds with lies and prevarication. The sergeant raised the counter flap and ushered her through.

The room was small and rather dim. Situated on the north side of the building, the light coming through a small window behind his desk was cold. And clear as a spotlight. Fay guessed the DCI to be the clever sort, moving on a fast track to promotion. Dark hair was cut close to his head, the eyes focussed on the woman before him adding to the impression

12

that his interest was more than just a routine enquiry into a death on the railway line.

She sat down, placing her bag on the floor, wishing she had worn something more formal. Roger Hayes made her defensive. She declined his offer of coffee and, without more ado, he launched into what seemed all too much like an interrogation.

'Shall we start with your full name and address?'

'Frances Mary Browne, Glebe House, Bucks Hill, Stamford.' She quoted her telephone number. 'I am a solicitor.'

'And can you say exactly when you arrived at the station last night?'

'About ten to ten. I had a late session at the Law Centre in Fenner Street. I normally finish at eight but once a month we have a committee meeting after closing.'

'You went straight to the station buffet,' he said smoothly, looking at her under dark brows, his face shadowy, outlined by the frigid sunlight from the window at his back.

Fay nodded.

'The woman serving mentioned it. A regular, she said. Knew you by sight, of course. Even knew your tipple, Mrs Browne. Professional pride, I expect.' He smiled.

She drew back, affronted, but he continued without pause. 'It was a chilly, wet evening. I am in no way critical. Please go on, Mrs Browne. In your own words.'

Biting her lip, she struggled to refocus the details, aware that it was imperative to get her story right first time.

'There were several young men in the buffet. It was noisy ... I finished my drink and decided to wait at the end of the platform.'

'In the rain? Beyond the canopy? With no raincoat or umbrella?'

'I'd had a bad evening. A slight headache ...' she muttered.

'Who else was waiting?'

She shrugged, momentarily confused. What was he implying? Hayes knew the circumstances exactly. He must have put the same questions to the nurse.

'The girl – student nurse, you said? – was standing along the platform. She had some shopping,' she floundered, as if this had anything to do with it.

13

'Go on.'

'The other . . . er . . . woman was . . . er . . . too near the edge. It occurred to me she might be knocked over if someone opened a door as the train came in. It happens...'

'Quite so. You went up to warn her?'

'No! Actually, I didn't register it was a woman at first. She wore a black or a dark grey plastic mac with the hood up. And trousers, I suppose. I don't remember. I was only on the platform a few minutes when the train was signalled. I moved in close and the boys from the buffet crowded in behind us. It was suddenly very noisy. The train came round the bend and there was a sort of surge forward. Then I dropped something and as I bent down there was jockeying from the back. You know how it is when everyone's trying to push forward.'

'You dropped something, you say. Could it have been a bottle? There was glass on the platform. Yours or the victim's?'

'Mine.' Fay's eyes met his and she knew he was confirming his own assessment of the situation. He jotted notes in his book.

'More whisky,' he said without looking up.

'It was a present. A grateful client at the centre.'

'I thought gifts were not acceptable? You are a volunteer, I take it?'

'Strictly speaking we don't take presents,' she answered coldly. 'But sometimes it's difficult to refuse without giving offence. I prefer not to elaborate on the particular circumstances. Our work is strictly confidential.'

He laid down his pen and leaned back, smiling in a thoroughly disarming manner – almost up to Robert's standard, Fay acknowledged with a bitter smile of her own. It must be a quiet patch on the criminal scene, she decided, to grab the interest of a senior officer.

'Tell me about this voluntary work of yours, Mrs Browne. All very commendable, I'm sure. How long is it you've been taking a weekly surgery at Fenner Street?'

'About six years. Not always there, previously we had rooms in the centre of town. It gets me away from the house. My husband's business is based at home, you see. It's a bit like living over the shop.'

14

'Ah, yes. Sergeant Mollis was telling me all about it. A great enterprise for sleepy little Stamford. The return of the native with a vengeance, one might say.'

'Robert was at school there. He has a soft spot for the place.'

'But you don't?'

'Indeed I do,' she retorted, flushing. 'But there's very little industry in Stamford, it's just an overgrown village. The mail order business has been astonishingly successful. I like to get away from time to time. Do something entirely different.'

'You yourself are not involved in the Browne & Suskind warehouse operation I take it?'

'Not directly. The office is in London. Robert's partner, Hugo Suskind, deals with the antiquarian side and Robert does the travelling and the sales. It works very well.'

'An absolute boon to local employment no doubt.'

'Hardly that. Only a score or so on the regular payroll. But it brings visitors to Stamford – foreign tourists even – and Robert is continually giving the place a lot of publicity one way and another. The annual book festival with lectures and VIP authors' signing sessions brings in hundreds of people. Local shops and even the hotels in Renham benefit. It put Stamford on the map, one could say. For a place with few attractions.' She stopped, aware that she had probably said too much. 'But I really don't see what my husband's business has to do with the accident!'

'No, of course not. I'm new here, naturally curious, Mrs. Browne.' He picked up his pen and said sharply, 'Do you always use the train to attend your legal surgeries in Renham?' This sudden change of tone took her by surprise.

'Er, no, of course not. I usually drive, in the summer anyway. But when there's a monthly committee meeting after hours and in the winter I occasionally go by rail. I dislike night driving, Inspector, and the evenings are drawing in. I knew last night would be a late session. There was a lengthy agenda...'

'Ah, yes, of course. I took the liberty of speaking to your chairperson, Ms Cheryl Baker, last night. She confirmed the monthly committee involves a little supper party, a few glasses of wine. A longer meeting than usual she said.'

Fay's hands clenched in her lap, the oblique reference now inescapable. Hayes reread his notes. The silence was unnnerving. Without looking up he continued. 'We have a slight problem here, Mrs Browne. You see, you are the only real witness. We need to be quite sure of the facts. The nurse, Miss Bixell, has only a sketchy account of events, and the men from the buffet insist the woman jumped on the line as they were moving across the platform. You were immediately behind her, Mrs Browne, and with your legal background I have to rely on your statement. You are our professional observer one might say.'

'I know what I saw.' The words came stiffly, her eyes averted like an obstinate child determined to stick to an unlikely story.

He shuffled sheets in his file and tapped on the desk as if to insist on her complete attention.

'I have here your remark last night when it was suggested the victim was a suicide. "She didn't jump", you said.'

Fay felt things were getting out of hand and coldly insisted, 'May we allow this poor woman some identity? A name? We can't keep referring to her in this abstract way as if she were merely another statistic in your file.'

'By all means. Her name was Barbara Leah Hertz, age forty-six, recently widowed, employed for the past two months as an assistant at Renham Central Library. You must have seen her there in the course of your research work for the centre. I gather from my sergeant you are a frequent user of the newspaper files here in Renham. The deceased lived in Israel most of her adult life. Came to Stamford and moved in with her sister when her husband died this summer. You didn't know her?'

Fay was startled. 'Of course not! Why should I?'

He shrugged and went on. 'You took a grave risk trying to save a total stranger. I congratulate you, Mrs Browne. An astonishingly quick reaction.' His manner was cool, the compliment delivered without warmth. 'Mrs Hertz had no connection with your husband's book repository then? Never applied for a job, for instance?'

Fay shook her head in a vague refutation of the enigmatic line his enquiry was taking.

'Where were we? Ah, yes. You were saying there was a surge

16

of activity, you dropped the whisky bottle and the woman toppled over the edge. She didn't jump, you said. Are you implying you were pushed from behind and inadvertently bumped into the victim, unbalancing her at the edge of the platform?'

'No, I am not!' Fay jumped up, anger sparkling fiercely in the grey eyes. A typical redhead's temper, Hayes decided.

'Inspector, before we go any further I think it necessary to eliminate certain factors which seem to have crept in here. Yes, I do enjoy a tot of whisky from time to time. And I have been known to order a drink at the station buffet in Renham Junction after my weekly stint at the centre. My work is often discouraging and recently the tone of the service has changed, become more strident. The bottle of whisky was an unfortunate accessory to this tragic episode which seems to have coloured your assessment of my recall of events. I smelt strongly of whisky because it splashed up at my coat when I dropped the bottle. I am not an alcoholic, Inspector Hayes.'

He rose, raising a hand in a mild gesture, a veiled apology.

'Please, Mrs Browne, please go on. *You* say what happened. I am merely here to record your own words, to pre-empt any queries.'

Fay grudgingly sat down again, searching for the exact sequence of events.

'The signals had changed and the buzzer announcing the oncoming train had sounded. Mrs ... er ... Hertz was already at the edge of the platform, she seemed determined to be first on to the train. The other woman – the nurse – and I were also quite near the edge, but when the train was announced the buffet boys crowded in, there was some jostling and I got the impression just as I bobbed down to save the falling bottle that a hand shot out and touched the woman in front of me.'

'Pushed her?'

'I couldn't say that. I was trying to save the bottle which I had stupidly let slip. The paper was wet. I should have been more careful. But you know how it is, even in a split second when one's mind is intensely focussed, other things crowd in. I thought an arm shot out over my shoulder.'

'One of the youths?'

'I don't think so. They were all in a bunch, on the move certainly, but all together.'

'The porter says two other passengers pushed through just before the train was due. In the hubbub obviously someone could have scrambled into a carriage without declaring himself. I'm sure if there was another witness he or, she will come forward.'

He closed his notebook with a sigh of resignation.

'Accidental death I would say. I agree with you, Mrs Browne, but I had to be sure. From the enquiries I have already made there seems absolutely no indication Mrs Hertz was a potential suicide. But recently widowed, in a new country, feeling the cold of her changed circumstances? Who can tell? I spoke to her twin sister last evening, a lady called Millicent Ambache. Barbara Hertz came here to share her cottage on the road out of Barstow. Cheyney's. You probably know it.'

'What did you say?'

'Cheyney's.'

'No. I didn't mean that.'

He rose, fixing her with that quizzical stare which had been so unnerving at the start of the interview. 'Sorry?'

'The sister's name.'

'Oh, er, Ambache. Millicent Ambache. Yes, unusual, isn't it? You've met her?'

'No, I'm confusing her with someone else.'

Hayes paused, eyeing his informant with interest. 'A strong-minded woman. Her sister too, I would imagine. Resourceful lady, Mrs Hertz, setting off on such a long and arduous road at her age, wouldn't you say?'

'What?'

'Her evening class. Didn't I say? Barbara Hertz was waiting on the station after attending an evening class. She was studying law.'

He ushered her out, promising to have a typewritten statement ready for her signature as soon as she had finished her shopping. Fay breathed a sigh of relief. It would all be well and truly under the carpet in no time at all.

Three

Arriving home, Fay was relieved to find her cleaner had finished downstairs and could be heard vacuuming to the disco beat pounding in Luke's room. Roger Hayes' polite grilling had left her with a feeling of disquiet which would not be improved by the perceptive eye of Rose Barton, a woman who attracted a certain notoriety in the village for clairvoyant – if not downright witch-like – abilities.

She dropped her string bag on to the kitchen table and called upstairs. 'Luke?' The racket continued, unremitting. Fay shrugged and padded back to the kitchen. Wasn't nine a bit young for hard rock? She was probably out of touch. 'Must ask Maeve,' she muttered.

Glebe House was the largest house in the village and, according to local folklore, built by an unfrocked priest. His specifications had included a private chapel. Originally sited well away from any other dwellings, the Victorian house had escaped any gothic influence and the renegade priest had planned his bolthole on old-fashioned lines. The house was therefore hard to place architecturally and appeared to be much older than in fact it was. Its quiet dignity had survived behind a high brick wall while Stamford steadily expanded all around it like a moat, drowning the woods and meadows.

Rose Barton clumped through the door holding out a bag of assorted boots and shoes.

'None of this lot fits him no more.' She dropped the bag on the floor and reached for the kettle. 'Reckon you'd better get new trainers but the rest should do a turn till Christmas. Still some name tapes missing though. And two pairs of running shorts belonging to some poor kid called Unwin.'

'OK. I'll wrap them separately.' Fay smiled. 'How's the soul travel going, Mrs B?'

She swivelled to take in Fay's grin, smoothing the front of her overall. 'Do you the world of good to relax a bit more yourself, duck,' she said, pouring boiling water over a tea bag and carefully adding milk. 'You think I'm crackers but you'd be amazed at what I've seen – and no whisky needed neither!'

Touché.

Fay chatted on, light-heartedly quizzing this stout party sitting at her kitchen table sipping tea. An out-of-body experience for such a commonsensical old trout was hard to imagine. She looked unequivocally earthbound with her frizzy grey hair bundled into an untidy knot and eyes placid as a rock pool. Fay wondered, not for the first time, how old she was.

'Well, this won't do, Mrs B. I think I'd better get started on Luke's box.'

Fay cleared the table and flicked on the light. Already the sky had dulled under a misty haze and the leaves of maple in the milk bottle hung like rags. Abruptly, she turned away and with a few loose strides reached the hall and bounded upstairs two at a time.

She spent the afternoon sorting through her summer clothes and adding some to the pile of Luke's outgrown things for the jumble. Unfolding winter skirts and dresses, the muted tones of brown, green and pink seemed unfamiliar after months put away. Robert, so vain and finicky about his own clothes, managed on so little. A few suits in his dressing room and spares at Hugo's London flat for emergency trips, like this forthcoming ten days springing from nowhere just when she had hoped for a few quiet days together after Luke was back at school. Well, life with Robert was always full of surprises. She laughed, thinking back.

'And what's so funny, Rusty?'

She started up, his voice unnerving her as he stepped soundlessly into the bedroom. Robert Browne was a large man, tall and heavily built with a quiet footfall which seemed oddly out of character. In every other way he was a man intent on making his presence felt. His hair, greying early, now assumed the substance of steel wool. Perversely, it accentuated the boyishness of his smile and a jaunty energy completed the illusive paradox. The Browns were an interesting-looking pair, hard to place. Another dealer had been heard to say with an edge of malice that Browne had cultivated this strong image to cap the genuine scholarship and integrity of his partner, Hugo Suskind.

Fay guessed that Robert's latest project had been the last straw for Hugo. Another of his marketing brainwaves, a runaway success despite everyone else's recessionary tactics: a series of pocket books on specialized subjects, lavishly illustrated, printed cheaply abroad and distributed directly from Glebe House with the normal mail orders and requiring no extra staff. It was a far cry from Hugo's antiquarian bookshop where they had started. And already Robert was pushing him to agree to a new academic book club idea. Hugo's resentment smouldered. It was foolish of Robert to heap coals on the fire. The man had a flair for going too far.

Fay let a dress flop into the crook of her arm as she embraced him and rubbed her cheek against his sandpaper jaw. 'I wish you wouldn't creep up on me like that, Robert! I didn't hear the car. But I *have* missed you,' she added, glad to have him home. A hint of garlic and cigar smoke hung in the air. A promotional lunch, she guessed..

'Bit late for a spring clean, isn't it?' he said, eyeing the piles of jumble.

'Just sorting out a dress for this evening. And packing up the tee shirts – the weather's really changed all of a sudden. I only take it in when Luke's gone and once the house is empty it seems never to stop raining. You haven't forgotten we're going to Maeve's tonight?'

He drew back, affecting a melodramatic blow to the head.

'I had. I had. Maeve would never believe it. To forget an invitation to dine with the queen of the leprechauns, bejesus!'

'Don't play the fool, Robert. You haven't organized something else this evening, have you?'

He slumped on the bed, meeting her sharp gaze. 'I don't suppose it would be possible to squeeze out of it, do you think? I've brought back a mountain of reading to be got through before tomorrow. You know I'm off to Houston in the

21

morning? Good God, I asked that babysitter to write it on the calendar last night. Didn't she tell you I'd phoned?'

'I saw the scribble across ten days all right but I thought she'd probably got it wrong. You should have phoned me at the centre – you know leaving messages with Cissy's just asking for trouble. Anyway you promised to take Luke back to school in the Mercedes on Monday.'

'Out of the blue, my darling. Can't put it off. I meant to speak to you about it but I've been up to my eyes for the past week.'

'Well, a phone call wouldn't have taken much effort and—'

'Needs must, sweetheart. This museum bloke wants to see stuff I bought from Renfrew in the spring and I've got to nip in quick. Too good an opportunity to foul up. Hugo would never forgive me.' He carefully placed this last shot knowing Fay's sensitivity to Hugo's problems and pressed his advantage. 'I've got to fly out there before this American guy cools off. You know what these Texans are like ... The only flight Meg could get is tomorrow, and even so I've got to go via Paris. Hardly gives me time to draw breath here and there's a pile of stuff to go over with Goldsmith.'

'Honestly, Robert, you're the absolute bloody limit,' she snapped. 'I can't possibly cry off at an hour's notice. Maeve would be furious. It's a very small party. Ted's invited his Tory agent and needs the support of a few "respectable locals" as he puts it. He's not with the Monster Raving Loony Party, you know.'

'Could fool me.' He raised both hands in a mock gesture of surrender but his mind was elsewhere.

'I'll make an excuse for us to leave early and you can always fit in a couple of hours before breakfast and still have time with Goldsmith before you go for the plane. I thought that was the whole point of having that chain gang working in the chapel right on our doorstep.'

This last jibe was a regular which Robert didn't bother to counter. There were occasions when a strategic withdrawal was called for. 'OK, boss,' he said. 'You win.'

Fay relaxed, affectionately touching his cheek as she went into the bathroom to run his bath. 'But Robert,' she said, pausing in the doorway, 'you simply must make some time for Luke this evening before we go out. He's hardly caught a glimpse of you these holidays.'

'No problem.' He followed her and bent over the mirror, running fingers over the faintly perceptible stubble. 'Do I have to shave again?'

'Not really.'

She stood beside him as he frowned at their reflection in the glass.

'But please, darling, no nonsense with Ted tonight. He's serious about this political shot and doesn't need you to set him up to make an ass of himself.'

'Not with Maeve at his side, he doesn't.'

Swiftly she added, 'Please, Robert. Play fair.'

He shrugged and, whistling, started to unbutton his shirt.

Fay went downstairs and was laying a tray for Luke when the telephone rang. The fork in her hand clattered to the floor. Five past six. Fetching a clean fork, she ignored it. Robert shouted to her over the bannisters.

'Get that, would you, darling? It's probably Hugo. I'm just about to get in the bath. I'll call back.'

The moment Robert appeared in the house the phone never stopped ringing. But Fay was willing to bet that this time, the call was for her exclusive attention. Considering Robert's mania for computerising the business, his dogged determination to restrict the telephone outlets at home and not even instal an answering machine never ceased to amaze her. She pushed away the sour suspicion that it kept Robert's contacts at arm's length, leaving less scope for inconvenient calls at home where every word might be overheard.

She went into the hall and lifted the receiver, holding it stiffly an inch from her ear.

'Hello?'

Silence.

'Hello,' she croaked, her throat as dry as the leaves in the withering garden. No one spoke. No sound but the rhythmic dripping of a tap. She dropped the phone back in its cradle and stood irresolute, gripping the newel post.

Luke bumped downstairs. 'That another wrong number, Mum? You should complain to the exchange. Cissy said so. There were two last night when you were out. Just rings off without a flippin' word.'

The boy watched her. 'Last night on TV there was this loony who rings up this blind girl and—'

'Shut up, Luke. You watch too much television. What was Cissy doing letting you see all that rubbish? What time was it, anyway?'

'*Tales from the Everglades*. It goes out about eleven but Dilke lent me this video and I—'

'The phone call, dumbo! What time was the phone call?' Fay pushed him into the kitchen and tried to curb the edge in her voice as she cut some bread.

'Cissy got one when she was watching the boring old news at six and I answered the other one when she was trying to fix up the video just after.'

'Nothing later?' She turned some burgers under the grill, keeping her tone light.

'No. I told whoever it was everyone was out 'cept me, so they didn't bother. I said you'd be at the law place in Renham till late.'

She dropped a can of Coke on the tray in surprise. 'He spoke?'

'No, Mum, I told you. Not a flippin' word. I wanted to see the Everglades video without having to answer the phone all the time so I just said that in case it was the same dopey caller.'

She decided to drop it. Luke was far too perceptive for his age. She banged down a bottle of ketchup followed by a jar of sweet pickle and a tumbler for the Coke. 'This is your very last Junk Special, my lad. And no more horror movies while I'm at Maeve's tonight. No wonder you look so washed out.'

He giggled, grabbing the tray to scoot off just as the telephone resumed its jangling peal.

'Blast!'

She leapt at the instrument as Luke disappeared into the sitting room with his TV supper.

'Yes?'

24

Nothing but the noise of a dripping tap. Was someone out there conducting a survey on the effects of Chinese water torture?

She lost patience with the whole charade. 'Look here, mate. Just read a girlie mag or something. Find something else to amuse yourself with apart from ringing this number.' She slammed down the receiver, feeling better for the burst of temper, and made a grimace at Luke's freckled face peering round the doorway as she ran upstairs to get ready for Maeve's dinner party.

She had decided to tell Robert nothing about the accident on the line at Renham Junction. He was off to Houston in the morning. It would only complicate things if he knew she was involved. He might even insist she be legally represented at the inquest, build something out of absolutely nothing. She thrust the whole shocking business to the back of her mind and hoped it wouldn't crop up in conversation at Maeve's.

Maeve MacMillan was, Fay supposed, what passed for a best friend. Although there were a few mutually dusty corners neither wished to explore, a comfortable off-hand familiarity had seasoned since Robert had moved back to the place where he had grown up. Stamford was miles from London and on the face of it a hopeless backwater for a business of the scope he had in mind. It was Ted MacMillan, a commercially astute estate agent but an otherwise dull dog, who had persuaded Robert to consider Glebe House as a practical extension of the Pimlico operation. Not only would it double as a home but the property included this unconsecrated chapel ripe for redevelopment. Buying the most imposing house on his old stamping ground was an offer hard to refuse. It was no fluke that Ted MacMillan had made a mint with such a knack for putting his finger on clients' little weaknesses. Holding out the chance to shine in the muddy puddle in which generations of Brownes had been very small fry indeed caught Robert's fancy and grew more alluring the more he thought about it. It was, as was hinted at the Crooked Billet, a case of the biter bit. MacMillan had struggled to offload the empty old ruin for nearly three years before netting the local boy wonder himself.

In his own field Ted was as smooth an operator as Robert.

25

Unperceptive in many ways, he had shrewdly assessed his client's secret vulnerability. Robert Browne, quite simply, desired status. The transfer and expansion of his business to a place where he could make a splash was a tempting gamble which had paid off handsomely. In his wilder imaginings he secretly admitted a desire to set up a family base for Luke, a dynasty even ... That there was only one egg in the Brownes' basket was, Ted ironically observed, their bad luck. Robert, much to everyone's embarrassment, made no bones of the fact that he had bought the house for a Victorian-sized brood. Sad really, Fay making such heavy weather of her side of the bargain. But as Ted repeatedly reminded him, Glebe House had proved a sound financial investment all round.

The MacMillans themselves occupied a neo-Georgian residence complete with stable block – for cars – and an indoor swimming pool. It lay outside the sprawling encroachments of Stamford and had been built to Ted's exact specifications. Already the bald facade had veiled itself in Virginia creeper and as their car swung into the drive Fay was surprised to find herself warming to the house. The saplings had grown and, blurred with rampant greenery, the place seemed less offensive in its landscaped setting though, admittedly, the floodlit garden was a bit much.

Maeve was welcoming the Minters in the hall as they arrived and, hearing the car, flung open the door as Robert and Fay stepped through the porch. His arm swung around Fay's shoulder and he pulled Maeve to him as they entered, clasping both women in a bear-like hug, whispering, 'I hope we are all going to behave ourselves tonight, girls.'

Maeve smiled absently, drawing away, playfully slapping his arm as she disentangled herself. Really, Robert was getting to be a bit of an old ham these days.

She reached out for Fay's coat and they greeted each other with affection and an underlying complicity. It was likely to be a sticky evening one way and another. But what were best friends for? Maeve was almost as tall as Fay but with a softly rounded figure and none of the other's gaucherie. She dumped the coat on the hall sofa and beckoned them through, hazel eyes shining with puckish laughter. Fay glanced at Robert, hoping a stiff drink would dampen the heightening anxiety which had clung to her since the appalling accident at Renham Junction. She felt as if the spectre of the unknown woman had attached itself to her like a shadow, blaming her in some way. She shook her head, damning these neurotic fancies, determined to put the whole incident out of her mind – for tonight at any rate.

They followed Maeve through to the drawing room where Ted was pouring aperitifs for Charlie Minter, a local antiques dealer and his wife, Sally. Robert visibly expanded in company.

Ted, smoothly prosperous in a dark suit, wore his cricket club tie with the confidence of a man well into his professional stride. He exercised daily in his basement gym and had recently installed a sauna. Only a receding hairline refused to comply with his requirements and wispy curls defied the hairspray to fluff his temples like a cherub's. He passed champagne cocktails to the Minters and greeted Fay with a moist kiss. Robert made himself at home and mixed a kir for himself while Ted fussed over Fay.

'You're looking as gorgeous as ever, Fay,' he said warmly, admiring the pale skin which remained untanned summer and winter despite Fay's love affair with her garden. 'You don't deserve her, Robert old man, jetting round the world six months of the year the way you do. Can't think why you don't take Fay with you.'

Robert grinned. 'Like taking your own sandwiches.'

Ted responded wanly, jarred by Robert's wry humour. The chap was becoming insufferably cocky. One never knew which way to take his so-called jokes.

'Anyway,' Robert smoothly continued, 'Fay hates flying and I'm never in one place for very long. She would find it awfully dull. Mind you, before Luke, we used to pitch in with Hugo in London. What a trio. All girls together.'

He flipped into a campy pose and slopped kir down his jacket, dabbing at the dark stain with a handkerchief as Maeve, leaning elegantly against the chimney piece, drawled in her soft, barely perceptible brogue, 'What Ted really means, Robert, is he wouldn't dream of leaving *me* alone in Stamford to guard the family reputation.' She wrinkled her nose. 'Though if Ted does get adopted and eventually gains a seat, presumably I'll be hauled to Westminster for the season or whatever you call it. Ho ho!'

Charlie said, 'With a beautiful wife like you at the hustings, Ted's halfway there. You can knock on my door for a vote any time, Maeve.'

They were still discussing Ted's political chances when the doorbell rang and Maeve stepped out to greet Ted's potential agent, Harvey Cresswell and his wife, Norah. Ted determined to keep the banter on more mundane levels for the rest of the evening and hastily refilled Robert's glass before the two new-comers were ushered in. They entered, closely followed by a large dog which tried to slip in behind Maeve. While Ted effected introductions, the animal padded up to Charlie and slumped against his chair like a tired swimmer, rolling blood-shot eyes to the bowl of peanuts at his elbow.

The party settled round the fire and Ted noticed the dog for the first time, leaping to his feet to grasp its collar.

'Now then, Harold. Outside, old son.' It lifted a paw to Charlie's knee and assumed an air of weariness, bracing its considerable bulk more firmly against the upholstery. Ted flushed and made a move which Maeve swiftly intercepted, taking the dog in one hand and a handful of peanuts in the other and leading it from the room. Ted recovered his compo-sure only to find he had dismissed the only subject of con-versation which in any way animated Norah Cresswell.

'That's a very unusual dog you have there, Ted. I don't think I've ever seen one quite like it,' she prattled.

He grasped at this straw. 'Nor likely to, Norah. Not this side of the border, It's what's called a kirtle hound. Ancient breed, almost extinct, in fact. The boys wanted a pet and I needed a dog for shooting, so Maeve scouted round and came up with Harold.'

'Shooting,' Robert interjected, 'is exactly the right solution for Harold if you ask me.'

Ted glowered but Norah was not to be outflanked on this and as Maeve re-entered, called on another dog lover for support. 'You should show him, Maeve. A fascinating animal like that would provoke publicity for Ted. Babies and dogs always help a political campaign.'

'Well, you see, Norah, Maeve's not really a doggy lady and to be perfectly frank, Harold's none too easy to handle. No good as a gundog either,' Ted conceded.

'As a Tory I'm not surprised you can't control that dog,' Robert said. 'Not one called after Harold Wilson.'

Ted rose to the bait, all consternation. 'No, Rob, you've got it all wrong. MacMillan, see? Harold MacMillan – one of the party's founding fathers, a political giant. "You've never had it so good", remember?' He spread his hands in emphasis. 'One of Maeve's brainwaves. Those droopy eyelids, of course. A type of bloodhound, I imagine.'

The dog reappeared and slumped down again as if knowing itself to be the centre of attention and unlikely to be ejected a second time. It farted with deep satisfaction.

'The peanuts,' Maeve murmured, utterly straight-faced, avoiding Fay's eye.

'Interesting,' Harvey ponderously added. 'But I should keep quiet about the beast if I were you, Ted. Background interviews are a minefield. We don't want any jokes in *Private Eye*, do we?'

Fay glanced from one to the other in disbelief. They were all perfectly serious. She said, 'I can't see that Robert's in any position to amuse himself with a dog called Harold MacMillan having called our pet rabbit Lady Otteline Morrell.'

Ted and Charlie burst into great whoops of glee and Ted's agent saw the joke at last. Sally and Norah smiled blandly, uncomprehending, but Maeve remained entirely unmoved. When the hilarity had subsided she archly enquired, 'And to put the seal on my dismal convent education who the devil is this Lady Otteline?'

Robert leaned across, taking her hand. 'Was, Maeve darling. Was. Lady Otteline was a glorious literary tart with lots of famous protégés. She considered herself the artistic inspiration of the age. Not a patch on you, of course.' He raised her fingers to his lips.

'But what,' she wailed, 'has that to do with a rabbit? Did Lady Otteline have buck teeth? Lots of unofficial babies or something?'

Laughter resurged. Fay butted in. 'Ottie sort of thrust herself on us, you might say. Took us up. Our cleaner won a rabbit as a prize at a whist drive. When she went to the butcher to collect it, he jokingly said he'd have thought her to be a vegetarian and—'

'Our Mrs B,' Robert explained, 'has a local reputation for being mixed up in one sort of barmy thing after another. And this butcher, considering himself something of a wag, invited her to go round the back and choose a rabbit for herself from one of the hutches. He breeds them for sale in the shop. Rose Barton assumed, of course, he would slaughter it for her and so—'

'He would have done, too, if she hadn't got so huffy. She's a funny old thing, Norah, reads tea leaves and claims to have conversations with people on the other side.'

'Look, Fay, are you telling this story or am I?'

She shrugged.

'So Ridgeway fetches one of his live rabbits and stuffs it into a plastic bag. "Freshest meat in Stamford", he says handing it to her over the counter. Not to be outdone, our Mrs B sweeps past all the cackling old biddies with the bunny jumping up and down in her shopping trolley and trundles home with it.'

'She brought it to the house next morning to ask Mr Goldsmith, our warehouse foreman, to butcher it for her. But we couldn't bring ourselves to ask him. Ottie's very small, hardly a meal for a cat even now, poor little thing.'

'Like a bloody rat it is.' Robert tossed down the rest of his cocktail and took up the story which seemed to hold both Cresswells in thrall. 'And you know how the script goes after that, don't you, Ted? "No need to get a hutch for it, Robert, it'll be perfectly all right living in the outhouse under the Metro."' He grinned at his captive audience. 'Just like that wild cat Maeve got hold of. "It's not stayin', Ted darlin'",' he mimicked like a stage Irishman, "I'm just feeding the poor starvin' creature till I can find a nice home for it."'

'Four years ago now,' Ted agreed, 'and incontinent still.'

He rose and, unperturbed by Maeve's cool glance, took Norah's arm to lead the party into the dining room.

Four

Dinner was served by a stolid middle-aged woman who communicated with Maeve by a series of nods. She was a deaf mute and Maeve's treasure. Living in a hostel in Stamford, Dottie worked as their daily and helped with the entertaining and to babysit. Maeve's children adored Dottie, especially Flora, the three-year-old.

Talk around the table was animated, Maeve and Robert delving into a local story involving the visit of the bishop to a dried-up well to investigate a so-called miracle cure. After Dottie had left the room Fay whispered in Ted's ear, 'It must be five years since Dottie came to you. She's here so much, I wonder Maeve doesn't have her live in.'

'Oh, you know Maeve. She's got this thing against live-in help. Between you and me, Fay, I wasn't all that keen on having her around at all at first, especially after Flora arrived. All sorts of dangers having someone in the house who's stone deaf. But the woman's obviously intelligent, has an instinctive communication with the kids and is fiercely loyal. We had to have all sorts of visual aids set up in the kitchen to warn her when the front door or dining room bell is ringing for instance, and the only thing she's really useless about is the telephone.'

He leaned back. 'Still, at least we can't complain that Dottie jaws to us all day as I gather does your Rose Barton.' He nudged Fay, lowering his voice. 'I hear she's all the rage at the table-rapping circle that's been set up in Renham, so Maeve tells me.' He gave a knowing wink.

Fay hastily changed the subject to ask about Maeve's art classes at the local evening institute.

'She's taken on a new lot this term since the course was

transferred to the old grammar school. There's a proper studio there with far more facilities and the county has shunted a small group from the psychiatric place in Renham to join with the existing lot. They come with a minder, of courser – all harmless nutters. Its a scheme to give them the chance to mix with the locals before they let them loose.'

'How about the regulars? Aren't they a bit fussed being used as some sort of guinea pig environmental group?'

'Well, you know Maeve. One or two of the old-stagers complained but the number of students has been doubled so that helped a lot. She buttered up the moaners with some rigmarole about "a new artistic dimension of untrammelled minds" or some such tosh. They've done a couple of terms without any trouble so far. These schemes soon shake down quite successfully.'

Fay could well imagine Maeve disarming the dissenters with her sweet steel will – her powers of persuasion were on a par with the Mafia.

They were all invited to return to the drawing room where Dottie had laid out coffee and liqueurs.

The remainder of the evening passed smoothly, the only hiccough occurring when Harvey brought up the subject of 'the suicide on the line'. Fay started up, slopping her coffee. Maeve, anticipating an unpleasant downturn in what was supposed to be a light-hearted occasion, changed the subject. Every party had its ups and downs and this one had not been an unqualified success. Distinctly dodgy actually, but being lumbered with the Cresswells *and* Robert in a tricky mood wasn't exactly a piece of cake. Ted had hinted that the Browne & Suskind operation had hit a sticky patch but everyone had business problems these days. The trouble was, Fay bent over backwards to protect the wretched man – couldn't she see it only made Robert more prickly?

As they were leaving Fay realized Robert was more than a fraction unsteady. They made a noisy farewell and she slipped her hand under his arm and murmured, 'Shall I drive, darling?'

'Certainly not,' he snapped. 'You can't wait to get your hands on this magnificent piece of engineering, can you?'

Fumbling with the keys, he opened the doors and immediately she was seated, set the car in a wide swift arc and off down the drive. He drove fast and confidently and became unusually expansive about his forthcoming Texan trip – putting up a strong case for the need to take his assistant, Meg Heffer, along. Fay's mind wandered, inevitably drawn back to the forthcoming inquest on the poor Hertz woman. She tried to shut it out and concentrate on Robert's trip.

'. . . and I may go on to Boston for a few days while I'm over there. I'll let you know when I expect to be back. More than a week but I can't say for sure.'

'Shall I meet you in London? We could take in a play or something?'

'Christ no! You know how busy I am before Christmas. By the way, I've decided to swop cars tomorrow. Yours is really squalid. Not at all decent to take Luke back to Huxtable on Monday. The bloody burser'll want *two* terms in advance if he catches sight of that four-wheeled pigsty. I'll take the Metro and leave it near the airport at that garage I told you about. There's no point in parking a brand new Merc for the mechanics to take joyriding. You might as well use it while I'm away.'

Fay inwardly groaned. Robert's car was a nuisance to park and was the last sort of vehicle for the muddy lanes around about. Also, being Robert's pride and joy it must be treated with kid gloves. No chance of collecting that bag of peat she'd ordered – even the boot was pristine.

He swung the car viciously round a narrow bend and they were both temporarily transfixed in the glare of oncoming headlights. He braked hard. A lorry skimmed past with barely inches to spare. He pulled in. Switching off the ignition he lurched out and moved towards the verge and she vaguely wondered if he was going to throw up in the hedge. That would put the finishing touch to his suit, already spattered with kir. But he wrenched open the passenger door and jerked her into the lane.

'You're right. You're always bloody right. *You* drive. You could certainly do with the practice.'

He stumbled on the rough ground and she instinctively

grabbed his arm. To her surprise he pulled her close, stared into her startled eyes, then kissed her violently, invading her mouth with a rigid tongue. She swayed under this unexpected burst of passion and found herself responding, caressing the wiry curls at the nape of his neck, absorbing the faint musky scent of sweat and cigar smoke and alcohol which seemed infinitely more appealing than his aftershave.

'Darling, darling tiger,' he muttered, moving his hands under her coat and across the smooth silk jersey of her dress as he pushed her into the back seat.

Next morning Robert woke early as usual, clear-headed and insufferably jolly. Fay prised open heavy eyelids to the sound of his tuneless rendering of 'Pretty Woman' and sleepily observed him check the contents of his suitcase. He had already showered and was spruce and ready for the day.

Raising herself on one elbow, the bedside clock swam into focus. Hellfire, it was only six fifteen! She fell back on the pillows.

'Have you had coffee, Robert?'

'Not yet, Rusty.' He grinned in that lopsided way which had clinched a million sales. 'I'll bring you up some tea if you like. I'm not leaving till nine but I have to check some details with Hugo before I go. I'll take a mug to the study.'

She swung her legs over the side of the bed and slipped on a housecoat. 'We could snatch a quick breakfast together in the kitchen if I pop down straight away. Then I'll bring the paper and a cuppa back to bed while you're on the phone.'

In the wake of the unprecedented frolic on the back seat of the Mercedes, Fay felt a surge of tenderness for Robert, regretting having allowed the habit of staying home on these trips of his to establish itself. If she gave up her weekly stint at the Law Centre and with Luke boarding ... Lurking at the back of her mind there was the irritation of Robert's personal assistant, as she called herself these days. Meg Heffer. Almost indispensible according to Robert. She decided to phone Cheryl and cancel her sessions at the Law Centre for the rest of the month at least. She could do with a break.

34

As she prepared the grapefruit, she considered the possibility of persuading Robert to take a holiday before Christmas. Morocco? She stared out of the window, A pink dawn lurked behind rainclouds. She *had* to get away. With or without Robert. Why not spend a couple of days with his father after dropping Luke back at school? The old man's isolated cottage would be bliss after the hustle of the past few days with that suspicious detective, Hayes, breathing down her neck, not to mention the impending inquest. Even to herself Fay dare not acknowledge a growing fear of being alone in the house. All those anonymous phone calls hadn't helped. She shrugged. Anyway, a visit to Pa was long overdue. A sick relative. A perfectly valid excuse to sheer off.

They dawdled over breakfast, Robert elaborating about marketing in Australia, almost forgetting the dwindling time in which to settle dispatch problems with his warehouse fore-man, Goldsmith, before leaving. Pure chance had thrown him into the book trade. Hugo and Fay teased him about being a non-reader, which was almost true. To Robert Browne books were a commodity, marketable like fast food or computers. Hugo Suskind winced at Robert's success: it seemed almost like cheating.

The telephone rang. He abandoned the table to answer it. Fay sipped her coffee and thought, not without pleasure, of seeing Pa again. Perhaps Bernard Browne *was* just a shade peculiar by regular standards – no need to mention to Robert about the complaints from Bernard's neighbours and those interfering social services busybodies. Even old Goldsmith was a bit odd these days ... She made her way upstairs, passing Robert sprawled at the table in the hall embroiled in a tele-phone wrangle with Hugo.

Wryly she listed the number of things she kept from her husband: the funny phone calls, her involvement with the death on the railway line and, unaccountably, the increasing eccen-tricity of poor old Bernard. Robert had only himself to blame, getting a measured response from him these days was just asking for the moon. Hugo must be finding Robert's spiralling pace more than enough to cope with, especially with business recession taking its toll worldwide. Why couldn't Robert let up a bit? Coast along for a while? Hugo probably welcomed his partner's frequent trips abroad if the truth be known.

After changing into a skirt and sweater she rustled up Luke, prising him away from a model aeroplane kit he was busting to finish before going back to school. Fay, deciding it was imperative to give the Metro a quick clean-out before Robert took it over, filled a bucket and slipped out to Ottie's barn.

The rabbit generally appeared as soon as the doors opened but no rustle under the car gave it away. Fay peered under the chassis and poked about. Ottie had definitely scarpered. 'I suppose Luke's been tinkering about in here and the silly creature got out,' she said to herself.

Flinging a collection of plastic bags out of the car, she briskly set to with a handbrush on the murky upholstery. In a few minutes she had wiped the steering wheel and rubbed up the shelf and door handles, noting with satisfaction that it would just about pass muster if Robert was in a rush to get to the airport. She started the engine and circled the house to park on the drive. As she switched off, she saw Rose Barton trot through the gate and was astonished to realize it was already almost nine.

Fay followed her in, passing Robert still sprawled by the phone, listening intently, scribbling figures in a file in front of him. He urgently tapped his watch in frantic mime as she passed to go into the study. A few moments later she emerged carrying his briefcase and was surprised to see a girl with her back to her talking with him in the hall. The woman turned.

'Why, Meg, it's you!' Fay laughed. 'I hardly recognised you in the hat and sunglasses. Have you time for a coffee before you go?'

'No, she hasn't.' Robert was firm. 'We should have left ten minutes ago. Sorry to rush you, Meggy, but Hugo has problems. By the way, Fay, he's got to come down here tomorrow to sort out some stuff for dispatch. Oh, and darling, could you send that suit I had on to the cleaners? I spilt something on it at Maeve's.' He moved to the bottom of the stairs and shouted, 'Luke! I'm off now.'

Meg Heffer looked embarrassed, jerking her head awkwardly aside as Fay chatted about not hearing the doorbell. Her turn-out was as immaculate as ever, tiny feet in their gleaming lizard-skin Manolos swivelling on the waxed floorboards in a very un-Meg-like nervous fandango.

'I got a taxi and Robert let me in,' she said. 'I've already put my case in the Metro. Is that all right?'

'Yes, of course.' Fay glanced at the cream gaberdine suit and added with a smile, 'You're quite safe. I swept it out a bit. You won't have to sit on any rabbit droppings.'

Luke jogged downstairs, making jarring thuds on the bare oak treads, swinging round the brass newel post at the bottom.

'Hi, Meg.' He smirked. 'Smashing shiner you've got there.'

Robert's Girl Friday uttered a nervous laugh and he shot a murderous look at the boy. Fay's eyes zoomed in and she realized that the hat and sunglasses concealed a painful bruise high on the girl's cheekbone. And Luke was right. Meg had a black eye.

'I walked into a shelf at the shop. Just like me. Always clumsy.'

Fay hastened to reassure her. 'I wouldn't have even noticed if Hawkeye here hadn't spotted it.' Luke, unmindful of the conversational undercurrents, was already following his father out to the car.

'In a day or two,' Fay went on, 'it will have completely vanished. Anyway, dark glasses look glamorous any old time. They suit you, Meg. Make you look quite film-starry.'

She slipped her arm through Meg's and they went outside. Robert had lifted the car bonnet and was fiddling with the engine while Luke kicked at the tyres.

'Just checking. I'll get some petrol on the way.' He glanced at his watch. 'Come on, Meg, hop in.'

He put his arm around Fay and pecked her cheek. 'Bye, Rusty. Be good.'

He affectionately punched Luke's arm before swinging into the driver's seat. Fay grinned as she and the boy waved them off. Robert looked like a gorilla crouched behind the wheel in Fay's little runabout. A gorilla in a mantrap.

In the house, Rose Barton had just finished vacuuming the sitting room. 'All off, are they? That clock-changing lark must play up your stomach something chronic. Rather them than me,' she said, pushing the Hoover back into the cupboard. 'Too early for a coffee? Sure we could all do with a nice sit-down to catch our breath a minute.'

Fay nodded and reached for the still unread newspaper. She hoped the old woman was not wanting to gossip about the death of the wretched Barbara Hertz, which must have featured in detail on local radio, Mrs B's favourite source of information. Luckily the dead woman was a stranger to the area: Mrs B's interest rarely extended beyond her own village. Luke bolted upstairs back to his model Spitfire and Fay drifted into the sitting room where watery sunlight shafted through the long windows making a rusty pool on the brown carpet.

She dropped on to the windowseat and found herself gazing into the front garden. Two girls passed through the gate and, deep in conversation, disappeared through the shrubbery towards the chapel warehouse. Her eyes dropped to the headlines and she was just starting to comb through the home news as Rose Barton entered, placing a cup of black coffee on the side table.

'Here you are, duck. Bad for your nerves this stuff but it'll buck you up. You should persevere with that herb tea I brought you, much better than all this caffeine.' She peered at Fay, noting the dark smudges under her eyes and the tremor as she reached for the cup. 'You seem a bit down this morning. Some bother with hubby's trip or something?'

Fay winced. One could have too much of all this kind consideration.

'All organized down to the last detail thanks to Meg Heffer I imagine. Though, now you mention it, she didn't look her usual unruffled self. She had a black eye – walked into a shelf apparently.'

Mrs B tossed her head and vigorously rubbed at the piano lid.

'Walked into her dad's fist more like.'

Fay looked up, startled. 'Surely not. She's a grown woman.'

'Makes no difference to Syd Heffer. Always dotting that poor wife of his before she got fed up and pushed off.'

'I didn't know you knew them.'

'Knew them? Bless me, I should say so. I practically brought up Maggie myself after her mum left. "Meg" is a new handle since she moved up to London, I bet.' She continued dusting but her movements had slowed to a mild caress, her mind elsewhere.

'Heavens Mrs B, Meg's worked for Robert for years and she's never once mentioned knowing you. And she's seen you here dozens of times.'

She sniffed, tossing her head. 'Too grand these days to want to remember the likes of Rosie Barton. Secretive little thing. Always was. Got so used to keeping her mouth shut at home it become an 'abit, I reckon.'

'How on earth did you get involved with the Heffers?'

The older woman eased on to the arm of the sofa and leaned forward with all the horrid fascination of the Ancient Mariner.

'I used to work in the school kitchens, see – it was a boys' school in them days like when Mr Browne went there. Anyway, Syd Heffer, he got the job of caretaker and he and his Doreen moved into the caretaker's flat up at the school just before Maggie was a year old. Young Doreen was a silly sort of girl and quite the wrong one for Syd, who was always a bit of a bully.'

Fay was intrigued, fascinated by the ragbag of information Rose Barton so often upended for her.

'Well, I could see right from the start that poor Doreen couldn't cope, head like a sieve for messages and that and Syd never had an ounce of patience with women. Can't think why he got married in the first place. Should have been a monk, my Fred reckons. When Maggie was nearly two Doreen did a flit with a policeman lodging with Florrie Duke who used to live next door to me them days.' Her eyes rolled dramatically. 'Any rate, to cut a long story short, poor old Syd was left holding the baby good and proper. And me and the other girls in the kitchen used to take turns to help him out. To give Syd his due, he wouldn't hear of Maggie going into care or going to live with her gran. Not likely! Doreen disappeared like a puff of smoke, never set foot in the village no more from that day to this. Syd Heffer brought that kid up himself, no joke in a boys' school. And made a pretty good job of it, too. That Maggie had everything of the best, lacked for nothing. Would have given her the top of the Christmas tree he would. Timid little soul though,' she added. 'And a terrible fibber.'

'But if her father's so fond of her what makes you think he'd give her a shiner?'

The old woman shook her head. 'Well, you know what fathers are with their girls. Think they're angels and half the time they're worse than the boys. Syd was always finding her out in something or other and he just couldn't stop himself. Never get away with it these days. Raise your 'and to your kids and you've got social services on your 'ead like a ton of bricks!' She sighed, shaking her head. 'Maggie left him flat as soon as she was old enough. Did a runner just like her mum 'cept this time she 'ad no policeman in tow. Had bigger fish to fry even at that age, and who can blame the girl? I heard she'd gone to London to ask your hubby for a job. Funny kid. Wouldn't say boo to a goose one minute and brassy as you please the next.'

She rose like a galleon breasting the waves. 'Glad she made it up with Syd after all these years though. I heard Maggie was back at the school this week, stayed over at Syd's flat 'n all, so I was told. Blood's thicker than water when all's said and done. Pity she didn't make it up years ago. Still, if she's got a black eye already I reckon neither of 'em 'as changed for the better.' She pursed her lips. 'Typical man! Thinks time stands still. Forgets she's had a life of her own all this time, stupid old fool. Mind you,' she laughed, 'Fred told me they was killing themselves at the Crooked Billet the other week listening to Syd raving about the school going mixed. Driving 'im barmy it is; can't stand bits of girls messing up his cloakrooms. And all them women teachers telling him what to do. And now they've stuffed evening classes an' all on top of it! Gave Syd a young assistant, I heard, but he couldn't keep a civil tongue in 'is 'ead so he's doing the whole lot on his own, poor old devil. His own worst enemy and no mistake.'

Fay quickly broke in as Rose Barton paused for breath, fearing the reminiscences were likely to flow indefinitely. 'By the way, Mrs B, I shall be going to Devon for a few days next week. Old Mr Browne's unwell so I'll drive straight on from Huxtable and spend a couple of days with him to sort things out.'

'Not serious, is it?'

Fay grinned. 'Oh, no. You know how tiresome he can be at times. Probably a fuss about nothing. You'll be able to cope all right if I'm not here for a bit?'

'Don't you fret about a thing, ducky. Do you a power of good to get away.' She opened the lid of the piano and rubbed between the keys making loud jangling dischords, wide hips swinging from side to side. Fay's head ached. She wished Mrs B would do her polishing elsewhere. She made another attempt to read the paper but the old girl had stopped and was regarding her enigmatically. She rumbled on again like a leaky faucet.

'Not that I would have liked to see you go off with Mr Browne this morning.' She closed the lid with a thud. 'I had such a strong picture last night which I felt sure was about you, lovey. You definitely must *not* cross the water while there's a full moon.'

That did it. Fay's irritation evaporated on a gale of laughter. She was unable to contain herself and the expression of affront on the old woman's face made things worse. Fancy coming out with a fortune-teller's cliché like that! Be bringing her crystal ball to work next. Maeve knew a thing or two having a deaf mute to do her hoovering.

Rose Barton stood four-square, determined to have her say.

'You may laugh but I saw it as clear as I see you now. This person lying face down in the water with her coat floating all round her – 'orrible! I don't often get these pictures but when I do I take notice all right. It's no joke, you mark my words, Mrs Browne.'

Fay made a supreme effort to keep a straight face. 'But if this woman you saw in your dream was lying with her face in the water,' she persisted, 'how did you know it was me?'

'Hard to explain, dear. But I came home with your name

41

going over and over in my mind and this awful picture of this poor soul in a brown coat drowned and lying on the bottom.' She shook her head as if to shake off the whole episode. Then her expression transformed with a sly smile. 'Don't worry about it, my duck. You're not going swimming this time of year, are you?'

'Not bloody likely,' Fay muttered to herself, taking a long sip of coffee. 'Anyway,' she said aloud, 'it couldn't have been me. I can't swim.'

Rose Barton shrugged in disbelief and made for the door. Dropping her newspaper, Fay called out, 'There is one other thing, Mrs B. I'm worried about Ottie. She got out yesterday. Could you keep an eye open if you're outside? I'll get Luke to scout round and mention it to Mr Goldsmith. He can ask the girls in the chapel. I doubt whether she's gone far.'

'Soon turn up, you'll see. That rabbit's too timid to fend for itself, I'd say.' She shut the door firmly behind her.

After a few minutes Fay went upstairs to phone Maeve, drearily noting her leaden feet. She promised herself an early night. 'I'm letting these sodding phone calls get me down. Ridiculous.'

She got through immediately.

'Fay, how extraordinary. I was just about to pick up the phone to ring you.'

'I wanted to thank you for the lovely party. Delicious eats, of course.'

'What did you think of the Cresswells? Harvey's a bit heavy, isn't he?'

'You can't expect much sparkle from a Tory agent, you know.'

'And poor old Norah only sparkles about twice a year, I imagine. And then only when her dog's on heat.'

'Naughty. Remarks like that will *not* ease another MacMillan into number ten. You'll have to watch yourself, my girl.'

'Mother of God, won't I just? Ted seems to think I'll be vetted as well as himself.' Her voice lowered. 'What a terrible strain that'll be, poor ignorant sinner that I am.'

'Maeve, they'll be eating out of your hand.'

42

'Well, before I put myself away in a box there's one little favour I need to ask, Fay darlin'.'

'Ask away.' She was apprehensive. Maeve had a knack of involving her in all sorts of disastrous schemes.

'It's Flora. Could you be an angel and give her lunch on Monday week?'

'That'll be OK, I think. I have to go down to see Robert's father but I shall only be gone a few days. Can't Dottie stand in?'

'Oh, Dottie's all right but awfully nosey. And I don't want Ted to find out I'm not taking Flora with me.' Maeve hesitated. 'It's a tiny bit complicated, Fay. I'll explain when I see you.'

'Monday week, you say? A pleasure.' She was glad to have escaped so lightly.

'You're a darlin' girl.'

Fay noted the relieved tone, the lilting accent as soft as Irish rain. Minx.

'I'll ring you when I get back from seeing Bernard, Maeve. Must rush now. I've got to get Luke's show on the road, name tapes to sew on and goodness knows what else. And Hugo's coming to stay over the weekend. Bye now.'

A breeze sifted through the open window. Fay stretched, rose from the bed and walked across the room to look out, scenting wood smoke on the air.

I'll make a start on clearing the dahlias this afternoon, she promised herself. By the time I get back from Pa's it may be too late.

The curtains suddenly billowed inwards like a ghostly intrusion.

Five

Hugo arrived early next day. The crunch of tyres on the gravel before nine on Saturday took her by surprise. So unlike predictable old Hugo. Usually he drove down from London, arriving just before lunch and stayed overnight – or sometimes for several days at a time. He kept a change of clothes in the guest room in the same way that Robert had a pied-à-terre at the Pimlico shop.

She hurried out to greet him as he was uncoiling his crane-like legs from the Morgan. He grinned, tilting his head towards Robert's new Mercedes.

'Rob mentioned he was lending it to you to play with. But I never thought he'd actually go through with it knowing his distaste for your disgusting little runabout.' He walked towards her, swinging a briefcase and looking the same old Hugo. But beneath the banter an underlying strain had taken its toll.

'Well, you've seen it all now. He insisted on it, I promise you!' She laughed. 'It's lovely to see you. Robert didn't warn me you were making it a dawn raid. You must be starving.' She dragged him through to the kitchen. 'Scrambled eggs do?'

'Please, Fay,' he protested. 'I've already breakfasted. Really!'

'But that must have been hours ago.'

'Just after eight as a matter of fact.' He relished her evident disbelief. 'Honestly, love, it's quite simple. I stayed in Renham last night at the Prince of Orange. All very swish.'

Her dismay was almost comic. 'But that's only a stone's throw from here, Hugo. Why on earth book into an hotel? Not "swish" enough for you here any more?'

He smiled but the cheerful facade was paper thin. He looked

jaded. His face had a greyish hue, the old panache overlaid with tension.

'Come on, Fay. You know me better than that. Actually, I've been staying at the Prince for a few days. I had some business in Renham on Wednesday and Robert mentioned you would be dining out Thursday night, so I thought I might as well stay put. I had some quiet thinking to do.' He brightened. 'As a matter of fact, it's very comfortable. I've been feeling a bit run-down lately so it seemed a good idea to stay on an extra night. In any case I had to see Goldsmith this morning so it suited me to get here early. He's got a gang working overtime for me this weekend.'

He perched on the kitchen table and swung his foot. 'Tell you what. When I've had a couple of hours with Goldsmith I'll take you to lunch at the Prince and you can judge for yourself.'

'You're on! Only thing is, Luke's still home. He doesn't go back to school till Monday. He's out in the woods, searching for Ottie.'

'Marvellous.' He stood up, loosening his stiff shoulder muscles and began to look more his old self. 'I haven't seen Luke for months. I promise I won't say any corny things about how big he's grown or how like Robert he's looking!'

'With that red hair! Buckets of Robert's confidence though. I'll walk over to the chapel with you, Hugo. I've been keeping my head down lately, I'm afraid. One can easily get sucked in if Bill Goldsmith thinks there's another pair of hands going begging, and October's always the busiest time for him.'

They strolled through the garden, pausing by the pool to watch the fish darting in and out of the reeds. It was a natural pond fed by a stream, an idyllic spot well secluded from the house. It had become her favourite hidey-hole and water lilies had been planted to pretty up 'Fay's muddy puddle' as Robert called it. The place had a hypnotic appeal and Hugo, who had planned a full schedule that morning, found himself drawn by the circling rhythm of the fishes' course between the broad leaves which obscured much of the surface.

'Is it deep, Fay?'

'Actually, yes. Very. At least eight feet in the middle. I'm not sure how deep exactly but I used to keep it fenced until Luke went to school, and it's still out of bounds when it's frozen over. I should have got it filled in I suppose, but he's old enough to be sensible and it attracts all sorts of wildlife.'

'Did Robert get off all right yesterday?'

'Yes, of course.' She looked up sharply. 'But you were speaking to him just before he left. I had assumed from London. Slyboots!'

Hugo shuffled about in a nervous way she found disconcerting.

'Robert *thought* I was in London. I phoned from the hotel. If I had mentioned being in Renham he would have insisted on getting me over before he left.' He avoided Fay's puzzled stare. 'Robert can be very exhausting, Fay. I've learned to keep my distance when necessary.'

He turned his back on the pool and faced her. His suit was crumpled and under the tie his shirt collar gaped, the top button missing. Hugo Suskind was looking uncharacteristically frayed at the edges.

'He obviously hasn't mentioned anything to you, Fay, but we had one hell of a dust-up last week.'

'Oh, there have been rows before, Hugo. He explodes then looks all astonished when anyone has the audacity to be upset by it. He's probably gone to Houston assuming it will have blown over by the time he gets back. Robert's really an awful coward, Hugo. You know that.'

'Good grief, business rows! We've had hundreds of those. But this was on a personal level and I told him on Thursday that it was time I moved on.'

He stood poised at the edge of the water, tense as a wading bird.

'You can't do that! Robert doesn't mean half of what he says. I can't begin to imagine the firm working out at all without you.'

'Fay, I've made up my mind. Really, it's been simmering for a year or two. I've just lacked the energy to get out.'

He started to walk away and she hurried after him.

'Robert's pushy. I know what you mean. He seems to drain

the colour from everyone around him. Poor man, it's not deliberate. I've assumed something of a sepia tint myself in the last few years. The bloom of inertia you could call it.' Her laughter was thin.

'I shall make some definite arrangements before he gets back. I've allowed myself to be talked out of it before but I know it's time to split. We've changed too much. And to tell the truth, Fay, this high-powered stuff scares me stiff.'

They passed through the orchard, their feet crushing a path through grass dotted with toadstools. Cobwebs spangled the bushes and the air was damp. She shivered.

'Have you anything else in mind, Hugo?'

'Not really. I phoned the accountant last week and asked him to draw up some preliminary figures which Rob and I can go over later. Fortunately, old Goldsmith keeps the stock list in tip-top order. I imagine it can all be sorted out quite quickly.' He squeezed her elbow. 'Rob will always make a success of things, Fay. You have absolutely no worry on that score.'

'But what will *you* do?'

'I haven't really decided. I've been offered something interesting at one of the new universities but I've been away too long. I shall probably take a holiday for a couple of months and then start again.'

They reached the chapel and stood on the worn stone step.

'There's plenty of scope for both of us. I might even keep the shop if Robert's agreeable. We could always cooperate, of course. But I must be independent.'

They stepped inside. Brilliantly lit by fluorescent tubing set along the old oak beams, shelves reached from floor to rafters on every side. Pews had been removed, leaving a large central area where four metal desks were pushed together to form a dispatch pool. Six or seven men and girls were working, two on ladders at the high shelves. A man in his sixties hastily replaced the telephone receiver and rose from behind one of the desks, smiling broadly.

'Good morning, Mrs Browne. Mr Suskind. Mr Browne told me you had a big order to check over the weekend so I took the liberty of asking some of the staff to do a bit of overtime.' He waved towards his private army. 'They've already made a start with the lists you sent down.'

'That's awfully good of you, Bill. It's a rush job. As ever, eh? I shall probably work through the weekend but I'll see you on Monday to finalise transport.' He turned to Fay. 'It may take longer than I thought but I hope to finish by Monday night. May I stay over till Tuesday or Wednesday if necessary?'

'Of course. I'll ask Mrs B to look after you if you have to work over. I shall be away for a few days next week but your room's always ready.' In an undertone she added, 'Depending perhaps on whether something more tempting lurks at the Prince of Orange?'

He smiled. Waving to those at the far end of the warehouse, they linked arms and wandered outside. The sun had broken through, accentuating the foggy skirts which shrouded the trunks of the apple trees. The upper branches seemed to float a few feet above the ground, the fruit gleaming gold and pink.

Hugo drove Fay and Luke into Renham for lunch and they must have appeared a carefree, noisy family party. Afterwards, he brought work through to Robert's study and soldiered on till after nine. Fay felt much happier since he had arrived. She, of all people, understood his need to escape, understood it all too well. Robert's overriding ambition was unstoppable. No wonder Hugo had had enough.

But the germ of an idea began to take shape. Perhaps with Hugo and half the business gone there might be a place for her in a smaller operation. She could give up the Law Centre and work with Robert again like the old days. Pick up the threads. His success had shut her out. But Robert cut down to size might be more amenable to turning back the clock. Or was she being hopelessly nostalgic?

Her mental ramblings abruptly scattered when the anonymous caller telephoned just after ten. She had relaxed, thinking the nuisance had run its course. Nothing was said. Her imagination reached desperately towards the prospect of a few quiet days with Pa away from here. Perhaps by the time she returned her mysterious caller would have abandoned this senseless persecution. 'Why me?' Rationally, she argued it was madness to allow it to frighten her so much. But the fear was instinctive and somehow shaming. No smoke without fire? She said nothing about it to Hugo.

On Monday Fay drove the two boys back to school. They yacked in the back of the Mercedes, forgetting apprehensions of starting back late – if they were secretly harbouring any – leaving Fay free to sift her own problems. Pa's peculiarities were becoming a real headache, but losing Hugo loomed larger on her worry list. Presumably the London staff would stay on with Hugo but Robert would be totally lost without Bill Goldsmith to run the warehouse and the mail order side. But the foreman was bound to stay on in Stamford – he was as rooted in the place as Robert. Oh, she supposed it would all work out … At least the Barbara Hertz inquest could be mentally shelved till the end of the week. There was a limit to the number of things one could worry about.

Maeve had a theory about worry. She insisted that everyone had their own private quota which remained constant. The lack of any serious disquiet merely allowed minor considerations to jump the queue, and the congenital worrier lay awake picking away at things which in more stressful circumstances wouldn't get a look in. Fay smiled grimly to herself. She was under no illusions about the serious nature of her own current concerns, whatever Maeve's cock-eyed theory made of them.

Driving west, the trees seemed to grow in stature, straddling the fields like giants. The air was still and cows stood immobile like cattle in a painted landscape.

Disposing of the boys at Huxtable went smoothly and she made a rapid farewell, leaving them in the vaulted hall with Matron, their gear forming untidy heaps around them on the streaky marble floor. The place smelled inexorably of school: a whiff of over-cooked sprouts mixed with something like sweaty trainers. Unforgettable. She escaped to the car, her undignified haste masked by the smooth progress of the Mercedes as it circled in front of the building then surged back along the avenue of chestnuts.

She drove swiftly to Moreton, the car responding smoothly under her hands, devouring the miles with effortless rapidity.

Within a couple of hours it had passed through the high gates of the rural estate on which Robert's father rented a cottage. Beyond the gatehouse the road quickly deteriorated and soon split into two muddy lanes. Fay frowned, peering through the gathering dusk to avoid huge potholes and wishing, for the first time, she had the Metro. Apart from the stones that ricocheted loudly under the chassis, it occurred to her that an expensive car would do nothing to smooth relations with Pa's critical neighbours, who clearly considered his rightful place to be in Stamford. Me too, she ruefully admitted, but life's not as simple as that.

Fay stayed away until late on Wednesday and parked on the drive just after ten. Far from finding the visit exhausting, she felt refreshed. She let herself into the house and switched on the lights. It seemed enormous after Pa's cottage. It hardly seemed possible she had been away only three days. She made a pot of coffee and switched on the electric fire in the study. There were some bills for Robert which Mrs B had placed on his desk, and an open letter for herself propped against the inkstand. She dropped into the armchair and filled her cup before reading it. The note was from Hugo.

'My dear Fay, Thanks for the warm bed.' She wondered what Mrs B made of that! 'Finished Monday evening so I'm off. The phone seems faulty so I reported it. See you soon I hope. Love Hugo.'

There was a postscript. 'Mrs Barton seemed to think I should mention that the rabbit's still off, whatever that means. Sounds like salmonella.'

She went through to the kitchen and washed up. The house was unbearably quiet. After obsessively checking the doors and windows she picked up the radio to take upstairs, consoling herself that a voice of any kind would be company, even that of the newsreader. The hairs on the nape of her neck rose as another thought mocked the first. Not *any* voice, surely? Switching out the lights, she resolutely took the receivers off *all* the telephones, putting paid to the dreaded attentions of the practical joker. She slept badly nevertheless, tossing and fretful, a thousand useless anxieties coming home to roost.

Next morning everything seemed less dismal and Fay decided to spend the day outdoors. Make a final onslaught on the untidy autumn borders. Keep busy. She made a start on the dense shrubbery behind the chapel warehouse.

She worked for an hour, systematically clearing and forking round the sagging outhouse, hoping to catch a glimpse of Ottie in the bushes. She felt better already, relaxing into a strong rhythm, cutting the foliage down to stubble with wide swings of a lethal-looking machete. A spike of brilliant scarlet caught her eye and she hesitated, parting a clump of irises. Fat seed pods bursting with berries were revealed, obscenely vibrant in the dying undergrowth. Like gaping wounds.

Bill Goldsmith's shout startled her. He called to her across the grass and, straightening, she saw he was accompanied by a familiar figure. The foreman started to exclaim from twenty yards away, waving cheerfully as he limped towards her.

'Mrs Browne. So you *are* there. Couldn't get any reply from the house and came to the chapel to see if you were with us.' As they drew level he confidently added, 'I told him I'm sure I know where to find Mrs Browne, if she's at home at all that is. Plenty to do at this end of the year if you're a gardener like this lady. That's true, isn't it, Mrs Browne?'

Fay nodded, but before she could speak Bill Goldsmith was off again. 'Detective Chief Inspector Hayes,' he said importantly. He didn't seem to grasp the possibility that she was all too familiar with the man. 'Parking on yellow lines again, Mrs Browne?'

The policeman made no attempt to interrupt, standing quietly aside, watching her as she stripped off her gloves and pushed back her hair, embarrassed by his stare, the composed manner. She thought the Hertz case had been all wrapped up. No loose ends he said. Surely Hugo's complaint to the telephone engineer had merely reported a fault, not set another police investigation in motion?

While they warily eyed one another Bill Goldsmith rattled on, explaining the need for more security at the warehouse.

'As I said to Mr Suskind, it's not good enough leaving the gates open at night.' He turned to Roger Hayes, appealing for support. 'Security's very important these days, isn't it, sir? And the stock's under-insured if you ask me. Arson's no joke in this trade – some lads from Renham have done—'

'Absolutely,' Fay interjected. 'We must have a serious talk about it when Robert gets back, Bill. But perhaps the inspector is too busy to chat about our security arrangements just now.'

Firmly fixing Hayes with, 'Shall we go inside, Inspector?' she started back to the house, waving curtly to the foreman as she stepped out.

'I'll be off then,' Goldsmith said, a note of disappointment in his voice. 'There's a mountain of work waiting for me,' he lamely added, turning to shuffle back to the warehouse.

Hayes followed Fay to the back door. It was not until they stood in the sitting room that he spoke for the first time. His words were formal, no lead-in, no pleasantries, no reference to the forthcoming inquest. Fay listened without comprehension. She must have looked blank. He patiently repeated the question.

'Mrs Browne, do you own a car with the registration number FAY 23JB?'

'Y – yes. Yes, I do. A Metro. But it's not here, Inspector.'

'I regret to inform you a car bearing that number was involved in a collision on the M4 on Tuesday night.'

Fay sat down, shaking her head.

'I'm afraid you've been sent on a wild goose chase. There's some mistake. My husband left the car at a garage near Heathrow on Friday before flying to Paris and on to the States. Banks Hill Garage. He rents a space there, uses it regularly.' She indicated a chair. 'May I offer you some coffee, Chief Inspector?'

He remained standing. 'No, thank you. There's no mistake. I've confirmed the details. It's not really my case but I heard about it at the station and, in view of our involvement over the past few days, I felt it necessary to speak to you personally.'

Fay raised her eyebrows, his formality doubly irritating since they were, as he implied, by no means strangers. In an odd way the tragedy of the woman on the railway line was a bond, the nightmare details raw as a blood ritual between them.

'In that case, someone must have stolen my car for a joyride. Though why anyone would choose an old banger like that I can't imagine.' She smiled in mock reproof. 'My car's no hotrod, Chief Inspector.'

His expression did not flicker. 'This is no laughing matter, Mrs Browne. The driver was killed.'

Fay felt the colour drain from her cheeks. 'My God, how dreadful. Who was he?'

'Not he, Mrs Browne. The driver was a woman. When they couldn't get in touch with you it was at first assumed you were driving the car yourself. But the lady's handbag was locked in a suitcase in the boot. It contained information which Thames Valley Police followed up, and the deceased was finally identified by her father last night. It was Margaret Heffer, who was, I understand, your husband's personal assistant.'

Shock cauterized her speech. Hayes' eyes narrowed. When she eventually spoke the words came in a gasp.

'Was Meg alone?'

'Yes.'

She slumped with relief. 'What a terrible thing. She was booked on the plane with Robert. Perhaps she felt ill and came back to Heathrow after Paris.'

'Perhaps.'

'Is there anything you need from me? Papers, insurance, something like that?' Her voice had regained its normal level tones.

'The latest MOT certificate and details of your insurance cover would be helpful.'

'Oh, dear. My husband deals with those things and he generally locks papers like that in his safe. I'll look in the study and bring them to the station if they surface, but you may have to wait until he gets back.'

'I noticed another car in the drive. Yours, Mrs Browne?'

'The Mercedes. No, that's Robert's car. But he left it for me to use while he's away.'

'Do you have a contact number in America? There are some questions I need to ask. A mobile telephone number would do.'

'I'm afraid not. He usually travels about a good deal on these trips. But a list of places where he can be reached is left at his office in London. He doesn't use a mobile when he's abroad, he always phones me – it's easier to keep in touch that way. He's always in meetings if I try to speak to him. Normal wifey moan.' The feeble attempt to lighten the conversation fell on deaf ears and she hurried out to fetch one of Robert's business cards from the study. When she came back, Roger Hayes was still standing on the same sunlit patch of carpet, frankly appraising the room.

She handed him the card, which he carefully placed in his notebook.

'I'm sure Hugo Suskind can give you any further information you may need.' She thought for a moment. 'May I ask if Miss Heffer had actually left the country, Inspector?'

'No passport or air tickets were listed in the personal effects. In fact, there was very little to go on, and until the dead woman was identified, the fact that you yourself had apparently disappeared muddied the water in no small measure. Did Mr Browne make a habit of lending your car to his secretary?'

'Oh, everyone borrows my car. Even Bill Goldsmith if necessary. Do you have any details of the accident? How it happened, I mean?'

'I understand Margaret Heffer crashed into the back of a lorry slowing down to enter a filter lane beside road repairs. Driving too fast presumably.'

'How odd. She was such a careful driver, the very last person to be speeding. Robert used to pull her leg about it.'

'Did you know her long?'

'Oh, yes. Meg's worked for us for years. She used to live in Stamford and approached him for a job when she moved to London.'

He continued to make painstaking notes. Fay watched him turn the page and was wondering how to speed things up when he raised his eyes and said, 'Did you know Miss Heffer was twelve weeks pregnant?'

Fay gasped. 'Of course not! Why the hell should Meg tell me her personal business? She was employed mostly in London. If she confided in anyone it would have been Robert and he didn't mention it.'

'Has the name of a man – a boyfriend – cropped up?'

'I hardly knew her. She wasn't the sort of girl to talk about her personal affairs. Certainly not to me at any rate.'

'Did you *like* your husband's secretary?'

Fay shrugged. 'Not much. But she was extremely efficient. A career girl. Robert relied on her a great deal but he never mentioned Meg's love life and I was never sufficiently interested to enquire.'

He said nothing and Fay continued, the words carefully chosen, the tone impersonal.

'I didn't see much of her actually. Meg came to Stamford only occasionally, there was very little reason for her to work at this end of the business.' She waved her hand vaguely towards the garden. 'The chapel is used as a warehouse – for dispatch and storage – as you've probably gathered from Mr Goldsmith. But negotiations are conducted in London. Buyers don't come here.'

Roger Hayes looked at her curiously, waiting for some elaboration she guessed. What was he getting at? Fay rose and found herself holding open the door, confused by his line of questioning.

'She shared a flat in London. Fulham, I think. I haven't the address but you could ask Hugo Suskind. Her flatmate would know more about her friends.'

He put the notebook away and loitered in the hall as she opened the front door. He seemed in no hurry to leave, frankly looking about, taking everything in. The sunlight etched fine lines about her mouth and the shadows under her eyes stressed the exhaustion which had dogged her for days. The Mercedes stood on the drive. In the sunshine the mud-caked wheels and spattered paintwork looked almost like vandalism, at best deliberate carelessness. They both regarded the car and Fay felt her conscience lurch when confronted by Robert's pride and joy in such obvious disarray.

'May I ask where you've been for the past few days, Mrs Brown? We've been trying to reach you.'

'I've been staying with my father-in-law in the west country. Not that it's relevant, surely? I wouldn't want him troubled in any way. He's an old man and already in a confused mental state. I shall be at the Hertz inquest tomorrow – I won't run away, if that's what's worrying you. My statement was entirely satisfactory, wasn't it? The accident ...?'

'Oh, yes. Of course. It seems to be a bad time for you all round, Mrs Browne. Two accidents, both women you barely remember. Never rains but it pours as they say.'

She abruptly stepped back but remained composed. He admired her self-control. The woman was a cool customer, he was prepared to admit that, not one to be caught off balance. A quick thinker too. Trying to save that Hertz woman was a lightning move. Even so ...

'You won't forget to let me have the MOT certificate, will you? Leave it on the desk at the station if I'm not there.'

'I can't promise to lay my hands on it immediately. As I said, you may have to wait until Robert can open the wall safe in his study. I'm careless with cars but Robert's clever with engines and keeps a very close watch on the mechanical side of things. The Stamford Motor Company has records of servicing, I'm sure.'

His gaze slipped behind her shoulder as she stood at the front door. The telephone was still off the hook from the night before, the receiver laid on the hall table.

'I wondered why I could only get the engaged tone, Mrs Brown. All the phones off the hook?'

She replaced the receiver. 'I had had a long journey yesterday and preferred to sleep undisturbed. No night calls ...' she limply added.

'Even from your husband?'

He buttoned his jacket and, making a half-salute, passed Robert's car and unlocked his own. 'Till tomorrow then. The inquest at Renham.'

Just as if she could forget!

Fay didn't wait to see him drive off. She closed the door and leaned against it, thoughts whirling inside her skull like snared birds. What was that snide remark he made about 'two women you barely remember'? A sneaky barb about a secretary was one thing, but why imply she had known Barbara Hertz?

56

Six

When the doorbell rang shortly before eight the following morning, she assumed it to be the postman. It came as a shock to find Hayes back on the doorstep. The same neat dark suit and the same sober expression. But this time he had another plain clothes policeman in tow. Her spirits sank. She moved aside to allow them through, surreptitiously replacing the telephone receiver as they passed. Surely she was not being taken to the inquest under escort? Did he really think she would abscond? His prime witness?

'Good morning. Please come in, Chief Inspector.'

They all trooped into the sitting room, Hayes taking up the same place on the carpet as the day before. It was as if they were caught up in a whirlpool, inexorably passing the same spot, circling a vortex. He introduced the other man. A Sergeant Bellamy.

'Won't you sit down?' she said.

'No, thank you, Mrs Browne. Shall we get on? There's a lot to do today.' The sergeant stood by, a silent onlooker.

Fay took the window seat again, her face obscure, any expression that might cross her grey eyes shadowed. Two could play at that game.

She said, 'I'm afraid I was unable to find the insurance papers you were asking for. Robert will be home in a few days if that isn't too late.' Within the sunny framework of the window her red hair flamed, brightly rimmed like stained glass.

'It's not urgent. I was able to get most of the information I needed from the garage in Stamford. Did you know that a new car is there for you? The manager tells me it's only waiting for the paperwork concerning the transfer of your personalised number plate from the Metro.'

Her surprise was evident.

'No, I didn't. But then Robert never consults me about cars.'

'Perhaps he meant it as a peace offering after this trip?'

She frowned. 'That would be an extravagant gesture even from Robert. You've got a funny idea of my husband's business trips – they're not foreign frolics for which he has to apologise. He travels all the time, and believe it or not, all that flying and living out of a suitcase is no fun.'

'A surprise then?' he conceded.

'That's more likely. I certainly hadn't expected a new car.'

'Did you complain about the Metro?' the sergeant put in. 'Was there any mechanical fault you'd noticed, Mrs Browne?'

'Nothing. Nothing at all. It was a scruffy little runabout but perfectly satisfactory. Surely the garage confirmed that? It was serviced only recently.'

Hayes took back the initiative and said, 'By the way, I've been unable to trace Mr Browne's whereabouts. Have you been in touch yourself?'

Fay shook her head. 'Have you asked his partner for Robert's itinerary?'

'Yes, indeed. Mr Suskind has been very cooperative. I called to see him in London yesterday and he kindly agreed to search Mr Browne's desk to see if the car insurance papers were at the office.'

She felt herself flushing with irritation. 'But I told you! He keeps all those things locked up *here*.'

'I like to make quite sure, Mrs Browne. I did notice that your husband had a local appointment in his business diary for two o'clock on Friday afternoon.'

'That's impossible. He left with Meg Heffer that morning. He would have been on the plane at two.'

'I checked with the airline. He caught a plane to Paris in the early evening, but alone. Miss Heffer did not accompany him.'

'Oh, I understand,' she said bleakly, understanding nothing at all, or even why these two policemen were even here.

'The appointment was with a Dr Meredith at the Shane

Clinic, which is less than forty minutes' drive from Stamford.'

'But Robert's never ill. He doesn't even have check-ups.'

'The appointment was for Miss Heffer.'

'Checking up on her too?'

'The appointment was made in your name, Mrs Browne, and your husband saw her admitted.'

The silence was electric. After a pause she blurted out, 'Perhaps she was embarrassed to use her own name for a gynaecological consultation. Presumably the Shane was monitoring her pregnancy. A scan? Some sort of test?' That this pedantic flatfoot could lead her to bumble on like this, to sound prudish and censorious, was intolerable.

'Miss Heffer was not seeking medical advice. She was seeking an abortion,' Hayes said. The sergeant coughed.

'Oh.' The monosyllable summed up her bewilderment. Everything this man said about Meg was totally out of character. He might as well be discussing a stranger. Meg did *not* drive recklessly. Also, she was not the sort of girl to become carelessly pregnant and then have second thoughts about it. And even if she had, Meg would certainly not be too shy to use her own name at an abortion clinic. The Shane had a certain reputation, the last place to encounter disapproval. If this was one of Robert's jokes, it was in pretty poor taste.

'Mr Browne made the arrangements himself. Margaret Heffer was to enter the clinic on Friday the sixth and afterwards to travel to an hotel in Gwent to recuperate. It was not her first visit. If he made the arrangements on an office phone he may have used his own surname to prevent any gossip about his personal assistant – walls have ears as they say. If he left here shortly after nine, they must have stopped for lunch or on a business call before they arrived for the appointment at two. The medical director confirmed the facts of her case, Mrs Browne. Your husband paid the clinic, and also the hotel bill. In advance.'

Her hands flexed in her lap as he remorselessly continued. 'As it happens, Heffer discharged herself from the clinic half an hour after Mr Browne left, and there's no record of her movements after that. Up to the accident, of course.'

Fay took a deep breath before launching into a desperate effort to salvage something from all this.

'I'm not sure what inference you are inviting me to draw but I am completely in the dark. Robert, as I told you, employed Meg Heffer for years and no doubt felt it necessary to assist her in a discreet way. If he helped her to cover up these arrangements at a time she was assumed to be in the States, and if he loaned her the money to pay the medical expenses, he was only acting as any sympathetic employer would. As soon as he gets home he will, most definitely, be able to confirm what I say.'

'But you have absolutely no idea where he is, do you? Or whether, in fact, he intends to come home at all?'

Even the sergeant choked on this last shot in the dark. Hayes had gone too far this time.

Fay refused to rise to the bait and crossed the room to show them out. 'I won't even bother to answer that, Inspector Hayes. If there's nothing else, I really do have a lot of things to attend to. You seem to be making the most impertinent investigation of what is, to put it bluntly, just one more appalling traffic statistic.'

The two men made no move to leave, Hayes smoothly stating, 'Merely pursuing the normal enquiries following a suspicious death, Mrs Browne. I have here a copy of the vehicle engineer's report and there are conflicting views on the mechanical standards of your car as given to me by Stamford Motors. Are you absolutely sure, Mrs Browne, you hadn't noticed any looseness in the braking system before you loaned the car to Margaret Heffer?'

'No. No. I've already told you. It ran perfectly, and in any case I didn't lend the Metro to her. Robert used it to drive to the airport.' She scrabbled about in her memory for the tiny confirmation she sought, snapping her fingers as the picture cleared.

'Yes, I do remember. I went to Renham just before Robert went away. It was the Thursday morning, the day I came into your office to give my statement. In fact, that was the last time I drove it. A cat ran out and I had to stop suddenly. Perhaps someone in the new houses heard the screech of brakes or saw me pass? The owner of the cat maybe?' She relaxed. 'No, Inspector, there is absolutely no question of the brakes being faulty and,' she added in triumph, 'the tyres were almost new.'

'According to the police report there is mild corrosion on the supply pipes which might have caused a braking failure. Brake fluid had been seeping, possibly caused by a loose nut.' He quoted directly from a typed sheet. 'The engineer notes that a nut on the brake pipe was shiny as if it had been recently tampered with, but was slightly soiled with use. He was unable to give a definite opinion whether the leak had occurred through wear or was caused by the nut being loosened manually. As you maintain, Mrs Browne, the brakes were entirely safe the day before handing it over, can you recall anyone fiddling with the mechanics *after* that?'

Pictures slotted slowly across Fay's inner vision like old-fashioned lantern slides. One remorselessly repeated itself as if some blip had fouled up her recollection: Robert hung over the Metro checking the engine the morning of his departure. She fought to dispel it, worrying at the location of this brake pipe Hayes was talking about. Surely that must be *under* the car? Struggling to control rising panic Fay made a supreme effort to concentrate as he continued.

'Will you please think back carefully? You say your husband regularly checked your car himself. Did he overhaul it between the last service and the day he took it away?'

'No. He had no time to look at the car. Between my emergency stop to avoid the cat and Robert's departure next morning he was fully occupied. He had urgent business arrangements to discuss with Hugo between getting home after an evening with friends on Thursday and leaving the next morning. He was on the telephone for an hour before he left at nine.'

The ensuing silence seemed final and Hayes slowly refolded the police report and clipped it inside his notebook, nodding to the sergeant. Fay opened the door and went into the hall without a word. He followed closely and they faced each other under the porch.

'I think that concludes my questions at present, but I shall need a statement from your husband before the Heffer inquest.

Until we can fill in Margaret Heffer's movements after she left the clinic, Mr Browne would seem to be one of the last to see her alive.'

He smiled grimly. 'We shall require Mr Browne's opinion of the braking system when he drove the car himself, although as the clinic is only a short distance from here he may have experienced no anxiety on that score. Depends really if they had a little ride round before lunch, doesn't it? The receptionist at the clinic confirmed that the Heffer woman retained the Metro and the receptionist ordered a hire car to take him to the airport. She remembers it all very clearly. Quite a problem for her to persuade a driver to go so far at short notice. Mr Suskind told me he had a message to say his partner would be with an American colleague on a hunting expedition in Texas for several days, so it will be a little while before we can get in touch. But, of course, you know all that.'

Her blank response confirmed his hunch. Robert Browne had simply disappeared.

Hayes said kindly, 'You look exhausted, if I may say so. I should try to relax if I were you. Nothing can be done until he turns up, and there's this inquest on Barbara Hertz to get through today.'

'Y–yes,' she stuttered. 'You're right. Actually, I haven't been sleeping well lately. There have been several anonymous phone calls and I've stupidly let it play on my nerves.'

He stared as if a fresh thought had struck home.

'Of course! I queried the number with the exchange when I couldn't get through and apparently there was a complaint about a fault on the line. But there was no suggestion of a nuisance call.'

'No. A friend reported it. He'd been staying for the weekend, as a matter of fact. Hugo Suskind. I didn't tell him about the anonymous calls and he assumed it was a mechanical defect of some kind.'

'But you were away.'

'That's right. I left on Monday to stay with my father-in-law. I mentioned it to you.'

Hayes reassumed his formal tone, the fleeting moment of

kindness evaporated. 'You should have informed the police, Mrs Browne. You must have the occasional disgruntled client at the Law Centre. Ms Baker told me there was trouble there the evening you last attended, the night Barbara Hertz died. Did this anonymous caller of yours make any improper remarks?'

'No. Nothing was ever said.'

'Are you sure no one is threatening you?'

'Of course not,' she snapped. 'It's just a stupid person with nothing to do in the evenings. Kids select phone numbers from the directory and amuse themselves by ringing up – it's not uncommon. You must have dozens of complaints about this sort of nuisance behaviour. It's a modern version of Knock Down Ginger, I suppose.'

'These calls only occur at night?'

'The phone rings about six o'clock and then two or three times after that. It's really not that important, Inspector. It's very silly of me to get so jumpy.'

'If these calls continue, perhaps you would ring me at the station? It's possible to put a trace, and from what you say the timing seems predictable. All incoming calls can be intercepted as you well know.'

'Yes, of course. I'll bear that in mind.'

From the corner of her eye she glimpsed Bill Goldsmith and Mrs B deep in conversation near the shrubbery. The comings and goings of the police would not go unremarked in a place like Stamford. She hurried inside and closed the door, shutting out all the scrutiny, feeling like a butterfly on a pin.

Fay drove into town to get the car cleaned, taking the same route through the estate as before, the last time she had driven the Metro. The day had clouded and the new houses looked shoddy, robbed of the sparkle of that other morning which now seemed an age away. Perhaps it was her own mood – a sense of indefinable dread overlaying her every thought like mildew.

Did Hayes really believe Robert capable of causing a leak in the braking system and then take himself off? Virtually disappear while the investigation took place? Anyone could have tampered with the car. Nobody knew where Meg had gone after leaving the clinic on Friday afternoon. She had obviously gone somewhere for a long weekend – with someone? The man in her life? Hayes was implying Meg presented some sort of threat to Robert. Perhaps that overzealous detective thought those silent phone calls were a blackmailer's reminder. Maybe he even thought *she* had some motive for wanting Meg dead. Or Hugo? Or the father of Meg's baby, whoever that might be.

The pregnancy was the crucial issue. Robert's reputation as a charmer had come home to roost with a vengeance. There was only one way to stop this fearful investigation. The spectre of old sins rose in her mind with all the clarity of a neon sign proclaiming, 'I told you so'.

Fay manouvred the Mercedes down the side entrance of the Stamford Motor Company's repair shop. Cars for servicing and new cars for the showroom jammed the narrow entry and, in despair, she abandoned the vehicle in the forecourt. Leaving the keys in the ignition, she hurried through to the office. The switchboard girl continued reading and after a minute Fay pressed the buzzer in exasperation. She looked up petulantly and slammed down her magazine but as Fay was about to speak the service manager appeared from the workshop.

'Mrs Browne! You haven't come for your new car, have you? It's not quite ready – all the red tape about the number plates and—'

'No. Not that.' She drummed her fingers on the counter and the girl on the switchboard regarded her with bored indifference. The man looked confused.

Fay said, 'It's not the new car. I don't think I'm meant to know about it, Owen. Perhaps we could leave that for my husband to sort out. A surprise. He didn't mention it, you see. Someone else told me.' It all sounded a bit vague.

'Sorry. Trust me to let the cat out of the bag.' He lit a cigarette. 'Truth is, he only ordered it last week – wasn't fussy about the make or anything – and I had this sudden cancellation, and as it's such a funny colour and with dark windows 'n all, it might have been difficult to place. You might not even like it, Mrs Browne. It's certainly more of a goer than your old Metro. But I thought I'd better give Mr Browne first refusal as he seemed to think yours was no cop. Funny thing that. Knocked me sideways when that police bloke come in here and says it's a write-off on the M4 only days after Mr Browne decides to change it. P'raps your char, old Rosie Barton, tipped him the wink, eh? Saw it in her crystal ball?'

Fay gave a nervous laugh and the switchboard girl's shoulders twitched. Everyone found it wonderfully amusing. How sick to joke about a fatal accident like that. Probably some sort of defensive reaction. Like touching wood.

She changed the subject, briskly bringing them all back to the matter in hand. 'It's the Merc, Owen. I'm using it myself while Robert's abroad and I'm afraid I've got it in a bit of a clart. It needs hosing down. Come and see.'

He lifted the flap of the counter and led her through to the forecourt where the Merecedes was parked. The mud had dried to a khaki haze on the dark blue paintwork and the tyres were caked like a tractor.

'Blimey! You should have a Range Rover, Mrs Browne.'

He threw away his cigarette and bent down to examine the wheels. 'And you want it to look good as new before the old man sees it, I s'pose?'

'Well, er, yes,' she muttered. 'I know you don't usually do this sort of thing, and you're obviously busy, but I'd never be able to get off all that mud even in a car wash. It needs cleaning properly. I've been in the country. If you've got a lad spare perhaps he could wax it for me afterwards.' She bit her lip. 'I really don't see how I can tackle it myself.'

He squeezed her elbow. 'Just for you, Mrs Browne. I'll ask Gary to do it for you. He's a bit simple but makes a smashing job of car washing and sweeping up.'

Fay grabbed her jacket from the passenger seat. 'Owen, you're a godsend! I have to go into Renham. When can I pick it up?'

'The lad's due back any minute. I'll put him on to it this afternoon but it won't be ready till after three.'

'Could you possibly let me have a small hire car for the day?'

'Take the red Escort in the forecourt. Madge'll give you the keys.'

'Marvellous. Our little secret, Owen, not a word to Robert about all this. Make out a bill for the valeting and the hire expenses today. I'll pay this afternoon. Don't put it on the account.'

She flung a brilliant smile at him before turning to hurry back to the front office. He stared after her, admiring the sheer tights and smart black suit. All very formal. He guessed where she was off to. The inquest would be in all the local papers. That poor cow who threw herself on the line. Bad luck Mrs Browne being the only decent witness. Still, at least she hadn't been the one to top herself in the bloody Metro. Been worried sick since that inspector bloke had him over the coals about the brakes. Rumours like that could ruin any repair shop.

Fay drove straight to Renham. The inquest was adjourned pending further police enquiries. She was stunned, as was the stationmaster. Hayes seemed non-committal but Fay's evidence that 'she did not jump' came across loud and clear, a statement she had imagined would have tipped the balance on the side of 'misadventure' or whatever was the official stamp in accidents like that. But her remark had evidently planted the impression that Barbara Hertz had not deliberately thrown herself on the line, and that some darker cause had yet to be investigated. Fay had never expected her gut instinct to be given such weight. What a stupid thing to say! She should have kept her opinion to herself, a remark made under stress about someone she didn't even know. But it seemed unfair to offer no lifeline – a suicide verdict would have left a bitter aftertaste for the family.

Afterwards, Fay caught sight of the Hertz woman's sister, a severe-looking party in a purple coat, stern and untearful. Millicent Ambache spoke to no one and departed swiftly, as anxious to get away as herself. Fay was almost disappointed. Her firm evidence had disposed of any lingering impression that Barbara Hertz had thrown herself on the line, but she had half expected a kind word from the sister.

But Miss Ambache seemed almost to blame Fay for the accident, casting a vengeful shadow from the well of the court-room, her dark eyes riveted on her as she gave evidence. For a fleeting moment Fay felt sure she had seen the woman before.

Then she remembered. No wonder the white features seemed familiar: they were twins. The face she recognized was the same white disc that had swung up at her as she had tried to grasp the plastic of Barbara Hertz's raincoat. She shuddered, hurrying away, keeping her head averted from the curious bystanders waiting outside.

Seven

Hayes reported straight back to his superintendent, who was impatient for a briefing on the Hertz inquest.

'What next?' he spluttered. 'A full enquiry into every bloody speeding offence?'

Supt Waller was a bull of a man, fiftyish, and none too enthusiastic about adding to an already formidable workload. Renham was a nice little manor in his view, crime mainly restricted to burglary, a fair bit of vandalism and the inevitable call-outs to wife battering and pub brawls. No rapes, no murders and no mysteries requiring the nit-picking attentions of his overzealous new chief inspector.

'It's a suspicious death, sir. The Browne woman says she didn't jump and the sister, a Miss Ambache, insists the victim was not suicidal.'

'Motive?'

Hayes shrugged.

'Suspect?'

'Mrs Browne was behind her and the obvious witness, and despite what she says *did*, according to the sister, know Barbara Hertz. It was in my report.'

'Years ago, Hayes! Met the victim years ago! Why drag all that in? Believe me, getting on the wrong side of Robert Browne and his lot is a dodgy game. If you took the trouble to make yourself familiar with the local politics here, you'd realize that Browne and his cronies are a sight more important than a woman intent on claiming her sister's death was no suicide. Catholic is she?'

'No, definitely not.'

'What's your problem, Hayes?'

68

'Gut feeling, sir. There's more to this than the Brownes are willing to say. Funny business, the Browne's PA dying in a car crash, the brake failure is still under investigation and—'

Waller broke into a guffaw. 'You're not dreaming up a double murder, are you, Hayes? Mrs Browne shoving some poor woman in front of a train while her other half polishes off his secretary? Or maybe the wife did both of them in? A serial murderer?'

Hayes stiffened. 'No harm in checking it out, is there, sir? We don't want to be accused of sweeping anything under the carpet just because a local bigwig's wife's involved?'

The phone rang. Waller snatched up the receiver and after a few moments dismissed Hayes with a curt wave of the hand.

After the inquest Fay drove to the council car park. The library was stifling and she loosened her jacket before approaching the desk. The assistant looked up with a myopic stare.

'I want a medical directory if there is such a thing. Something which lists addresses if possible.'

'Local? Those are on the computer over there.'

'No. London. A directory like Crockford, only for doctors not clergy.'

'Upstairs then. These directories are not always up to date you know. There's one in the reference section, left of the oversize art book shelves.'

She hurried up the stairway and found herself in a gloomy long gallery with a row of tables set along the window side and books everywhere else. In a way, not unlike the warehouse at home she decided, but more holy. The chapel was always noisy with laughter and shouted conversations, Bill Goldsmith fussily orchestrating, phones constantly ringing. Her eyes slowly accustomed to the inadequate lighting which was due, she imagined, to council economies. As there was only one other person there their budgetary priorities were spot on.

The other browser was also poring over the medical books. It seemed rude to stand so close to the woman while all the other shelves stood unattended. They fastidiously avoided each other as if the printed medical symptoms were contagious. Fay pulled a volume from the shelf and took it to one of the tables. She rustled the pages. Sutton-Brookes. Her sluggish memory unwillingly churned as she shook it like a kaleidoscope to reproduce the old pattern. An unusual name. It couldn't just vanish.

She turned back to the introduction and one sentence leapt from the page: 'The names of untraceable practitioners are not included.'

An unbearable desire to lay her head on her arms across the table came over her. Despair or exhaustion? What's the difference?

Replacing the directory, she knew she had to get out of there. The overheated study area with its air of dust and disappointment was insupportable. She spun round and made a rush for the stairs. The colourful book spines spiralled, dizziness whirling her like a top. Clutching at a shelf she waited till everything gradually settled back in place then tottered back to the table and sat down, slowly feeling the blood seep back to her clammy temples.

No lunch, that was it, she decided. A stupid panic attack. Not sleeping hadn't helped, not to mention the beastly telephone calls. And Robert never being home. On top of everything else, the black, accusing eyes of Millicent Ambache. A suspicious death? Inquest postponed pending further police enquiries? Had the sister implied she had somehow *pushed* the poor woman? Why? A wet night, a greasy patch of oil on the platform even? A crowd shoving from behind? Why pick on her? What had this bloody Ambache woman got on her mind?

With hindsight, the sensible thing would have been to keep her opinion to herself. For all she knew the Hertz female *had* jumped, others on the scene were keen to say so. A suicide verdict would have gone through on the nod if she had kept her mouth shut. 'Say nothing'. Wasn't that the advice she was always giving her clients? And now, presumably, there was yet another inquest on the horizon.

The other person in the library eyed her across the empty tables, frankly curious as Fay made an unsteady exit. Probably thinks I'm drunk, Fay thought as she crept downstairs, gripping the handrail like a convalescent. I should be so lucky!

Outside, the afternoon was luminous with the threat of rain. It occurred to her there was plenty of time to take herself for a cup of tea before the Merc would be ready. She was always happy to postpone going back to the house these days. She fastened her coat as the first raindrops fell and drove back to Stamford. Pulling a scarf from her bag she tied it over her hair before setting off down a side street to the small bakery which was the nearest approximation to a teashop. As she turned into the entrance she almost collided with someone coming out.

'Why, Mrs B!' she exclaimed. 'I didn't know you came here for your bread. A bit off your usual track.'

Rose Barton was, as usual, laden with shopping, and they stood blocking the doorway, sheltering from the rain.

'Oh yes, duck. The only bread my Fred'll cat. Smells ever so lovely.' She edged past on to the pavement to let a customer through. 'Glad I bumped into you, Mrs Browne. Tried to phone but it was engaged. Would it be all right if I had the morning off on Monday? Make a long weekend of it with my sister? Thought I'd see her off at the station on Monday as she don't come down that often. Put her on the right train an' all.'

'Yes, of course. Take the whole day. I shall be looking after Flora.'

'Dear little mite.' The older woman looked wistful. 'Wouldn't like to miss seeing her. Nice to have kiddies round the house, I always say. No, I'll come on later – there's always a pile to do on Mondays. After me dinner all right?'

'Just as you like, Mrs B. I'm likely to go away myself at the weekend. The house seems awfully empty now Luke's gone back.'

'Not the seaside?' Mrs Barton's look of anguish was almost comic. Fay laughed.

'Don't worry. I haven't forgotten what you said about swimming. No deep water involved, I promise. I shall probably just pop up to London and do some shopping.'

'Best thing. Bill Goldsmith's worried sick about security up at the warehouse. Needs seeing to. We was talking about it only the other day.' She moved back under the shelter of the shop doorway and Fay shivered, hoping Mrs B was not off on another psychic rigmarole. Once running there was no holding her back.

'Bill said not to worry you about it, he'd tackle your hubby when he gets back. Nearly caught someone lurking round the back last week when he was working late. Took off smartish but Bill reckons he knows who it was. Local. Wouldn't tell me who but says he'll nab him if he tries it again. Stubborn old fool'll get hi'self hurt. Should leave things like that to the coppers.' She patted Fay's arm. 'You get off for a nice break and forget all I've said. Should have kept my mouth shut like Bill said. But being stuck there all on your own like you are its best to be on your guard. You get the place properly locked up at night. Just to be sure.'

After a further brief exchange, Fay escaped into the shop, passing through a bead curtain to the back. Two of the small tables were already occupied, little posies of marigolds adding their own sharp scent to the bakery smell. Fay sank on to a chair as a spotty teenager in a frilly apron moved in to take her order.

The tea lifted her depression and she returned to the garage revived. Gary had effected a transformation to the Mercedes. It stood in the forecourt gleaming as expensively as a gold tooth.

Fay drove home via Barstow to satisfy her curiosity about Millicent Ambache's cottage. Cheyney's. She drove past slowly, intrigued by the drawn curtains which gave the house an air of solitary confinement, withdrawal from the world at large. Cheyney's was bigger than she had imagined, two cottages converted into one, a substantial house attractively set back from the road in a well tended garden. A fine home for two single ladies. She shrugged. It was impossible to guess people's circumstances. She had just not imagined the library assistant in the plastic mac living in such style.

Once home she decided to relax in a hot bath. Generously lacing the water with lavender oil she lay in the scented water sipping a glass of wine, mulling over the problem of the missing doctor, Sutton-Brookes. Afterwards, wrapping herself in a towel, she lay on the bed and closed her eyes. And slept, utterly zonked.

The noise woke her. A jangling peal, an unrelenting attack on shrivelling nerve ends. Her brain re-engaged, adjusting to her overreaction to the very ordinary sound of the telephone by the bed.

'Hello.'

Silence.

Fear tingled her scalp, electrifying as a shot from a live wire. 'Who *is* this?'

Someone cleared his throat at the other end and Fay waited in the certainty that he was finally about to speak. Her fingers shook and she gripped the phone, not daring to breath while the little alarm clock ticked the minutes away. Ten past six. She had slept for nearly two hours.

Then he hung up. The shock of this was almost one of disappointment, as if she had been jilted, robbed in some way. Cheated.

She had *always* been the one to sever the connection. Why the change? She rolled over, replacing the receiver, knowing she had been on the brink of an answer. Holding the bath towel to her, she dialled Maeve's number.

'It's Fay. Have you heard this ghastly news about Meg Heffer?' she blurted out.

'Hey, take it easy. There's no fire.'

'I've just had another of those crazy phone calls, Maeve. I know it's stupid – probably only kids larking about – but this silent treatment is really getting to me. I flinch every time it rings. I can't leave it off the hook any more, Hugo complained to the telephone engineer. And anyway, I must be here in case Robert tries to ring. I've got to speak to him first. Before he talks to the police.'

'Slow down, sweetie. Being alone in that mausoleum doesn't help. Why don't you come and stay with us till Rob gets back?'

'I can't. I *must* be here when he calls.' Fay consciously put a brake on her fear. 'I'm OK really. Don't worry. I just needed to hear a friendly voice.'

'This is silly. You're working yourself up and it's nothing to do with you. Ted told me the news about Meg's accident. Tragic. But these things happen. There's no need to protect

73

Robert – nobody could possibly hold him responsible. Jesus, he wasn't even in the country when she was buzzing along the M4. Robert is perfectly capable of dealing with the police on his own without consulting you about it. Road accidents are just part of living in this lunatic world, darling. You can't blame yourself just because it was your car.'

'It's more complicated than that.' She hesitated and then went on, 'I'll tell you about it when I see you on Monday.'

'You don't have to leave it till then, muggins. You're obviously driving yourself potty in that great empty house. If you won't come to stay the weekend, why don't you spend the evening with us? I've been bullying Ted to come to one of my students' exhibitions. Come along, do. You know what they're like. Guaranteed to cheer up Job himself, I promise you. A more untalented bunch would be impossible to gather under one roof.'

It was tempting.

'All right. What time?'

'Can we call for you about seven? Bring your cheque book. I shall force you to buy the most hideous exhibit for Robert's study. Serves him right.'

Fay rang off and searched for something to wear. She was dabbing some scent along her throat when she heard the doorbell. Pulling a jacket from the closet she hurried down.

'Hello, Ted. How sweet of you to ask me along.'

'Nonsense. What could be nicer? Ready?'

He slammed the front door behind them, all the lights blazing inside the house like the *Marie Celeste*.

Maeve was waiting in the car. She questioned Fay about the telephone calls and they touched briefly on Meg's accident. Maeve was too tactful to ask about the Renham inquest. The death of Barbara Hertz was a subject no one seemed inclined to dwell upon, least of all Fay Browne. It was as if the whole world had an unspoken assessment of the death of a library assistant under a train as being unimportant.

Within less than ten minutes they were parked in the playground at the back of the old grammar school. Fay shrank into her seat.

'Maeve, I can't go in there.'

'Why ever not?' Maeve was worried. Perhaps all this telephone harassment had tipped the balance, been the last straw on top of the inquest and Meg's car smash.

'When you said one of your exhibitions, I assumed it was still at the old village hall. I'd forgotten your classes had transferred to the school. There must be hundreds of people in there. The entire Evening Institute!'

'But Fay, it's really spacious. Not stuffy or crowded like the old place,' Ted assured her. They both peered from the front seats. Fay sat hunched in the back looking cornered.

'N–no, Ted. It's not claustrophobia. It's Meg, not to mention the woman who died on the railway line. It was in all the papers. Being here enjoying myself seems utterly callous. I know these people, they're very narrow-minded.'

She scrambled out of the car. 'Don't worry about me, you two. My own stupid fault. Go on in. I can easily walk back.'

'Rubbish,' Maeve said as Ted locked the ear. 'People don't care a fig in any real sense. Just nosy. Ignore them.'

'Maeve's right, old dear. Anyone would think you expected to be accused of something.'

Ted took Fay's arm and they escorted her – almost frogmarched her – inside. Knots of people stood gossiping in the brilliantly lit hall. No curious glances came her way. She was becoming neurotic, Fay chided herself. Conceding defeat, she accepted a glass of sherry. The sherry was quite as dreadful as Maeve had predicted. They raised their glasses.

'Out with your cheque books, folks – all in a good cause!' Ted said, encouraging the room at large. He was expansively at his best at local functions. Soon the place was crowded. Maeve had cajoled students to donate their pictures and the MacMillans' social set had been roped in in force.

'Marvellous lady,' the rector enthused, his eyes following Maeve's progress round the room as she greeted her chums with whoops of laughter, whipping up sales. The paintings were, at best, mediocre. Maeve had given three of her own pen and ink drawings, which glowed like pearls against the panelling. Many of the pictures were already sold and Fay rapidly decided she must choose something quick.

'Ted was telling me Maeve has more new students from St Barnabus's this term, Rector.'

'Yes, indeed. It's quite a success already, I think. Come over here.' Reverend Stevens steered her through the crowd. 'Look at these – things they have done already. They love to get out and about, of course, and Maeve is so encouraging.'

They stood before some bright collages stuck over with pieces of felt and net, feathers, silver foil and scraps of wool. Suddenly, the clumsy efforts of Maeve's new students, which at first seemed facile, took on an appealing vitality. Fay moved along, alternately amused and touched by the simplicity. One sketch irresistibly drew her. It was a long ribbon of blue card on which a series of firm strokes depicting a duck – or maybe several ducks? – led the eye to a duck-sized daisy in a splash of green. Here and there a roughly defined wing or beak was haphazardly placed and triangles of feet hung unattached as if in rapid motion. Underneath, 'I love you' was roughly scrawled, the spiky lettering almost disappearing in the jagged strokes of painted grass.

Fay flipped through the typewritten catalogue and found the artist's name. Daisy Meadows.

'Please excuse me, Mr Stevens, I'll be right back.'

She pushed her way to the desk where an elderly woman was patiently marking off references on a sheet and pushing bank-notes into a metal box. Ted appeared as she was about to speak to the cashier.

'Hello, Ted. Be with you in a minute.' She leaned over the desk and pushed across her list. 'I want to buy that one.'

'Number 72? Do you like it?' The woman peered over her bifocals and betrayed disbelief.

'I do. It's charming.'

'When I first saw the list I thought Daisy Meadows was the title!' She laughed, a high, trilling chortle. 'That will be twelve pounds fifty, I'm afraid. Framing's expensive, Mrs Browne.'

Fay felt a stab of surprise hearing her name. She flushed. She had never set eyes on this woman before. An overwhelming feeling of being the focus of curious attention engulfed her and she drew Ted to one side.

'Ted, I've had enough. I must get out of here.'

'OK old girl. I'll get Maeve.'

'Oh, no, don't do that! I'll get a taxi if you can tell me where the phone is. Please don't let me spoil your evening.'

'Come on,' he said, leading her towards a side exit. 'I can run you home myself and be back here before Maeve even notices I've gone.'

She followed, drawing deep, grateful breaths as they found themselves in a grassy cloister. Clasping her hand in the darkness, he led her along a back path and through the kitchen yard to the floodlit car park.

'Clever old Ted.'

He unlocked the car and they slid into the front. Fay wondered if cheap sherry on an empty stomach was wise. She felt distinctly light-headed.

'Smooth exits are a MacMillan forte,' he snorted. 'I've been escaping Maeve's cultural shindigs for years.'

Fay felt his hand on her shoulder.

She stiffened as his other arm swung round to enclose her and she felt the soft brush of his moustache. Her mind surged back to that last evening with Robert. Good grief, what was happening to these guys? Suddenly finding herself wrestling in a car twice in one week! His mouth brushed her cheeks and hair, his arms pinning her against the leather seat.

'Ted! Please, Ted.' Her voice came out squeaky as a girl's and she giggled. 'It's that poisonous sherry. Maeve was right!'

'Come on, Fay. Be a sport.'

She started to laugh in a wobbly, nervous hiccough as the ludicrousness of the situation struck her. Patting his knee she struggled to control gathering hysterics as his confused expression swam into focus.

'Ted,' she gasped, 'you're a sweet, darling man but you don't have to go to these lengths to cheer me up, you know.'

He placed both hands on the steering wheel and after a momentary silence started the engine. He wound down the window to edge out of the parking space and glanced at Fay, clearly illuminated in the car park floodlighting, vainly trying to stem her laughter. It was infectious. He joined in. They were both launched on an upsurge of glee, rolling against each other, lifted up on a wave of sheer relief that a farcical situation had been averted. The cold air rushing through the window was like the very breath of sanity.

'Clot,' he spluttered. 'I wasn't cheering *you* up. If anything I was cheering myself up. It was so bloody boring in there. And the merest whiff of the old bike sheds always makes me randy.'

She patted his arm, grinning to herself. 'Lucky I know you so well.'

The hilarity subsided. Headlights swept the blackness of the playing fields and the Jaguar swung in a wide arc before surging through the main gates and back to Glebe House.

He dropped her at the front door. Fay leaned through the driver's window to touch his cheek.

'Night, Fay. Robert's a lucky sod.'

'I'll tell him that if ever he gets back.' She waved in royal dismissal before he drove off, back to Maeve's art show.

She unlocked the door and flipped the receiver off the hook before sprinting upstairs to her cold, solitary bed. If Robert rang her tonight he'd be out of luck. Tough. Maeve was right. All she needed was to get out of the house for an hour or two to quell the heebie-jeebies. Tomorrow was time enough to extract Robert from the main shaft of Hayes' suspicions. 'And another fine mess you've got us into,' she said grimly, not that Laurel and Hardy had ever been faced with a tragicomedy on Robert Browne's scale.

Fay woke early and lay in the grey half-light thinking about the two women who had died. She tried to assemble the facts logically, to cast aside the panic that had persisted for days.

But it was no baseless panic which convinced her that the Thames Valley police, at the instigation of Hayes, were seriously investigating Robert's involvement in Meg's death. Or even Fay's own complicity in it. If the Hertz accident had not thrown her into Hayes' path, the chances of him interesting himself in the Brownes were minimal. It was as if the death on the line was merely a cruel device of fate to bring them down.

Did the police seriously imagine Robert capable of cold-bloodedly engineering a motor accident while he was safely abroad? And yet, was it really so outlandish? A successful businessman, threatened by the impending break-up of his firm and personal exposure by his pregnant girlfriend ... Her demands could well trigger not only an expensive divorce and the possible loss of his son, but also the loss of his home which was also his place of work. Short of money? Desperate? Were there deals Robert could no longer hide once the accountants took things apart, halving the assets, checking his wheeler-dealer methods? Something only Meg Heffer, his personal assistant, knew about? And all this compounded by Robert involving himself in the wretched girl's abortion? Stupid. Meg was more than capable of taking care of herself. But Hayes wouldn't know that.

Robert's fidelity was a painful spot that Fay chose not to explore. To any casual acquaintance his flirtatious manner and obvious charm might seem to cast him as a regular ladykiller. But Fay had never had any real cause for alarm, and since Luke had completed their close family unit, harbouring nameless suspicions was a dangerous game. Keeping himself on board was clearly Robert's recipe for an uncomplicated life and who was she to make an issue of what might be, in his mind, merely a temporarily amusing dalliance? They had been married well beyond the fabled 'seven year itch' and passions had inevitably cooled to something else, something more solid and possibly less heartbreaking than the early days, but an enduring relationship bonded by their child.

Fay banked down any incipient anger. Loving Robert had settled into a careful avoidance of the stones along the way. Protecting Luke was imperative: an unfaithful husband was one thing, a father accused of murder was something completely different.

But there was no question about one thing. Robert was entirely capable of tinkering with the brakes and had ample opportunity. The police vehicle engineer's report was conclusive. At least she could prove that Robert was not the father of Meg's baby. That would destroy the most obvious motive. The rest of the case against him would fall apart once she could indicate the existence of another man in Meg's life. There *must* be another man. If Maggie Heffer had always been as devious and secretive as Mrs B intimated, Fay herself might winkle out the mystery man, even if Hayes did not.

She must drive to London in search of the one person who could shatter the case against Robert – a name she had never mentioned to him, a secret Fay hoped had been buried for ever. She leapt out of bed, and within forty minutes was leaving the outskirts of the town before the shops were unshuttered.

The first thing was to locate Maureen Sutton-Brookes. The doctor's evidence would be an ultimate weapon with which to fend off the police if it came to the crunch. But such a double-edged weapon might destroy everything she had endeavoured to protect. It would be walking on a knife edge.

She must also speak to Hugo. He had known Meg for almost as long as Robert. Surely Hugo must know something about her personal life. No one could be that secretive. Except Meg? Fay determined to question the flatmate. Someone was keeping something back. In one way Robert disappearing into the blue had alerted Hayes' suspicions but, for the present, he was safer out of it. If she could get to him first, unearth further evidence before Robert opened his big mouth, the truth need never come out.

But where on earth was he?

Eight

S he arrived in the city only to get caught up in a maze of Marylebone streets without even remembering the approximate locality of Sutton-Brookes' old consulting rooms. If only she could recall the name of the street it would be a start. Her mind seemed to have drawn a veil over the whole thing, a sort of amnesia. The only course was to get out and walk. It had to be around here somewhere, provided the place hadn't been redeveloped. She was sure to recognize it once she started pounding those vaguely familiar pavements. She parked in the basement of one of the larger stores.

It was crowded with Saturday shoppers, the stuffy atmosphere closing in as she stood on the escalator, carried up as if on a giant conveyor belt. Not another library black-out she prayed, bolting into a cloakroom to hold her wrists under the tap. The pallor of her reflection looked artificial, painted on. Coffee might help.

She trailed through the coffee shop and took a tray to a corner table, mercifully near an open window, and stared at the sandwich on her plate. She yearned for a cigarette, having not smoked for years. Perhaps this sudden craving was some sort of bulwark against the fear she was struggling to ignore. The horror of unravelling Robert's secrets, being faced with the truth about the man who, she must admit, had become something of an enigma over the years. Her glance roamed desperately round the cafe and she wondered if all these people were, like herself, deliberately blind.

A woman was speaking into a wall phone by the door. An idea filtered through, obvious really when you thought about it. Sutton-Brookes must be in the phone book. If she was still in

London. Or hadn't remarried. Or given up her practice. Or was ex-directory. Gathering up her things, Fay quickly took the woman's place and searched the phone book for both Sutton and for Brookes. Nothing. Directory enquiries couldn't help either.

The disappointment forged itself into a goad, driving her out into the street again. Pushing her way out through a side exit she turned a corner, immediately experiencing a waft of famil-iarity. She took in the elegant terrace and the proliferation of brass plates. This was it. Or certainly a street just like the one she remembered. At least she had stumbled upon the medical quarter. Fay walked slowly down one side examining the number plates and dredging her memory for a number. She paused by one house. Pettit. She stared at the worn lettering. Pettit? As she was about to ring the bell the door opened and a woman holding a bin bag struggled out.

'Doctor's not here this morning, love.'

'But I've come up from the country! It's urgent.'

The woman hesitated, her eyes flitting across Fay's bloodless cheeks. She dumped the bag on the step and said, 'Not for me to say, but Miss Stokes is working this morning. She might make an urgent appointment for you if you've come specially.'

'That would be such a help. I would be so grateful.'

Fay followed her in, waiting while she rebolted the door, then trailed behind her up the stairs and through to a waiting room on the first floor. The woman put a finger to her lips and motioned Fay to sit down while she rewound the vacuum cleaner cable which snaked across a dove-grey carpet. A door separating the waiting room from the inner office stood open and, beyond, another door was ajar, presumably leading to the consulting rooms. Fay took in the studied placement of house plants and a glass-topped table strewn with current copies of *Vogue* and *Country Life*. The window was obscured by roman blinds and nothing seemed as she remembered it. And yet...

A metal filing cabinet slammed shut and she heard whispered conversation percolate from the inner office. Another drawer closed and the door widened. A grey-haired woman appeared, the thick lenses of her spectacles projecting a fish-like stare. Her manner was cool.

'I'm afraid Mr Pettit does not hold consultations at the weekend, except in very exceptional circumstances – special patients, you understand.'

'My name is Browne. Frances Browne. I was a patient here some years ago. Perhaps you still have my case notes.'

'I doubt it, Mrs Browne.' She cast an impatient glance over Fay's gaunt appearance 'Files are not retained for more than five years if there is no treatment within that time – not here at any rate.' She nodded towards the open door. 'It would be impossible, you see. There just isn't the room. Old files are stored elsewhere. As it is I have a constant battle to keep my records up to date, especially,' she bitterly added, 'with the useless girls the agencies send these days. We are computerized now, of course, but you said you were here some time ago?'

'I'm sorry to be such a nuisance – you're obviously very busy. But my previous consultations were with Dr Sutton-Brookes. Is she still in partnership?'

The woman snorted, dispelling her air of arid efficiency. 'Sutton-Brookes a partner of Mr Pettit? Never!' She stepped close, bobbing her head confidentially, and said in a low voice, 'Dr Sutton-Brookes used to assist but we've seen nothing of her for simply ages. She had rather flamboyant feminist views, which Mr Pettit found embarrassing. No tact. Unforgivable in medicine, naturally. The patients don't come here to listen to that sort of claptrap.' She laughed, the rimless spectacles flashing under the fluorescent lights. 'Hardly bra-burning types!' Miss Spokes grinned widely at this outlandish notion, disclosing long yellow teeth.

'Did you say Dr Sutton-Brookes is no longer sharing these consulting rooms?'

'Absolutely not.'

'Oh. Have you any idea how I could get in touch with her? You see,' she hastened to put in, 'I would really prefer to consult Dr Sutton-Brookes. She knows my case.'

'I'm afraid we do not refer patients. Though I did hear she did a locum or two after leaving here. But she concentrated almost entirely on her political ambitions after that. Would you like me to make an appointment with Mr Pettit for you? I suspect Sutton-Brookes is no longer in practice. Have you checked the medical directory?'

'Yes, I'm afraid you're probably right. Thank you – er – perhaps ...?' Fay mumbled, confused and indecisive. The woman's eyes flickered to the wall clock and her temporary chattiness evaporated at the realization that she was going to be late for lunch.

Fay rose. 'You have been very helpful. I think I had better ring you next week when I've finally decided what to do. Thank you, Miss – er – Stokes.' She extended her hand. The doctor's secretary looked surprised at this gesture and briefly placed a passive palm next to Fay's before hurrying to the door. She held it open and said flatly, 'Just as you wish, Mrs Browne. I quite understand. I hope you are able to locate Dr Sutton-Brookes. Changing doctors is always upsetting, isn't it?'

Fay went back to the car and sat, trying to think what to do next. Maureen Sutton-Brookes seemed to have sunk without trace. It had been a long shot. But at least it had given her the incentive to get out of Stamford, to do something positive. She would have to deflect Hayes some other way. Looking for the elusive doctor had wasted precious time. Meg's current lover was the key to Robert's exoneration after all.

She unlocked the Mercedes and telephoned Hugo on her mobile.

'It's Fay. I'm in town for the weekend.'

'Sensible girl. Having a bit of fun while Robert's away? I hope you're spending a lot of money.'

'Not yet,' she parried. 'I'm near Oxford Street. Hugo, I've something I want to ask Meg's flatmate. You know about the accident, of course?'

'Yes. Tragic. Poor kid.'

'Could you give me the address?'

'Mm. Should be around here somewhere.' Hugo hesitated. 'I say, I hope you're not getting involved are you, Fay? I should leave it to Robert if I were you.'

'No. Just something I want to ask the other girl, if you have the address handy. If I go there now she may be at home on a Saturday afternoon.'

'Hang on. I'll look.'

She waited, idly regarding the passing crowd.

'Hello, Fay? Can you take this down?'

She fumbled with an envelope and urged Hugo to go ahead. He dictated an address in North Kensington and added, 'You might not catch this girlfriend of Meg's, you know. Her name's Jessica by the way. Meg used to complain about Jessica coming and going at all hours. She's an air hostess.'

'Bless you, Hugo. I'll see what's doing.'

'How about dinner this evening? Or are you already booked for the theatre or something?'

'Heavens, no. I haven't even booked a hotel room yet.'

'Fay, you're the absolute end. You'll land up on a bench in the park. London's always chock-a-block in October, conferences and suchlike.'

'Suppose you're right. I hadn't thought.'

'Have supper with me and if you haven't found a room by then you can doss down here at the shop if you like. There's always Robert's bolthole.'

'Hugo, you're an angel. Shall I come over when I've finished at Meg's? I'd like to have a shower and change. It's been one hell of a day.'

'Fine by me. Till then.'

Her familiarity with London was limited to two small areas: Knightsbridge, and the immediate vicinity of Hugo's bookshop. This was no help at all beyond Kensington High Street, and the one-way traffic systems added to her confusion.

More by luck than navigation she found herself in the street in which Meg Heffer had lived, a once genteel terrace now entirely given over to flats and bedsits. As she stood on the pavement checking the address, two men came out carrying an amplifier. They stumbled down the steps and shambled to a parked van, humping the equipment between them, leaving the door ajar.

This was it. Number sixty-one. She rang the bell several times. The men finished loading the van and drove away. She tried the bell again but this was clearly a waste of time, no one was going to answer. She stepped inside and made her way

85

upstairs and along an airless landing. Meg's flat was at the back. She knocked. The door had been recently repainted, the panels picked out with narrow brown brush lines. Rather smart. But what had she expected? Some sort of squat? Meg had been earning good money for years, after all. Fay knocked again, louder. She had come too far to give up now.

The door opened a couple of inches, secured by a chain. A head wrapped in a white towel peeped round, prune-black eyes unwinking.

'Yes?'

'I'm Fay Browne. Might I have a word with you? It's Jessica, isn't it?'

The half-glimpsed visage could have been carved in obsidian, beautiful and unyielding.

'It's about Meg,' Fay persisted. 'There's been an accident.'

'Yeah, I heard.' And then wearily, 'OK. Come in. But I'm way behind schedule already.'

The door closed and Fay waited while the chain was un-hooked and the door reopened, this time fully. She entered a brilliantly lit small lobby and waited while the girl shut the door. The walls, papered in same sort of jungle print, were covered with small paintings, silhouettes and snapshots in gilt frames. Propped on the radiator shelf was a message board criss-crossed with tape behind which several photographs, postcards and train timetables were jammed. Scribbled phone numbers and ribald messages leapt to the eye. It was like a collage.

For a moment, she had forgotten the girl standing behind her in the canary-yellow bathrobe, her glossy skin giving off a faint steamy scent like pineapples. She held the towel round her head. Without a word she passed Fay and went into a sitting room, pushing aside some dry-cleaning to perch on the arm of the sofa. Reaching into the pocket of the robe, Jessica took out a cigarette pack and Fay, mesmerised by the long brown fingers, watched her light up. Jessica inhaled deeply, fixing pansy eyes on the faded redhead who had blown in off the street like an autumn leaf.

'I am so sorry to ... er ... burst in on you like this,' Fay stuttered, waving vaguely at the assortment of clothing littering the room. 'I expect you're busy.'

'That's OK.' The black girl loosened the towel and rubbed her frizzy damp curls before throwing it on the sofa. 'I was having a shower and when whoever it was didn't go away I thought I'd better open up in case it was that nosy detective again.'

'You don't mean Hayes?'

'Sure. That's the guy. Tall. Dark. Eyes like lasers.'

'Good heavens. I had no idea he was making a full-scale investigation of all this – he isn't even based in London. He told you about Meg, I imagine.'

'Yeah. Poor daisy. Born loser from the day she opened those big blue peepers. What's your interest in all this?'

'Meg worked for my husband and as he's abroad I'm trying to tie up a few loose ends. It's all very confusing. Would you mind me asking what Hayes wanted to know?'

Jessica's attention shifted to her cigarette and she reached behind for an ashtray which she considered at length before using.

'Oh, the usual stuff. Who were Meg's buddies? Did she have a special boyfriend? Did I know the names and so on.'

'Did he mention Meg was pregnant? But I expect you already knew that.' Fay felt compelled to force something from Jessica, who seemed to shake off interrogation like an otter.

'Yeah.' Her eyes narrowed. 'Silly cow.'

'You must know who ...' Fay struggled to find a less oppressive phrase but it popped out anyway, 'was responsible?'

Jessica laughed, all white teeth and rosy tongue. Everything totally without blemish.

'Oh, my.' She continued to laugh, her shoulders quivering, exposing more glossy skin in the long V of her robe.

'Please, Jessica. Please help me.'

The laughter cut out. In one swift glance she perceived Fay's distress.

'I'll level with you, honey. I guess you think your old man's been with Meg, don't you? That's what that pig Hayes was scratching about for anyhow.' She hesitated, weighing Fay's ability to take the truth. 'You're probably right about that. I'm pretty sure he thought Meg a basic lay if you must know, but I wouldn't say so to that detective because I don't see it would help Meg one way or the other.'

Grasping the bathrobe to her throat, Jessica thoughtfully drew on the cigarette.

'Meg was a funny kid. We'd been sharing for over three years. Had lots of parties here. And in all that time she never dropped more than a hint of any special fella. We wouldn't have lasted the week out if I wasn't away most of the time. Meg and me were not naturals for sharing. I'm no housewife as you can see, and Meg was fanatically tidy. And how!' She grinned. 'We used to row about the mess I made. But on the whole we got along fine and, as I say, I was away a lot. But, you know, sometimes I'd get back and –' Jessica waved a hand, encompassing the room. 'Not a thread out of place – but there would be something in the air. Know what I mean? Something shouted MAN HERE almost before my key was out of the lock.'

'And she never said a word about it?'

'Like a clam. Dropped a word here and there if she'd been to a new restaurant or a show but never offered to bring anyone to a party. And no one ever picked her up from the flat either. Not when I was here anyway.'

'Perhaps he worked away from London. In the army perhaps. Did she have letters?'

Jessica shook her head. 'Nothing I ever saw. But there may have been someone. She played everything very close to her chest but,' Jessica stubbed out her cigarette with a final air, 'Meg was sharp as a laser once she got on a line with anything. And lately, since the summer, she seemed fixed on giving up all this and getting married.'

Fay jerked like a rag doll on a string. 'And she didn't tell you who?'

Jessica's hands opened in an empty gesture, the palms like milky coffee.

'Anybody! Absolutely anybody if you ask me, lady. A very old-fashioned girl, Meg Heffer. But she must have been saving up for a trousseau or something because for three or four months she had an extra job.'

'But she couldn't have! She was working full time for Robert.'

Jessica shrugged. 'Sure. But she had an evening job, too. She used to collect a manuscript from some author guy two or three times a week and type it here. I had some sick leave in June and was pretty damn mad with her beavering away in her room every night. She'd bought this cheap printer which clattered away like a woodpecker. It sure put the damper on any party. She said she was typing a book.'

'But Meg was getting a good salary from Robert. I know he looked on her almost as a partner, not just a PA. Did she say why she needed the extra money?'

'Told me to mind my own business.' Jessica raised an eyebrow. 'Fair comment. But she was so secretive, she even got me curious. You'd think she was moonlighting for the CIA! One night she was out and some aircrew buddies were here having a drink and we were joshing about Meg and her crappy book. Dave said it was probably porn and we all had some laughs – you know how po-faced Meg could be. I'd had a few martinis and had got pretty sick of her nagging so I flipped a couple of pages from her drawer and took them back to read to the others. But it wasn't any laughs. Didn't understand a word. All in Portuguese apparently. One of the fellas here said it was pretty boring stuff – archaeology, I think he said.

'There wasn't any trouble with the rent or anything, was there?'

'Not in a million years. Meg paid all the bills on the nail and once a month she'd show me this little notebook of hers with all the expenses and receipts of what she had paid. Always ticked off to the last penny. No, Meg was the last to get in a jam over cash. I think she was just making a bit extra – tax-free – to put aside for this wedding she was hinting about. I didn't take a lot of notice because it seemed a bit crazy to me, laying up a bottom-drawer when there was no bridegroom.'

'Was she fantasizing, do you think?'

'Lying, you mean? Meg wasn't George Washington, I know

that, but she was really happy for once. Up on cloud nine. But that was early summer, before she got pregnant. She never mentioned the baby to me but I'd found this testing kit in the bathroom and wasn't altogether surprised when that detective mentioned it. For someone who lied without batting an eyelid, Meg Heffer believed every note if some man was singing the right tune. Naive yet cunning. You know what I mean?'

Fay nodded, clasping her hands in her lap, sensing firm ground under her feet at last.

Jessica continued. 'But the poor kid got pretty moody lately. Been feeling rotten, I guess, but for the last few weeks she let things go here in the flat. Things she would have blown her top over before. So perhaps she didn't plan on staying much longer. We had a party here a week or two back and some fool burned a hole in the coffee table. Meg hardly noticed. And yet, she'd burst into flames over nothing at all. Like when an Aussie pal of mine called in and made a pass at her one night. She punched him in the face and had a screaming fit, shooting her mouth off about him being married and should keep his hands to himself and all that stuff. We bundled her into the bedroom and she went out like a light. Pissed, I guess. But vicious with it. Never known Meg to blow her stack in front of people like that before. Didn't drink as a rule. Miss Snowbum some of the guys used to call her.'

Fay made one last appeal. 'I must ask you, Jessica. I've no one else to turn to. Are you quite sure Meg didn't mention the name of a man – any man – she was fond of?'

Jessica's elegant brows knitted. 'She flung out junk like "neurotic women playing dog in the manger with husbands", that sort of stuff. I thought she was just bitching because she couldn't come up with one herself after this big build-up about getting married. But I think I would have remembered a name. There was Bobbie, of course. But that was her boss, wasn't it?'

Fay nodded, lingering in the dazzling little hall as Jessica fiddled with the door catches. Her brain fizzed in an effort to find something, *anything*. Hayes still had to prove that Robert had tampered with the Metro, but establishing he'd had a motive *and* an opportunity might tip the scales. There *must* be another man. Her glance fell on the snapshots on the message board.

'Are these yours?'

Jessica held open the door, edgy with the delay. 'Not all. Meg and I used to pop the odd thing there after a trip or something like that.' She snatched up the board and impatiently handed it over. 'Here. You take it home with you. You might find Meg's true love lurking amongst that lot somewhere.' It was surprisingly light, hardboard presumably, but awkward to carry without dropping the bits and pieces. Fay held it level like a tray and stepped out on to the landing.

'Thanks, Jessica. I'm sorry to be such a pest.'

But she was already closing the door.

Fay stood in the dim passage hearing the faint thump and twang of a stereo from one of the other rooms. She sighed and made her way downstairs. She really wasn't very good at this detective game, she decided.

Nine

Hugo's place was closed on Saturdays and Fay was surprised, as she drew into the kerb, to see all the lights blazing. The window was set out sparsely with a token display. The main part of the premises was cut off by a frosted glass partition, beyond which shelves – where only privileged buyers were permitted to roam – rose to the ceiling.

Dusk was drawing in as she peered through the shop window, rapping ineffectively on the door. The brightly lit maze beyond the partition glowed like a robbers' cave. She knocked more persistently. At last, Hugo's head bobbed round the frosted glass and he came through to unlock the door, affectionately squeezing her elbow as he pulled her through. A figure hovered in the shadows. Hugo called out.

'Hey, Carey! Come and meet Mrs Boss. She's fairly harmless.'

Hugo and Fay entered the harshly lit rear premises and a youth in jeans and a sweatshirt shuffled forward, shyly extending a hand.

'This is Carey Williamson – Fay Browne. Carey's doing some research,' Hugo explained. 'I'm trying to find some old memoirs of an Oxbridge expedition to Guatemala for him.'

'I'm putting up a thesis on the Mayan script.'

Fay laughed. 'Bully for you, Carey Williamson.'

Hugo poked him in the ribs. 'I hadn't realized it had got so late. Let's call it a day, boyo. If you like you can come in and have another stab at all this stuff in the morning.'

The lad reached behind a stool for a denim jacket and began to push notebooks and files into a plastic carrier bag.

Hugo laid a hand on his fraying cuff. 'No rush. Come up and have a drink before you go.'

She was surprised to detect a note of appeal in the invitation. She looked quickly from one to the other, then turned and made for the stairs leading to Hugo's flat. They followed.

Upstairs the rooms were in sumptuous contrast, redolent of comfort. Fay touched switches which simultaneously illuminated several lamps and discreet spotlights, lending the maroon walls a mellow antique charm. The seating was abrasively modern yet in a subtle way complimented the Turkish rugs and hangings. Giant Moorish floor cushions struck Fay as being new as she crossed the room to pull down the blinds.

'Told you she was a bossy lady,' Hugo said with a smile.

'Rubbish,' she retorted, dropping on to one of the sofas and patting the seat beside her. Carey sat awkwardly, his fair wispy beard soft against his cheeks. 'Hugo loves having me visit so he can show off his exquisite taste. Robert wouldn't even notice,' she added, faintly aware that things seemed a trifle strained. She smiled weakly at Carey sitting stiffly beside her.

Hugo joined them, carrying a tray of glasses and a bottle of burgundy.

'I know you prefer wine, Fay. OK for you, Carey?'

He nodded, shying away to lounge on a cushion pushed up against the wall. Hugo placed a bowl of nuts on a low table and started telling Fay about a Woody Allen season which had featured at a film club he frequented. They chuckled over favourite quotes, capping well-worn jokes with all the humorous subtlety of the 'Knock, knock, who's there?' variety. Eventually all three relaxed, sipping their wine in amiable silence.

'Are you studying in London?' Fay ventured at last. To discover this young man sprawling about Hugo's flat was unexpected: she had hoped to have him to herself.

'No. Cambridge. I've been doing a vac job here for the summer.'

'Carey's in his final year. He's considering joining us permanently when he comes down.'

The boy reached for the bowl of nuts, ignoring this.

'More wine, Fay?' Hugo offered the half-empty second bottle.

'Mm.'

'Carey?' He hovered in the centre of the room, his tone eager.

Emptying his glass, Carey gracefully uncurled and stood up, instantly seeming over-large in the carefully designed interior. 'No thanks. I'm off.' He pulled on the jacket, smiling as he made for the door. 'See myself out. Cheers.'

They listened to his footsteps on the stairs and finally the bang of the shop door.

Hugo refilled his glass and the two smiled across at each other, both visibly winding down.

'I can't believe you're serious about breaking with Robert.'

He shrugged. 'Had to come, old love. We really do get on each other's nerves these days. Makes it difficult for the staff.'

'He didn't say a word about it before he went to Houston, you know. I'm sure he doesn't take you at your word.'

'The trouble with Rob is he never remotely concedes anyone else *has* a point of view.'

Fay fingered the rim of the glass, her eyes averted. 'More so these days, I grant you. But I'm sure he thinks he's doing what's best for everyone.'

'Oh, yes, I don't dispute that. But I'm too old for all this bloody marketing nonsense. Let's drop it, shall we, Fay?' And that seemed to be his final word.

She sighed. 'Apart from all that, I'm dreadfully worried about the investigation into Meg's accident.' She leaned forward. 'You've met this policeman, Hayes. You know what he's like. Sounds crazy but I'm certain he thinks Robert's involved in some way or other. There isn't any financial quarrel with Robert neither of you have told me about, is there?'

'My quarrel with Robert is more personal.'

'I only ask because Hayes is making too many enquiries for a normal traffic accident and I don't want any nasties crawling out of the woodwork when he starts banging about. You see,' she paused, struggling to put it to Hugo without sounding paranoid, 'there's been a special report by a police engineer. Hayes suspects Robert tampered with the brakes.'

'Good God!'

'It's utterly ridiculous, we both know that. But Hayes is

insinuating all sorts of horrible things about Robert and Meg and the brakes and everything.'

Fay started winding her watch with obsessive concentration, staring at the dial like a woman with an urgent appointment. 'I'm at my wits' end, Hugo. I must come up with something to prove Robert's not involved before Hayes gets to him. You know what a small world this business is, and Stamford's no more than a village once a scandal's in the air. Thank the Lord, Luke's back at school. You heard about that other accident, I suppose? The woman on the line?'

'You mean the railway line?' Hugo looked nonplussed.

She shook her head. 'It's not important. A tragic coincidence but ... forget all that. It's Meg's death that's so dangerous.'

He took a small cigar from a box on the table and carefully lit it, avoiding her eyes. At last he looked up. 'I don't know what to say, my dear.'

'But it looks so black. You don't know it all.' She braced herself to continue. 'Meg was going to have a baby.'

Hugo shook his head.

'Well, she was. And Robert stupidly involved himself in helping her, paid for an abortion and for an hotel afterwards. Covering up while she was supposedly in the States with him. They must have planned to arrive back together and no one would have been any the wiser.'

Hugo paced the room, taking short puffs at the cigar and scenting the room with smoke.

'Hayes makes it sound so calculated,' she muttered. 'There *is* someone else, I know it. Surely Meg must have mentioned a man? She was working here most of the time, closely involved with you all.' Her eyes devoured Hugo's erratic progress round the small room. He turned abruptly to face her.

'Fay, I would do anything in the world if I knew a way to help you. We've been friends so long. Meg had problems. And she was desperate,' he added enigmatically.

'But someone must have called for her after work, surely? She wasn't a recluse.'

'There are always plenty of fellows in and out of the shop, not to mention extra staff in the summer. But she never featured in

95

office gossip like the other girls. Meg Heffer was a very private person,' he finished lamely.

'Oh, well.' Fay sagged against the cushions, utterly defeated.

'Why don't you have a nice hot shower?' he suggested, pulling her to her feet and leading her to the bathroom. 'And afterwards I'll take you to a jolly little Italian place in Fulham and we'll try to forget all about it.'

Fay paused in the doorway and pecked his cheek. 'My things. They're still in the car.'

'I'll get them. What is it, a weekend case or something?'

'A small airline bag in the boot and, oh yes, a message board.' She went back to the sofa and opened her bag to pass him her keys.

'Hugo, would you be a darling and fetch the lot while I freshen up? After all that lovely wine I need to clear my head.'

She heard his light step on the stairs as she rinsed the glasses in the kitchen, moving with familiarity about the flat. He returned, dropping the keys on the bed and placing clean towels beside them.

'OK?' He grinned apologetically. 'I'll sort out my kit from the bathroom when you've showered and then you can call the place your own. I'll use the staff place in the shop. No hassle.'

She closed the door, stripping off her creased suit in happy anticipation of one of Hugo's dotty little restaurants.

Breakfast next morning was a chatty, argumentative occasion, Carey banging at the shop door just as Hugo was carrying the coffee pot through from the kitchen.

'I'll go, Hugo.'

Carey followed her upstairs and shambled in. He looked less shy but just as unkempt, the raw edges of his denims forming a ragged frill above his trainers. Hugo pulled up an extra chair and took his jacket.

'You timed it exactly,' he said, removing the lid from a dish of sizzling sausages and bacon. Carey grinned and set to. Breakfast passed smoothly, the awkwardness of the previous evening forgotten. They split the Sunday papers, arguing fiercely over the news.

While she cleared up, Hugo searched through some old catalogues in his desk trying to track down the Mayan papers. Carey wandered about, quietly examining the rugs, fingering the small collection of fossils on top of a cabinet. When she came back into the room he was holding up the board from Meg's flat and had evidently asked Hugo about it.

'Ask her yourself. Hey, why on earth did you bring this, Fay?'

'It's not mine. It belongs to Meg's flatmate.'

Carey placed the board on the cleared table and she stood beside him, staring at the juxtaposition of postcards and holiday snapshots. Here and there a scribbled message, scrap of fabric or a foreign bus ticket varied the pattern, but in the main there were just random bits and pieces.

Hugo moved in and three heads bent over the table while Fay unpinned the lot, resting the hardboard against a chair. She regarded the disordered pile with vague uneasiness. It seemed to have expanded now it was all loose. She sifted through, snatching up photographs at random and scanning each one obsessively – like a panhandler looking for nuggets. Hugo and Carey stood aside, uncomprehending.

'You see,' she explained, 'Jessica and Meg both used to slip things under the tape and I'm hoping something will turn up.' She gazed hopelessly at Hugo. 'Can't you recognize *anyone* here who might have meant something to her?'

Hugo pushed his hands inside the pockets of his cardigan as if to touch Meg's things would be utterly abhorrent. He spoke to the boy. 'You remember Meg Heffer, Carey, Robert's assistant?' He pointed to one of the snapshots. 'That's her, the fair one.'

'Yeah, sure.' He studied the two girls in the photograph posed beside an open sports car. 'And the other one's Liz Deiser.'

Hugo looked closer and Fay grabbed the snapshot, peering fiercely at the sun-drenched scene. 'Who's she?'

'One of the girls who works here. Just one of the typists,' Hugo said. 'They went to Lisbon together, at Easter I think it was.'

'Do you know anything about this girl Liz, Carey?' She passed back the snapshot.

'Not much,' Carey replied in a bored tone. 'She was pretty lively. Much more fun than the other one,' he said, indicating Meg.

'Did the girls say anything about meeting any men while they were on holiday?' she persisted.

'By the time I got here at the end of June I expect they'd just about forgotten all about it.'

Meg touched Hugo's sleeve. 'Couldn't you ask this other girl, Liz, if Meg had a boyfriend? Perhaps someone they met?'

Hugo shrugged, detesting the continued interrogation.

'Heavens, Fay, if Meg had a man in her life her flatmate would know all about it. I can't see the necessity to drag the staff into this.' He turned apologetically to Carey. 'Meg had a tragic accident, you see. She was killed in a car crash a few days ago.'

'Jessica never saw *anyone* with her. But I'm sure!' She brought her hand heavily down on the table, scattering pictures in all directions. 'Robert's no saint, even I know that. But, he wouldn't kill anyone. I won't see Robert hounded over this. Just think of the effect on Luke!' Angry tears glittered.

Hugo slipped his arm round her shoulder. 'No one's accusing Robert. You're worrying unnecessarily.'

'Once people start talking it's a case of mud sticks, and then it hardly matters whether anything's proven or not. It's not just blind obstinate trust in Robert, Hugo, I've a child to think about.'

Carey knelt on the floor collecting up the scattered fragments. He rose, placing the snapshots back on the table, retaining one postcard which he was enthusiastically examining.

'The rain god, Chac. What a bit of luck.' He passed it to Hugo who looked distractedly at the picture of a squat little figurine and passed it back.

Carey said, 'It's a pottery incense burner from a shrine in Mexico, a place called Mayapan. It's from the Middle Post-classic period. Fay, do you think I might keep it? If she's

98

dead she won't care anyway, will she?' he added with painful logic.

'Some of these things belong to Jessica.' She turned over the postcard. 'But this was Meg's.' It was addressed to the flat and bore a Brazilian stamp. 'Are you sure this thing's Mexican?'

'I'm not stupid! It is my subject after all.' He rifled through the rest of the pictures.

'Only this card was posted in Brazil, not Mexico. On August 12th this year, actually.'

He grabbed it and scrutinised the small print on the back, then returned it. 'Can't help that. It's Mexican. Whoever sent the card must have been keeping it from another holiday.'

Fay peered at the cramped message then passed it to Hugo. 'I can't read it. What do you think?'

He held it distastefully and withdrew spectacles from his pocket.

'God knows,' he said at last. 'In Spanish or something. Meg was a linguist, you know. One reason Robert found her so useful on these foreign buying trips. Could gabble away like a monkey.'

Carey reached out lazily for the postcard and gazed fondly at the picture of the stocky little rain god holding what looked like a grenade in each hand. He flipped it over and drawled, 'Not Spanish. Portuguese. Says something like, "London in summer has no need of Chac." Roughly that, anyhow. And then there's a name which I can't quite decipher. Hyphenated. All that's clear is the last part. Maria. A girlfriend of Meg's on holiday in Brazil, at a guess.'

Fay had lost interest and nodded absently while re-sorting the rest of the snapshots. There was no familiar face apart from Jessica's with a flight of aircraft steps in the background. She nudged Hugo. 'That's Jessica, Meg's flatmate.'

'But she's black!'

'As a Nubian slave girl,' Carey said, grinning wickedly.

'Possibly,' Hugo retorted with asperity. 'Funny Meg never mentioning it.'

'But that's Meg all over! Tight as a clam.' She grimly shuffled the pictures neatly together. 'Dear Hugo, *please* ask the other girl, Liz, if she knew if Meg had a special man. Please. I must find out. It's all I need to get Robert off Hayes' hook.'

He grimaced but accepted the photographs and placed them in a manila envelope.

'Ask her if she recognizes anyone in those snaps.'

Carey held up the postcard. 'OK if I keep this one? A mascot for my thesis?'

Fay nodded.

'Thanks.' He pocketed it and moved towards the door, saying to Hugo, 'I'll carry on with the work downstairs if you don't mind?'

'By all means.' Hugo waved expansively. 'I'll join you in a little while.' He turned to Fay. 'After lunch, how about a visit to the Royal Academy? I meant to take you this morning – I'm a Friend – but I can't let Carey loose without some sort of supervision.'

'Of course you can't. That sounds fun. But not too late, Hugo, I think I'd better push off at teatime.'

'Just as you like, my dear. You know you're more than welcome to stay on here.'

'That's sweet of you, but I must get back. I've promised to look after Maeve's little girl tomorrow.'

Hugo moved off to join Carey downstairs while Fay settled with the Sunday papers.

Turning to the arts section, her eye was caught by what Mrs B would term 'a name from the past'. GROCERY KING DONATES A MILLION the headline announced.

Philip Lewis, head of the Sharon supermarket chain, cele-
brates the opening of a new megastore outside Bristol with a
cheque to the artistic director of the Old Vic.

Fay grinned. Well, well, well. Nobody would have pictured Phil Lewis as a patron of the arts when they became an item at that students' camp near Tel Aviv, Phil getting his knees brown and enjoying a taste of being a stand-in for his father on an excursion away from the check-out tills. He had also been part of the Sutton-Brookes' set in those balmy, far-off days when

Lewis Senior had sponsored some sort of medical centre. Dare she approach him after all these years? See if he's still in touch with Sutton-Brookes? Anything was worth a try.

She flung down the newspaper and ran downstairs calling to Hugo. He appeared from behind one of the partitions, looking harassed.

'Sorry to interrupt, Hugo, but I've had a mad idea. I'm going to ring Philip Lewis, you know the Sharon supermarket man? I've been trying to contact a mutual friend of ours. It's OK, don't look so stricken, he's an old mate of mine. Has very good reason to remember me, in fact. Have you got a *Who's Who* down here?' He passed it over.

'I could ring him at home on a Sunday morning. He must have a weekend place in the country. He'll speak to me.'

Hugo rather doubted that, but he let it go. Poor old Fay was off down every rabbit hole these days.

She rushed back upstairs, revitalized, sure she was on to something at last, and threw herself on the sofa. She found Lewis's entry. Everything was suddenly clear. There was no mistake. She read it again.

Philip Ambrose Lewis. Chairman Sharon Groceries plc m. 1970 Millicent Ambache (divorced 1978). m. 1982 Miriam Rosemary Stritch.

She closed the heavy book and it lay on her lap like her inevitable burden. Must she carry this load for ever? Now even that name had been added to her bag of scorpions. Now she *had* to find Maureen Sutton-Brookes. There was no one else who could help her.

Ten

S he arrived home late Sunday evening and went straight to bed, sleeping fitfully and waking in the dark, gripped by an irrational conviction that someone was in the garden. The wind had risen, whining in the old chimneys, causing the trees to lash about. She had always hated the wind.

Surveying the storm damage next morning, she equated the havoc with the chaos in her own life. Everything seemed to be falling about her ears. Maeve's car drew up outside. She hurried through the hall to open the door and was almost mown down as Maeve, her arms filled with bags and toys, almost fell inside. She was closely followed by a very small girl in a red jersey. Fay took some of the bags and they all trooped through to the kitchen.

Maeve dropped everything and flopped into a chair, Flora instantly climbing into her lap. Two pairs of identical hazel eyes latched on to Fay.

'Coffee?'

'Only if it's instant. I'm dashing off almost straight away and I've got to change.'

Fay took in Maeve's suede suit and raised an eyebrow.

'Don't give me that old-fashioned look, Fay Browne. I'm taking a day off. Sailing.'

'Well, hello sailor!'

'Cheeky. Ted's such an old maid about the sea, better if he doesn't know in the first place. So I said I was spending the day with you. Shopping.'

'Why didn't you change at home? Ted's left by now, surely?'

'Gracious, yes. Early worm and all that. But Dottie arrives at eight and if I'd togged myself up in sweaters and wellies she would have looked all sniffy, very Baptist and disapproving. Like you do now!' she added, giggling.

'May you be forgiven.' Fay poured coffee.

'Don't kid yourself Dottie thinks *you're* such an angel.'

'Whatever do you mean? Dottie hardly knows me.'

'Got you all sized up in that silent little mind of hers though. Hinted quite firmly only yesterday that you had your eyes on my husband, so there!'

'My God, what an imagination.'

'I nearly died of mirth when I finally got the drift of what she was trying to tell me. The sainted Mrs Browne of Glebe House no less. Poor old Dottie thinks she's the Delphic oracle, of course.'

'Don't they all! They must be putting some magic ingredient in the floor polish if every cleaner in the village is into ESP.'

Fay coaxed Flora on to a cushion on the floor and Maeve pushed one of the carrier bags across. The child peered into it, taking out small wooden farmyard animals and a fluffy toy rabbit.

'Dottie may have got hold of the wrong end of the stick with me, Maeve, but don't pretend you're launching yourself on the cold grey sea all alone in October.'

'Not exactly.' Maeve stirred her coffee, thick lashes concealing gold flecked eyes.

'Well?'

Flora started to chatter to herself, marching the little wooden pieces up and over the crumpled carrier.

'Murray Saunders is taking his boat out for a last flip before it goes in dry dock for the winter,' Maeve primly replied, 'and has been gallant enough to ask me to crew for him.'

'And how long will all this take?'

'Oh, it's only a little sail round the lighthouse, you might say. Just an hour or two. You know. I'll be back here by six and Dottie will stay on after the boys are back from school until I take over. Ted's out this evening in any case, some meeting at Harvey Cresswell's. He won't be home till late.'

'Who is this Murray Saunders anyway?'

Maeve laughed. 'The vet. Well, Starmer's Australian locum,

that is. I took poor old Harold down to the surgery a few weeks ago and this gorgeous suntanned creature beckons me into the surgery. Honestly, Fay, you *must* take that rabbit of yours. He's fantastic, no wonder there's such a queue in the waiting room – not just the dogs panting on the leashes, believe me! You can't imagine—'

'You are really mad, Maeve. If someone sees you, you'll have the devil of a job explaining.'

'Nuts,' Maeve said, downing her coffee. 'We'll be miles away. Who do we know who'd be tossing about in the Channel?' She jumped up and grabbed one of her bags, Flora eyeing her anxiously before going back to her game. 'OK if I change? I'll leave my things in Luke's room and change back again later. I can collect my sailing stuff another day.'

She disappeared upstairs and Fay smiled weakly at Flora who was putting the cows and pigs through manoeuvres. Maeve was the bloody limit. The turmoil of her own predicament forced its way to the surface and she found herself wearily tramping the familiar treadmill of possibility and counter possibility which Meg's death had set in motion. After yet another sleepless night even her own mangled brain was beginning to question the degree of Robert's innocence in all this. But murder? Robert?

Maeve reappeared in sailing togs, a brown gaberdine raincoat over her arm.

To her utter astonishment, Fay burst into tears, turning her back, gripping the sink as the agony spilled over. The child scrambled to her feet and clung to Maeve's coat. 'Fay, cut herself?' she whimpered.

'Yes, Flora darling. Sit there, sweetheart.' She gently pushed the toddler aside and put her arms around Fay's shoulders as she wept.

'Jesus! Whatever is it? Come on, love. What's happened?'

She shook her head, smiling bleakly at Flora who peered worriedly from one incomprehensible adult to the other.

'But what's the problem, sweetie? Not this railway accident surely? That's not still on your mind, is it?'

Fay blew her nose and impatiently brushed back a strand of

hair. 'It's Meg. The investigation's stalled, Maeve. Because Robert isn't here, I'm sure of it.'

'Just red tape. You know how country bobbies are. Nothing on the books for months and so they make a real production number of anything when it does come up.'

'You don't know the man who's in charge of the case. He's no country bobby. And there's more to it.' She tried to rationalize her fear. 'Meg was pregnant. Had you heard?'

'Oh, Ted mentioned some gossip at the pub, but that sort of situation isn't earth-shattering even in Stamford, is it?'

'Not in the normal way. But the brakes on my car didn't fail accidentally. It's all in the official report. Hayes is out to prove either Robert or I, or both of us, nobbled the car or, at the very least, passed it over to Meg knowing it was lethal. Someone else is involved and they are not even looking.'

'Balls!'

'The fact remains the police can put the finger on Robert the moment he steps off the plane. There's enough to go on to bring him in for questioning. "Helping the police with their inquiries" as they put it. It's ridiculous, we all know that. Who could possibly imagine him tampering with the brakes on the long shot of killing Meg? He even paid for her abortion and everything.'

Maeve sat back, staring at Flora who, losing interest in the adults now the tone of the conversation had lapsed into the drone of normality, was now rummaging through her mother's handbag. Without looking up, Maeve said, 'Why should Rob do that?'

'God knows. Paying by cheque and booking her into the clinic in my name looks pretty damning to the outsider, but it's just the sort of crackpot gesture Robert goes in for. Thinks he's fireproof. Of course, if there had been no car crash it never would have come out. It would never have come to light anyway if this local detective hadn't gone to such lengths to look into things. An ordinary traffic accident doesn't warrant a full-scale investigation by a chief inspector.'

'And you've been buzzing round trying to prove Robert's altruistic motives?'

Fay stared. Maeve's gaze was unblinking.

'Fay, for heaven's sake stop kidding yourself. Hayes isn't out to pin anything on Rob or anyone else. He's just trying to set out the facts for the inquest. He's thrown a spotlight on something you would have preferred to remain in the dark, and all this self-righteous hustle-bustle to find Meg's mythical boyfriend is your own frantic attempt to ignore the obvious.'

Fay gasped. 'How could you!' She half rose but Maeve grabbed her arm.

'Now, you listen to me. I'm the only friend you've got who has the guts to put it to you straight. And it's only because I'm fond of you I'm making the effort. I'm a lazy cow by nature and saying it like it is is not my style at all. But you, dear girl, are slowly driving yourself into a nervous breakdown over this. Forget it. Grow up. Let Hayes deal with it in his own way. Meg's accident is no longer important, the truth you have to face up to is that Rob's flesh and blood like the rest of us, not some plaster saint. If he slipped into bed with Meg once or twice he won't thank you for careering round the country shrieking his innocence. How can he come back and live with *that*? It's compassion he'll need, adult human sympathy. And I believe he has a right to expect it.'

'You would!'

Maeve was unperturbed. 'Take it how you like, love. But, believe me, the last thing Robert needs is you defending him like a tigress standing over a cub. Drop it. Acknowledge what is, after all, a small transgression by most people's standards these days. The poor sod probably had to spend hours alone with the dreary girl in all sorts of dreary places, all to keep you and Luke in clover.'

Fay's bitterness ebbed to low despair. Fresh tears welled up.

'There's more to it, Maeve. Hayes is on to something else. I said in my statement I had never met Barbara Hertz, the woman who died under the train. I thought at the time it was true. But I had, years ago, when I was a student. She and her sister were both on a visit to this medical centre in Israel. I hardly knew them as it happens, but I did a terrible wrong to Millicent Ambache, the Hertz woman's twin. I think she's the one behind all these mad phone calls I've been getting. The whole thing must have been raked over again when her sister came to Stamford to live with her and the two of them concocted this crazy persecution. To torment me, you see. Give me no peace. An eye for an eye. Retribution. But I didn't even remember her. Honestly. Hayes would never buy that! That I ruined Millicent Ambache's life and then totally forgot knowing the woman? She's the spitting image of her sister who died in the railway accident and she's been practically living on my doorstep for years. I've probably passed her in the street dozens of times!'

Maeve regarded Fay's stricken face, dredging for one word of comfort. At last she said, 'And you think this Ambache woman has told the police you lied? Why didn't it come out at the inquest?'

'That's the frightening thing. I don't know. It's a serious charge, lying to the police, especially in my profession. They would throw the book at me! The inquest is postponed but if Hayes has decided I might have pushed Barbara Hertz in front of the train it would be murder. Fancy that, two investigations, involving the husband and the wife!'

'If Ambache hasn't said anything so far she won't come out with it now.'

'Why not? She could hold it over me. Tell Hayes she has only just remembered where she'd seen me before, that we all knew each other intimately years ago. In his present suspicious state of mind he could even start thinking I had already been threatened by the Ambache sisters – the phone calls being painful reminders – and that I eventually pushed my persecutor under the train.'

'Utterly preposterous. You're really off your trolley with this one, Fay. Forget Millicent Ambache. After all, she's probably scared stiff it'll all come out about the phone calls. Poison pen letters and anonymous phone calls seem to be cornered exclusively by women living alone, nursing grievances. What did you do all these years ago?'

'Not now, Maeve. Forget it, please.'

'OK, have it your own way. But take it easy. Now, about sleeping? Are you still getting these crazy phone calls?'

No. But I've been thrashing about at night trying to sort things out in my mind. Started hearing footsteps round the house,' she ruefully admitted.

'Get some sleeping pills then. Who's your doctor? Old Rankin?'

Fay nodded.

'Why haven't you seen him about it before?'

'He won't give me anything.'

'Tosh!' Maeve stood up and put on her coat. 'Honestly, I sometimes think you're still in the Middle Ages. Taking the occasional sleeping pill isn't tantamount to being a dope fiend, girl.'

Fay blew her nose. 'It's not that. Rankin won't prescribe pills for *me*.'

Maeve stared blankly as Fay continued.

'My own fault. He gave me some tablets a couple of years ago when I got into that state after my sister, Prue, died. I accidentally took too many and had to go in for a stomach pump job.'

She faced Maeve's unbelieving response. 'Yes, really. It was a genuine mix-up. But Rankin didn't believe me and has marked me down as a fully paid-up member of the crazy gang. I saw what he had written on my case notes once. "Dosage cretin". In big capital letters.'

'Bloody cheek!'

'He told me I would never get so much as an aspirin out of him. Apoplectic with rage. You would have thought,' she laughed, 'I had dirtied *his* record, not just my own.'

'Doddering old fool. Should have retired years ago. Tell you what, I've got some looseners in the car – safer to keep things locked up there out of Flora's reach than at home. They're not dangerous, just some "don't care" pills I got last month to calm the "Irish frantics" as Ted calls them. They'll make you feel nicely relaxed. I'll get them.'

She darted out to the car and Fay and the child trailed behind, watching from the porch as Maeve rummaged in the glove compartment. Emerging triumphant, waving a small bottle above her head, she pressed it into Fay's hand.

'Sweeties?' said Flora hopefully.

'Yes, darling. Fay's sweeties. She's got some others for you. Mummy must fly. You'll be a very good little girl, won't you? I must go, Fay. I'm dreadfully late. Should have been in Renham half an hour ago.'

'Sorry, Maeve. Will he wait?'

'But of course!' She grinned. 'I'll park my car there and pick it up later. Mum's the word.'

Fay took Flora's hand and they stepped back inside to watch her drive away. Flora happily waved her toy rabbit until the car was out of sight. Drawing the child inside, she closed the door and bobbed down to touch Flora's rabbit.

'What very smart trousers he has.'

'Yes. He's called Rupert and I take him to bed with me every night.'

'Lucky Rupert. I used to have a rabbit once, a lady rabbit called Ottie. But she didn't have smart trousers like yours.'

'Did she get lost?' Flora's eyes widened with alarm.

'Not exactly. Ottie went off for a little holiday. Shall we go and look for her after lunch?'

'Rupert will find her for you,' she was gravely assured.

'Lovely. We'll do that.'

They went back into the kitchen and she cleared the table and began to prepare lunch. The child dispelled at a stroke the pall of dread which inexorably enveloped the empty house.

Eleven

They were just finishing lunch as Rose Barton trundled through the kitchen door, dropped her shopping and, massive in her tent-like coat, stood stock still miming amazement.

'Bless me, a little fairy visiting us today?'

Flora bobbed up and down in her seat, excitedly drumming her spoon on the table.

'It's me! Flora! I'm not a fairy.'

'Well I never, so it is. Gets more like a pretty little fairy every day, don't she, Mrs Browne?' She shrugged out of the coat and hung it behind the door, changing her shoes for bobbly slippers.

The old woman washed up, beaming over her shoulder, listening to Flora's prattle. She wiped the draining board, dried her hands and stood stroking Flora's hair.

'What next?' she asked.

Fay roused herself from her reverie and turned over a list of chores in her head. 'Upstairs, I think. Oh, and there's a coat of mine I've put out in the bedroom for dry-cleaning – it's got whisky stains on the lining and smells dreadful. I should have sent it last week but it slipped my mind. And could you check the pockets of Robert's grey suit, which is with it? Pack it all up in that large plastic bag the new sheets came in and I'll run them into town tomorrow.'

'Drop them in on my way home if you like. It's just by the bus stop. Be ready by the end of the week.'

'Oh, would you? That would be marvellous. I don't want to go out this afternoon while Flora's here.'

'No bother, duck. Leave it to me.'

She pulled the vacuum cleaner from the cupboard and

lumbered upstairs, trailing her own rendering of 'Yellow River'.

'I'm just taking Flora for a walk,' Fay shouted up the stairs as the strains of the performance receded along the landing. She pushed Flora's arms into her anorak and, putting on a heavy sweater herself, they set off, hand in hand.

They wandered through the fading autumn garden, making a detour to avoid the pool which, screened by the shrubbery, was still undiscovered by Flora. Guiltily, Fay remembered the half-finished clearance abandoned when Hayes had approached with Goldsmith across the grass, the tools presumably still lying by the path. She determined to complete the job next day without fail. They emerged from the orchard by a high wall which was crumbling in several places, held together only by strong tentacles of ivy.

They paused by a fence and a donkey approached, rubbing itself along the farm gate.

Fay lifted her up. 'Don't touch him, sweetheart. He's sometimes a bit nasty.'

'He's got flies on his eyes,' the child said, pointing a fat forefinger.

She put her down and they went on. As they scuffed in the fallen leaves a flash of grey caught her eye before vanishing into the undergrowth. Curious, she parted the bracken.

'A mousie! A mousie!' Flora trilled, jigging excitedly.

Fay plunged headlong into a tangle of brambles vicious as a thorn thicket. Flailing about in the bracken, first one and then another wild rabbit flew out, followed by a skinnier grey one which had first aroused her wild hope.

'Ottie!'

It hesitated, testing the air with delicate nostrils. Fay flung herself forward, falling headlong into the dry fronds, triumphantly grasping the rabbit with both hands.

'You've got one!'

Fay clutched the warm furry body, not daring to loosen her hold, feeling the flutter of a heartbeat in its narrow chest. The frantic wriggling suddenly ceased. Fay laughed aloud and emerged clasping her trophy.

'It's Ottie, Flora. *My* rabbit. We've found her again.'

111

'Rupert found her,' Flora reproved, taking a solid stand. 'I told you he would.'

'Of course you did. How extraordinary. Clever old Rupert.'

Flora sidled up, stretching out a tentative hand to feel the silky ears.

'A really real rabbit,' she murmured in awe.

'Yes, a very naughty lady rabbit. Holiday over now, Ottie, old girl. We'll take her home, shall we?'

When they got back to the garden the sun had dipped behind the house and Flora was shivering inside her anorak. They stopped off at the outhouse and secured the rickety doors before placing Ottie on the floor. Fay poked among the boxes at the back and found some hay.

'It's cold,' Flora wailed.

Poor kid's tired, Fay thought. 'I'm just making a nice bed for Ottie, darling, and then we can go in and have some tea in the warm.'

'Rupert's cold too.' Flora started to grizzle, rubbing a grubby fist round her eye, clutching her toy rabbit to her chest.

'Rupert can come inside with us and sit by the fire.'

'And Ottie?'

'Ottie likes it here. This is Ottie's house.'

'She doesn't like it! She doesn't. She ran away. She wants to be with Rupert,' the little voiced shrilled, a deep breath preceding a howl of ascending volume.

'Sod Rupert,' Fay muttered. 'OK Flora, we'll take Ottie inside for tea with Rupert.'

Flora's sudden squall evaporated and Fay acknowledged herself to be a woman of straw. 'Let's take this box for Ottie to sit in.'

The child flew to and fro filling a carton with handfuls of hay. The rabbit hunched in a corner of the outhouse twitching its nose, regarding the scuttling human efforts with interest.

Eventually, Fay, Flora, Rupert and Ottie plus a cardboard box were back in the kitchen. It was wonderfully warm. Rose Barton had laid a trolley with tiny sandwiches, salad and a covered plate on which half a dozen iced cakes were still moist and warm.

'Fairy cakes, Flora. She must have made them specially for you.'

She extracted the toddler from layers of woollies, made a pot of tea and pushed the trolley through to the sitting room.

A fire crackled in the grate while outside the sky had darkened to a thunderous slate. As she drew the curtains, rain began to splatter against the panes and Fay shivered. She pulled the sofa nearer the fire and as she did so Flora struggled through the door, Ottie wriggling violently in her arms, her chin set with determination. Fay swiftly crossed the room and grabbed the rabbit which promply sunk its teeth into her thumb.

'Ouch!'

'Ottie doesn't like being left out of everything,' Flora scolded, squatting down on the hearthrug.

'Close the door for me, darling, and then Ottie won't get out. We can have tea here.'

'And Ottie?'

'And Ottie,' Fay said with resignation. 'We can give her some of this lovely lettuce and after tea you can put her to bed in her box. Mummy will be here soon to take you home.'

She switched on the television, and while they ate, alternately watched a cartoon film and Ottie in her element at last in a civilized drawing room.

Flora climbed on to the sofa, Rupert once more restored to her affections, and lay in a mound of cushions sucking her thumb. Fay relaxed with a second cup of tea to watch the news. Ten minutes later the child was asleep, fat little legs splayed, her neck awkwardly bent against the armrest.

'Blast Maeve, I knew she'd be late back. I'll pop Flora in my bed for an hour.' Fay gathered her up and crept upstairs to slip the child under the duvet with Rupert. She switched on the softly shaded bedside light and tiptoed downstairs to clear the debris of rabbit droppings and shredded lettuce from the carpet. Pushing the trolley through to the kitchen, she sensed the rabbit hopping along in her wake and glanced round to see it easing behind the vegetable rack.

Fay grabbed it and pushed it firmly into the box together

with the scraps of left-over salad and some water. She hurried through the dark garden. As she was bolting the outhouse door, she heard the telephone ringing in the house and raced back.

Breathless, she lifted the receiver. 'Hello ... Hello? Who *is* this?' The scorpions in her mental bag of troubles lurched. 'Speak up, damn you. Why don't you say something? I *know* who you are.'

She slammed down the receiver and took the stairs two at a time, standing inside the bedroom shaken by her own pounding heartbeat. The lamp cast a honey glow over the rounded cheeks of the sleeping child, her imperceptible breath causing a loose feather to tremble on her chin. She crossed the room and took the phone from the extension and laid it aside.

Fay walked slowly downstairs and back to the kitchen. The open door swung wildly, squally gusts blowing dry leaves inside to whirl across the floor tiles. She closed the door, locked it and drew the bolt.

Pushing the leaves into an ash pan, she went through to the sitting room and, after clearing the trolley, noticed a note from Mrs Barton tucked under the traycloth.

Sorry I had to go before you got back but it was my bus. I took the cleaning and I'll bring the tickets next time. I found a wallet in his pocket – put it in the kitchen drawer. Love to little F.
Rose B.

Fay pushed the trolley back in place and opened the oddments drawer. There was a sizable morocco wallet she had never seen before. She held it to her nose, smelling the newness of the leather. But it wasn't a wallet. It was a small tool kit with screwdriver, pliers, wire and tyre gauge, all secured in individual pockets. Stainless steel, beautifully crafted and as neat and as effective as a surgeon's instruments. And this had been in the suit Robert had worn on the evening of Maeve's dinner party?

She sat down heavily, the thing open on her lap, staring at it numbly. Abruptly, she thrust it into her shoulder bag to obliterate the worm of doubt. Then the telephone started up its mad cacophony again. Raising clenched fists to her ears, Fay beat her temples. It rang on and on. Remembering the child, she stepped into the hall just as the racket stopped, the house pulsing in a silence as menacing as the mechanical trilling had been before. She should have got to it sooner. It was probably Maeve. Or Robert. One dare not ignore the phone.

Indecisive, she hovered in the hall, then went into the study for the decanter. Trailing back to the kitchen for a tumbler, her eye caught the small bottle of tranquillisers Maeve had left on the dresser. And why not?

She pattered back to the sitting room where the fire was now glowing gently and switched on the TV before settling down to wait for Maeve. She poured a drink and leaned back to watch the inane exchanges of a panel game. Where the hell was Maeve? Spilling half a dozen tablets into her palm, she smiled at the shade the chemist had contrived. Blues for the blue. Grimacing at her own feeble joke, Fay swallowed two and stretched out on the sofa.

An hour later she decided to ring Maeve's number and was relieved when one of the boys answered. Yes, Dottie was still there and could stay on, but what was happening? Fay fobbed him off.

She sprang at the phone when it rang again just after nine and slammed it down in exasperation when it turned out to be another from her mute caller. More heavy breathing and the inevitable dripping tap. She reached for more 'looseners' as Maeve phrased it. Fay was well into her fourth whisky when several unspoken calls came in a flurry, one after the other.

Her terror of the telephone had transformed into a tearful irritability, compounded by the unavoidable necessity to replace the receiver each time and lay herself open to fresh attack. Maeve would be sure to ring, explain the delay and they could concoct an alibi to placate Ted if necessary. It was as if a faceless accuser was trying to punish her for some unknown transgression and each was locked in bitter incomprehension of the other's failure to act out the allotted role. Who was the tyrant and who was the victim? Was there something she should say? Some password to appease this monster?

115

She swallowed another pill, lucidly aware of the comfortable baffle they erected. She *must* be awake when Maeve phoned, taking the receiver off the hook was impossible. She refilled the tumbler and resigned herself to a weary vigil.

At eleven, after several bouts of silent combat with her telephone assailant, she blearily took a call from Ted. Her clouded brain swam.

'Well, where is she, Fay?' He was cross and anxious, not at all his usual urbane self.

'I ... I'm not quite s–sure, Ted. You s–see there was some trouble with the car and Maeve had to call the AA. I got a taxi back here with Flora as it looked like being a long job. Hasn't she phoned you?'

'Like hell she has!'

'Oh, dear.'

'Where was this breakdown?'

'I ... I'm a bit hazy about the exact spot.' She floundered wildly for a likely location. 'Near Braintree, I think.'

'What the devil were you doing out there?'

'Some pottery place Maeve wanted to see.'

Ted sighed and, after a further brief interrogation, rang off.

Fay stumbled as she rose from the bottom step in the hall, bracing herself against the newel post. She shuffled back to the sitting room and crouched in front of the dying fire, too apathetic to renew it. A television film flickered soundlessly at her back and, staring moodily into the cooling embers, she reflected bitterly on the downside of friendship with Maeve MacMillan.

Gradually, she became aware of a painful recollection inserting itself like a scalpel into her befuddled brain. Delicately probing, she explored the tender fringes of memory. Painfully, the spot lay exposed. In anguish she remembered Mrs B's Cassandra-like warning: something about someone drowning she had said. 'Face down in the water'. That was it. The knife twisted. A body in a brown coat floating in the bright water. Maeve?

She leapt up, raking her hair, and paced the room, picturing Maeve that morning in the kitchen, putting on a coat over those ridiculous sailing clothes. It was brown. She was certain. Maeve had been wearing a cinnamon-coloured raincoat. She stared, unseeing, the newsreel churning mutely in the untidy room. Fay leaned her aching forehead against the mantelshelf and prayed in fervent despair. After a while she moved back to the sofa and lay there contemplating the terrible possibility of Maeve dead. First the woman on the line, then Meg and now Maeve? Didn't they say death always struck in threes? Then the phone rang again, it seemed for the hundredth time, and she staggered out into the hall to answer it.

'Fay, it's Maeve. Were you asleep?'

The demons receded and irritably Fay snapped back. 'No such luck.'

'Fay, I'm desperately sorry, poppet. Don't be angry. It's so complicated ... I'll explain it all later.'

'Are you all right? Was there an accident with the boat?'

'No, of course not. Whatever gave you that idea? Sorry, sweetie, you must have been frantic. Actually, we got stuck on a sandbank.'

'Where are you?'

'Outside Merryfield. Tried to ring you before but the number was engaged. I'll be with you in an hour or so. Did you manage to fend off Ted?'

'Yes, no thanks to you. I said we had had a breakdown near Braintree and I'd left you to call the AA while I came home with Flora in a hire car.'

'Is she all right?'

'Sleeping like an angel. I might as well keep her here and you can drive straight home and collect her in the morning.'

'No. I'll have to knock you up. To change my clothes. I'm soaked to the skin.'

'Oh, all right.'

'Bless you.'

Maeve rang off and Fay crept upstairs, guiltily aware that in her misery she had not looked in on Flora for hours. She leaned over the warm bundle under the duvet, still sleeping, quite unaffected by the strange surroundings and almost continuous phone calls. Fay lay on the bed beside her. Just for half an hour, she promised herself, tired to death and feeling rather sick. She lay rigid in her resolve to keep weariness at bay, to be awake for Maeve's return. Her eyelids flickered, then closed, her jaw sagged and heavy nasal breathing blended with the mournful hooting of an owl in the darkness outside.

She dreamed of floating, not drowning, not even in water, but floating in one corner of the bedroom, gently suspended above the open door, calmly observing her own and Flora's sleeping forms. Utter bliss.

But suddenly she felt herself jerked as if by a thread, drawn through a funnel of darkness down a screaming abyss. The noise deafened her, piercing her eardrums like the sound of a buzzer warning of an oncoming train.

She woke bathed in sweat, the continuous racket battering her brain. Fay lunged at the telephone by the bed and in the darkness feverishly felt about for an endless minute before discovering the receiver dangling at the end of its flex near the floor. Her mind spun in an effort to locate the sound, relentlessly pealing still. The doorbell! Not the phone, the doorbell. Glancing at the sleeping child, Fay swung leaden legs to the floor and lurched towards the door.

The floor undulated before her. Grasping the door handle she tried to control nausea and dizziness. A determined on-slaught on the bell launched fresh arrows of tormenting decibels as she staggered along the landing, her legs seeming to follow the messages from her brain like rubber appendages. The racket at the front door pitilessly continued. She tottered to the head of the stairs and hung there, clinging to the wall.

Drawing a deep breath as the noise began once more, she inched one foot forward like a reluctant swimmer testing a winter sea. It touched an oak tread but as she brought the other foot down to join it, her balance began to tilt and swirl. Her whole body contorted as she flailed the air.

Fay was conscious of falling, spinning in impenetrable black-ness, but it was if she was back in her dream, falling through space. But the blow which exploded through her head like a shower of sparks was no dream. She gasped, literally breathless. Then the soft dark mercifully claimed her.

118

Next morning, while Fay Browne lay in the narrow hospital bed, Bill Goldsmith sprawled undiscovered in the dense shrubbery behind the chapel warehouse. The machete lay beside him in the blood-soaked turf.

Robert's warehouse foreman was quite, quite dead.

Twelve

The room was dark. Exploratory hands discovered tender areas of bruising and bandaging of head and chest. Where was she? It was difficult to see, and the echoing sounds of heels on tiled floors reminded her only of school. Fay slid back into a doze. An hour later, feeling increasingly pained in every joint, she was violently startled awake as the door burst open.

Maeve stepped lightly into the room, juggling with an armful of yellow roses, several glossy magazines and something wrapped in gift paper. She left the door open and sunlight slanted into the curtained room. Maeve dropped everything on the bed and stood silently examining the figure in the iron bedstead, her eyes dark as peat in the half-light.

'Mother of God. What a bloody awful sight!'

Fay managed a weak smile. 'A bedside manner was never your forte, was it, Maeve?' In the temporary illumination, Fay absorbed the surroundings. Vague recollections of some sort of medical interrogation from a woman in a starched apron flooded back.

Maeve pulled up a chair and unwrapped the roses, lifting the plastic lid from the jug on the locker and jamming the stems into the water. A shower of droplets splashed on to the wall and settled in a pool.

Fay grimaced. 'The Nazi wardress in charge here will make painful reprisals when you've gone. I shall get the blame for all that mess. This is the local hospital, I presume?'

'Nearest for accidents, and if you are referring to the notorious Sister Menkes, she and I locked horns last winter when Anthony was having his tonsils out. God knows why the woman has got this ghastly reputation, she's actually very kind

120

when you scratch the surface.' Maeve tilted her head, taking in the rest of the room. 'You realize you've been thrust in a private room in the isolation wing? Have they given you your lecture on the evils of demon drink, you naughty girl?'

Fay shook her head and Maeve's laughter rang out in ascending decibels. Fay winced.

'Shut the door and sit down. Tell me what happened.'

Maeve perched on the bed, impish, relishing the dramatic details. 'Last night? Well, there I was, sopping wet and ringing your doorbell so long I thought Saint Peter himself would eventually open it. Frantic, I was. Stuck on the doorstep like an insurance salesman, getting nowhere fast. And I simply had to get back into the house to change before I could go home. Ted may not have a suspicious nature, but even he doesn't regard wellies and a kagoul as shopping gear. Then, of course, I heard this God almighty crash, and when I peered through the letter box, there you were in a heap at the bottom of the stairs, spark out. Nothing for it but break a window and climb in. The ambulance men were very decent about it after a bit of blarney – I said you'd been babysitting for me and fell down the stairs coming to the door. All true. But it sounded more than a bit iffy especially with you out for the count, lying in a pool of blood and vomit and reeking like a distillery. A very unlikely baby-sitter. I can tell you, I thought you'd had it. While they were putting you in the ambulance I slipped upstairs and, would you believe it, Flora had slept through the whole thing? Did you slip her a jigger, too? I threw my wet clothes in the bathroom, got changed and wrapped Flora in a blanket. The ambulance man fairly boggled to see me coming downstairs all dressed up. Lucky there wasn't time for explanations and I followed here in my car. They probably thought you'd had a party. There was no way of disguising the fact that you were boozed up to the eyeballs.'

'I suppose that's why the sister's so frigid. She was the one who did the stomach pump job on me before. Oh, God, Maeve, what a bloody shambles ... Is Flora OK?'

'Chirpy as a cricket. Rattling on about rabbits or something.' Maeve took Fay's hand and peered at her in the darkened room. 'I'm terribly sorry, sweetie. I really do land you in it, don't I?'

Fay grimaced, her scalp pricking as if her hair was bound up in a barbed wire hairnet. 'Not your fault I got plastered, was it?'

Maeve patted the starched sheet. 'Best idea you've had in weeks. Can't think why you didn't think of it before, stuck in that great empty mausoleum, getting yourself in a tizzy.'

'Tell me more about last night. It's all so muzzy.'

'Jesus, you really did crack your head, didn't you? Don't you remember me asking you to have Flora while I went sailing?'

'Vaguely. Go on. It's coming back by degrees.'

'Oh, Fay, it was all a disaster from start to finish. Murray was huffy because I was late meeting him in Renham, and by the time we got to the boat we had missed the tide or something. Eventually, we got out to the estuary and it was incredibly beautiful, darling, so quiet and still. We had some Bacardi and Coke and went below for a bit of a snooze. Next thing I knew we were stuck on a sandbank or mudflat or something. Couldn't move the rotten hulk for hours till it refloated itself. I nearly went crazy wondering if you would be able to keep Ted at bay till I got back. We tried ringing you on Murray's mobile but you must have taken the phone off the hook, it seemed permanently engaged.'

Fay giggled, shaking her head in disbelief and then wishing she hadn't. A hundred soldier ants began drilling inside her skull.

Maeve continued, now well into her stride. 'Murray and I started to bicker, me saying what a bloody awful sailor he turned out to be and how I didn't want his great red hands anywhere near me. You know, we'd been having a lovely romantic cruise till we got grounded, then it started to dawn on me – stuck as I was in that minute cabin – that those hairy forearms had probably been up to the elbows inside cows.' Maeve wrinkled her nose. 'Put me right off, I can tell you.'

'Randy bitch, serves you right.'

'Don't take that Calvinistic tone with me, Fay Browne. I've heard all about your fumblings with Ted in the school car park.'

Fay eyes widened in astonishment. 'With Ted? Your Ted?'

'Yes *my* Ted, my sweet innocent. Don't worry, I'm not going to come over all spouse-like.'

Fragments clinked together. 'Maeve, that was nothing. Just a friendly tussle in the car. You know full well Ted's crazy about you. He's never looked at anyone else, let alone me.'

Maeve's ringed hand flew up in a dismissive gesture. 'Don't give it a thought. I only mentioned it to give you a laugh, though, believe me, I put in an hour's solid brainwashing to scotch that rancid bit of local gossip.'

'Who told you all this? You haven't confronted Ted, have you?'

'Of course not. I'm saving that for a rainy day. It was my ever-faithful Dottie who put me in the picture. I told you before she's had her suspicions of your intentions towards poor Teddy. Who knows what set that little bird whirring in her primitive brain? Sometimes I think being deaf makes her slightly potty, too much strain on the imagination – always thinking she's missing half the action, I suppose. Anyway, I assured Dottie she'd got it all wrong but you know how she has this dogged dedication. And so when this chap living at her hostel told her about you and Ted snogging in the car park the night of the art show, she gets herself all worked up and lays this juicy bit before me as confirmation of her dire warnings. She came to help out on Sunday – I had people to lunch.'

'But there was nobody in the car park. We left early. Everyone was still at the exhibition, and in any case it was dark.'

'Don't fret, love. I wish now I'd never mentioned it but you know what a village Stamford can be when it comes to scandal, and Robert's success here keeps them agog.'

Fay smiled. 'Sorry. Go on.'

'Talking to Dottie at all is a bit of a strain. She's a marvellous lip-reader but you have to look at her directly and mouth your words clearly, and then she writes notes back. All very time consuming. It must have been pretty comic to see us having this slow motion argy-bargy about your morals. It seems that this man at Dottie's hostel does odd jobs about the school and they roped him in for the art show evening to help sweep up and so on. Presumably, while he was leaning on his broom, he saw you

123

with Ted and couldn't wait to pass on the dirt about these two prominent local citizens. Sod's law that it was the two people least likely to feature in any sleazy gossip who were being watched.'

'Poor Ted. How unfair. It was nothing at all like that, Maeve, I promise you.'

She sighed impatiently. 'I know that, juggins, but I didn't want this story drifting round town, especially now Ted's polishing his image for the Tory party. Eventually, I did manage to button up poor old Dottie. Threatened her with her marching orders if she let this bloke put about any more lies about her employer. She got pretty sulky about it, but being mute anyhow it didn't seem to make such a fat lot of difference. But I think she'll be simmering inside for a day or two.' Maeve grinned. 'It must be bloody annoying trying to put over the fact that you're not speaking on principle when you can't utter a single word at the best of times.'

Maeve laughed, slapping the bedcover and sending magazines cascading noisily to the floor. The door opened and Sister Menkes stood in the doorway.

'I'm afraid Mrs Browne must not be disturbed any longer, Mrs MacMillan,' she said coldly. 'She must be kept absolutely quiet.'

Maeve made a face and pecked Fay's cheek. 'Courage, *ma petite*,' she whispered and swept out. Sister Menkes watched her go, closed the door and approached the bed. She touched Fay's flushed cheek.

'That inspector, Hayes, wants to look in on you before you settle down. Is there anything you need?' she added kindly. 'Any pain?'

'N–no, n–nothing,' she stammered. 'Nothing at all.'

Roger Hayes passed Maeve on her way out and toyed with the idea of questioning her there and then. But if the Browne woman was really in a bad way it was imperative he got her story first. At least she was in no position to make a break for it. Being here was as good as being on remand.

He stood in no awe of Sister Menkes and, pulling rank, walked straight into Fay's room. The sight of the battered figure in the hospital bed was a shock – she looked as if she had done ten rounds.

After a bleak pause, he spoke, his low voice instantly recalling Fay to those other interrogations at the house. She wished her headache would go away.

'I was sorry to hear about your accident, Mrs Brown. Most unfortunate. I hope you don't mind me disturbing you, but Sister said you could cope with a few questions, and I must speak with you urgently.'

Fay stared at him wearily, wondering if her confusion was compounded by his stern manner or her concussion. She steeled herself to concentrate, fearful of her vulnerability – and Robert's.

He said, 'I understand you were brought to this hospital two years ago. A failed suicide.'

A nervous tic flickered her eyelid. 'That was an accident. I explained all that to Dr Rankin. Who told you this?'

He shrugged and sauntered across the room to bring up a chair. He seated himself by the bed.

'Last night you were brought here unconscious. Possibly the victim of an attack. A full investigation was called for and Dr Rankin tells me he was not altogether satisfied. Since your previous admission he has never prescribed drugs for you.'

'That's quite right. But I hadn't asked for any.'

'Then how do you explain this?'

Fay's mind went into a spiral. Was it going to cause embarrassment to Maeve if she admitted accepting tranquillisers from her? Best to gloss over that and act aggressive.

'You seem to be under some misapprehension, Inspector. I didn't throw myself down the stairs. Even without drugs there are more reliable ways of committing suicide. I fell. No one pushed me. It was dark. I had been asleep and . . .' she hesitated, 'I had had quite a bit to drink that evening.'

'That was obvious, I gather. But there's evidence of a drug overdose. In fact, the conjecture is that had you not been roused by Mrs MacMillan you might well have died of a fatal combination of alcohol and tranquillisers. Unbelievable as it may seem to you at present, falling downstairs was probably the luckiest chance of your life. If you *did* fall,' he added.

He wished he had had the chance to question the MacMillan female. The whole episode sounded distinctly dodgy. It wasn't helped by the superintendent's panic that Stamford's leading citizens, including the wife of a potential MP, were involved with the Browne case. Robert Browne, he had been warned, was a tricky customer, not likely to take kindly to uncorroborated accusations. And his wife was a lawyer, working with that thorn in the side of the local police, the Renham Law Centre. He'd better tread carefully. He sighed. Political manoeuvering was not his style.

'As I was saying, Mrs MacMillan's timely arrival was extremely fortunate.'

Fay winced. 'I'll take a lot of convincing that it was my lucky night. Even breathing is painful.' The mention of Maeve in all this made her nervous. What had she said to Dr Rankin, if anything? Or was Hayes just fishing? The tic danced under her eye, chipping away at her concentration. She plunged in, hoping for the best.

'There's no stair carpet you see, perhaps that's why I fell so heavily. I can't really remember.' In fact, searing recollections of the hurtling descent were burned in her mind. 'I'm sure I just overbalanced in my rush to stop the doorbell ringing.'

'Yes, that must be it. Why was she calling so late?'

'Maeve was fetching her daughter. I had been looking after Flora and she had been held up for some reason I can't quite recall.'

'Mrs Browne, I know you're still in a state of shock but I must pursue my enquiries. There have been tragic developments this morning.' He paused, then put his cards on the table. 'For a start, I think your Metro was tampered with and the wrong person died. Possibly your husband was the target, as he was seen to be driving. Then you yourself have this spectacular accident. Are you saying no one attacked you? No one broke into the house?'

'No. I was alone with the child. And if my car was tampered with it could have happened after Robert flew to Paris. Meg could have met someone. And falling downstairs was my own stupid fault brought about by clumsiness and whisky.'

He jotted down notes, his response carefully neutral. She stared at his fingers gripping the slim pencil and was disconcerted to find her concentration had again shifted. Her head began to throb with remorseless regularity.

'But you would agree that you have been in a highly nervous state for the past few days and have a history of unstable behaviour?' Waving aside her protestations, he continued. 'The anonymous phone calls obviously aggravated your state of mind and might have given you an irrational sense of persecution. You discovered that your husband had arrived back at Heathrow on Monday while you were looking after the MacMillan child. He booked into a hotel in London and went to several business meetings. Odd not to rush back home but there you go . . .' This was below the belt, he knew that. But he had to jolt some truth out of these people.

Fay heard this in shocked silence. Robert was already back? Had been in England since Monday morning? She dragged her scrambled thoughts back to Hayes' questions.

'. . . and so you see it's vital to discover if there is someone who would benefit from your death. Someone who, having failed with what would seem a car accident and knew you to be vulnerable to mental persecution, might try to stage a mock suicide. Did you dwell on this possibility yourself after the woman fell on the railway line? Do you still insist that Barbara Hertz was a stranger to you?' He paused before delivering the coup de grâce. 'Did you know that your foreman, Goldsmith, was attacked the very night you fell or were pushed downstairs? Killed in your own garden with a machete?'

'Stop! Stop it! Damn you!' she screamed, beating the air with clenched fists. He rose as Fay's hysteria swiftly brought Sister Menkes into the room. She frowned, pushing him aside and gripping Fay's shoulders, forcing her back against the pillows. Roger Hayes quietly withdrew.

'Shush now, shush,' Menkes said, smoothing her hair. She called a nurse and left the room to concoct a milky fluid which she insisted Fay swallow. Finally, Fay was alone, exhausted by

Hayes' pitiless onslaught, his summary of her own unacknow-
ledged fears. And Goldsmith? Was she going mad? Did he
really say it?

Tears glittered unshed as she lay allowing Hayes' insinua-
tions to slop back and forth inside her head.

Thirteen

Roger Hayes finished making his phone calls. He sat over his desk, scratching figures on a memo pad, juggling with hours and minutes, checking mileage calculations and keeping the superintendent in a state of acute agitation.

Two women. Two deaths. Both, on the face of it, accidental. And now a third, this time an unequivocal murder victim. Linked or unconnected? Goldsmith had apparently struggled with his attacker, but he was an old man, certainly unfit, the assailant need not have been any sort of muscle man. A woman could have wielded that fearsome weapon equally effectively. The fingerprint lads had drawn a blank: the machete was unmarked and even the Browne female had worn gardening gloves.

Hayes was not unfamiliar with accident victims and this was not his first murder investigation. But he was appalled by the vengeful brutality of this latest attack. It was a damn nuisance the search for the old man had been delayed for hours – everyone too busy chewing over Mrs Browne's near fatality to wonder why poor old Goldsmith was absent from work.

The body had been in the shrubbery since the previous evening, the doctor estimated. Had been there, unseen, in all those bloody evergreens where the woman had been gardening when he and Goldsmith had interrupted her that last time he had called at the house. Killed with that fearful implement too, poor old sod. 'A weapon conveniently to hand' – wasn't that the phrase so often used when explaining female domestic violence? A machete was hardly a rolling pin though, was it?

Hayes shook his head sadly and shuffled the figurework into a file. He lit a cigarette and watched the smoke curl towards the flyblown ceiling. The proliferating details were muddying what had already been a dirty puddle, and in his efforts to sift the flotsam before it all swirled down the drain, Hayes was all too aware that he was being overtaken by a flood of new information. His unfamiliarity with the locality, or even the people involved, was not helping. There was also the deliberate obfuscation by all the players. He suspected everyone connected with the Brownes was aiding and abetting in one way or another.

Robert Browne turning up in London on the quiet was a facer. Booking into a hotel on Monday morning without so much as a message home? Had heard the news about his secretary from Hugo Suskind, one assumed. Lying low. 'Sleeping off the jet lag', he had said when challenged by Sergeant Bellamy. Very laid-back, this Robert Browne. Hayes had him at the top of his list for questioning. Just as soon as he could lay hands on the bloody man. He grinned sourly, willing himself to look on the bright side.

Hayes' superintendent had his own problems. An urgent need for results must be weighed against the sensibilities of the local bigwigs, who fell into two distinct camps: (i) those who benefitted from Browne's entrepreneurial flair which had put Stamford on the map, and (ii) those who rubbed their hands in glee at the prospect of him coming a cropper. The super had reiterated the need to tread carefully and privately wished he could come up with a reasonable excuse to hand the whole investigation on to someone else, a local man, less ambitious than Hayes, more diplomatic. Roger Hayes, a divorcee, had been transferred, at his own request, from Oxford and his single-minded pursuit of lawbreakers was almost religious in its intensity. The superintendent was used to regular coppers. He needed no holy crusade on his patch. That he was worried was putting it mildly. But no doubt a kick upstairs – Hayes' promotion to some newfangled branch of the force? – would soon take this smart alec away from Renham. None too soon as far as he was concerned. No wonder the ex-Mrs Hayes had scarpered.

In her hospital bed Fay slept on and off, drifting on a balmy lagoon finally to wake at five the following morning, clear in her mind at last.

Hayes' strict orders that no one be permitted to discuss the details of Goldsmith's death until he was able to interview Mrs Browne in detail had been easily maintained in the isolation ward. Sister Menkes had been cooperative; there being enough potential hysteria already. She banned any newspapers and firmly put the staff in their place as to gossip with a patient already in trauma. In the meantime, Glebe House was closed and the warehouse staff dispersed, leaving only the police and old Rose Barton to sift through the mess.

Fay put on her bedside light knowing sleep was impossible. The wards were relatively quiet, free from the continuous daytime clatter, and even Hayes would not dare to question her again till after breakfast at the earliest. The remaining hour or two before the daytime hospital routine clanked into motion was only a temporary respite.

She lay back on the pillows and planned her escape. If Robert had indeed been in London since Monday she must speak to him privately before Hayes trapped him into any sort of admission. Hugo would know how to reach him and, as soon as she was free of this medical incarceration, she could put Robert in the picture, ask him if he knew about Meg's secret relationship or had been bamboozled into thinking himself entirely responsible for her pregnancy. As Meg's death was still notionally accidental – and the engineer's report was the only evidence which gave support to Hayes' suspicion of foul play – Hayes might have to relinquish his determination to nail Robert and concentrate his investigation on the murder of poor Bill Goldsmith. At least he couldn't blame Robert for that. Or could he? Arriving back in England on the morning of Goldsmith's attack was bad timing in the extreme. Did he have an alibi for that evening? She thrust aside her own ambivalent feelings about Robert's strange silence, the puzzling lack of contact, his not even ringing her from the airport to say he was in London. Fay clung to her one priority: Luke. The real necessity was to shield Luke. And protecting Luke meant shielding Robert. Till death us do part? Perhaps even that...

Fay leafed through the magazines Maeve had left, her

mind elsewhere. One of them was called *Better Half*, the centrefold sporting a coy male nude and featuring advice about multiple orgasms and enhancing female libido. She turned a page, marvelling at Maeve's idea of convalescent reading. Her attention was caught by a picture of women and children grouped outside a ramshackle house, its front door scrawled with graffiti. The women all looked defiantly cheerful, clutching their infants like survivors from a shipwreck, safe at last.

Fay peered at the woman in the centre of the group, her head thrown back in laughter, disclosing large teeth which even in print clearly sported a middle gap. 'Shows a generous nature' as Mrs B would say.

She squinted at the caption, a band of pain re-establishing itself behind her eyes. MAUREEN PATEL WINS ANOTHER ROUND. And underneath:

Doctor Patel persuades the council to allow her to take over one of their hostels for the exclusive use of battered wives and their children. Like a latter-day Barnardo, Doctor Patel refuses to turn away any woman in distress, continuing her relentless fight for women's rights despite local opposition in every district in which her refuges have been established.

Fay skimmed the rest of the article, growing increasingly excited by her own mounting conviction. The gappy teeth belonged to the woman she had known as Maureen Sutton-Brookes.

Her head jerked up as the door opened and a student nurse stepped in.

'Tut, tut,' she said, sending the trolley spinning out of reach. 'No reading allowed. Sister will hit the roof if she catches you.' The girl shuffled the magazines into a pile and slipped them under her arm. 'You're meant to sleep as much as possible, Mrs Browne. Doctor's orders.'

'Please,' Fay begged. 'Just one. Can't you leave the top one? It's very large print, nearly all pictures. You can take *Vogue* and *Country Life*.'

The nurse flipped through the pages of *Better Half* and grinned when she reached the centrefold, holding it up out of reach like forbidden fruit.

'Naughty, naughty. This the one you mean?'

Fay nodded, biting back a grin. The nurse joined in on an 'all girls together' snigger.

'OK. Just this one. But don't let Sister catch you with it.'

She slipped the offending periodical under the pillow and switched out the light, tucking the other magazines under her arm to read later. Fay smiled in growing confidence and reached for the telephone. Perhaps, as Hayes said, falling downstairs was lucky after all.

She tried Maeve's number and obviously woke her.

'Fay, whatever are you doing out of hospital?'

'That's the problem. I'm still here. That's why I'm ringing. I've *got* to get out of here. Could you possibly pack some of your clothes for me and bring them straight away? Don't tell anyone, make up a parcel, like a box of goodies – some sort of gift – and leave them at reception. But make sure they send them up immediately – before Menkes comes back on duty at eight. For heaven's sake be discreet, Maeve! And send a handbag and some money. A hundred if you can spare it.'

'Oh, I don't know about that, sweetheart.' She sounded flustered, on her guard, not at all like unflappable Maeve. 'Menkes said you had to stay in bed for at least a week and had to be very quiet.'

'Well, I haven't been certified yet, have I? They can't force me to stay here, for God's sake. That's just it. I can't possibly rest here. You know what it's like. And I can't go home. Hayes' men are probably all over the house. There's no treatment,' she added desperately. 'Just rest and painkillers. And Maeve,' Fay heard herself turn the screw with the barest flicker of guilt, 'you do owe me this favour, you know.'

Maeve capitulated.

At six thirty an orderly sidled into the room with a bulging carrier bag sealed with flowing ribbon bows. She seemed to speak no English but clearly regarded herself as some sort of fairy godmother, smiling broadly. God knows what story

133

Maeve had spun at the reception desk. The orderly left her to unwrap the 'get well present' and closed the door.

Fay threw off her nightdress and pounced on Maeve's lingerie, a tweed trouser suit, cashmere sweater and boots. Everything except the boots fitted but she fixed that problem with a pair of pink bedsocks over her tights. Maeve had even sent some make-up and a bobble hat like a tea cosy. She ransacked the locker for a brush then threw open the cupboard to look in the full-length mirror. Her first reaction was of utter disbelief. Who on earth was this battered creature whose reflection stared back at her?

Good grief, I can't walk out of here looking like this!

She closed in on the looking-glass. Swollen features wobbled as the cupboard door swung on its hinges. One eye was almost closed. The light was diffused but nothing could disguise the expanse of bandage round her head and bruising which extended from cheekbone to jaw. The flaming red hair hung like ribbons, almost lending a comic aspect to her injuries.

Painfully aware of the wrenching ache in her ribs as she raised her arms, she began to smooth stick foundation over the broken face. After a few minutes she had effected a passable camouflage and, brushing her hair forward to hide the puffy eye, she pulled the woolly hat over the bandages and hoped for the best. In fact, it didn't look too bad.

She checked the contents of the handbag. 'Maeve, you angel!' A bundle of notes was folded inside the purse and, most wonderful of all, a pair of sunglasses. She judged the effect in the long mirror. An improved version this time, mildly eccentric-looking in the ski hat and sunglasses, but not weird enough for her to be stopped as an escaping lunatic. On second thoughts, perhaps the sunglasses were a bit much. She would just keep her head down. Literally.

She gathered up her magazine and handbag and quietly left the room. Everywhere was still quiet. Perhaps she would pass off as a visitor of some sort – from the social services if the woolly hat was anything to go by. She gripped her bag and walked purposefully towards the lift.

Outside, on the stone steps, Fay was almost felled by the

clear, cold air which hurled itself at her lungs, bringing tears to her eyes. Bracing herself to step out she made it to the main road and rang for a taxi from a call box well away from the hospital gates. The cab picked her up almost immediately and, cradling her aching ribs, Fay leaned forward from the back seat and said, 'Greensbrook please. I want to get an Intercity.'

'Renham's nearer, miss.' He glanced back, startled by her pallor and the half-disguised bruises.

'No, the junction at Greensbrook. And hurry. I ... I'm meeting a friend there.'

'And none too soon, missus,' the driver muttered, swinging the rattling cab in a wide U-turn and accelerating north.

Later, seated at the back of a rail car full of early commuters, Fay smiled grimly as she wound her watch and planned the next move. Fortunately, no one seemed in the least interested in the jumpy redhead in the bobble hat and she hid herself behind a quality newspaper, tailor-made for escapees. She searched the home news for anything on poor Bill Goldsmith's attack but it rated only a mention as part of a columnist's crusade for stiffer sentences.

Arriving at the terminus, she wondered how to get to the women's refuge place. Suddenly feeling dizzy, she would have stumbled if a passing porter had not caught her elbow.

'Nice party, chick?' he said, swinging off in a rolling swagger before she could reply. Did she really look like a drunk staggering in to work after an all-night session? She scuttled out of the station – drawing attention to herself was the last thing she wanted. There was also the dreadful possibility that Hayes would send someone after her as soon as he heard she had run away from the hospital. Or could one discharge oneself by just walking out? No good worrying about niceties like that at this point, she decided, and made as much haste as her protesting ribcage would allow.

Coming to London, losing herself in the crowds, was really the best hope, no point in just sitting in an isolation ward waiting for Hayes to pop the all-important questions, not with Robert unable or unwilling to contact her. The queue for taxis was an obvious target if her flight had been discovered.

She boarded the first bus to come along, just to get off the street, longing to sit down, not even sure of its destination. She could get off at the next stop once she had got her breath. She asked the conductor if anywhere near Mafeking Road was on his route. 'Mafeking Road, Brixton?' she prompted without much hope.

He eyed her curiously but smiled and took the money. 'Sure is, love. I'll give you a shout when we get to the stop, shall I?'

She nodded. A bad move, the headache starting up again in concert with the grinding gears of the bus as it gained speed.

But luck was on her side at last and the bus carried her across the river and into the safety of the teeming suburbs.

Fourteen

After many stops she got off the bus at a street market and took out the dog-eared strip torn from *Better Half*. People passed on both sides, smoothly parting like the tide around a rock. Fay stared helplessly at vapid faces in the rush hour crowds, protected from each other by mutual indifference. Touching the rough fabric of a woman's coat to ask the way, the woman recoiled, her gaunt features accentuated by vulnerable dark shadows.

'Well?' It was more like a challenge than a question and Fay's stuttered enquiry came out in a croak.

'Mafeking Road?' The woman's mouth relaxed and she broke into laughter, her eyes focussing on the trail of bandage which had escaped from under Fay's woolly cap. She pointed to the corner. 'That's Glover Street, see, and if you turn down there Mafeking Road is on the left about halfway down. Number twelve, you can't miss it.'

She walked away almost before she had finished speaking and disappeared in the crowd, leaving Fay clear of one problem, its place immediately taken by another, confirming Maeve's theory about everyone's personal worry level. The nag in her brain was now, how had the woman known she was looking for number twelve?

She was right about it being easy to find. Fay recognized the house from the magazine photograph, the steps leading to a front door with 'Marty' aerosoled above the letterbox.

Her feet dragged the last few yards, exhausted by her escape, her spirit drained by this blind determination to prove Robert innocent of orchestrating Meg's accident. Did she even believe it? Her head ached, and with diminishing hope of anything in this ramshackle squat of a house actually working, she pressed the doorbell.

The shrill ring struck in a flashback of pain and she leapt back, pressing her hands against her ears, reliving Maeve's assault on the doorbell at home which had precipitated her hurtling spiral down the stairs. The door was flung open and faces seemed to swim and multiply before her. Fay leaned weakly against the wall and managed to blurt out, 'Dr Sutton-Brookes – I mean, Patel? Is she—?' before blacking out. She slid senselessly on to the doormat under the astonished gaze of the girl who, with a gaggle of small children, stood on the step.

'Christ Almighty! A goner!' she shrieked, pushing the kids aside to run back into the house. She shouted up the dark staircase, 'Linda! Linda, come quick.' A woman in dungarees raced down to kneel on the doorstep. Fay groaned. Her head rolled, revealing the long bruise along her jaw.

'She wants Maureen,' the girl whispered, making ineffectual gestures to fend off the children who pressed in, full of curiosity.

Linda pushed the nearest boy violently aside, sending him crashing on to the floorboards. 'Can't move a fuckin' elbow in this place. Give 'er some air, can't ya?' The kids scattered.

They exchanged anxious looks and Linda suggested they lift the unconscious stranger into the front room.

'Oh, I don't know, Linda. Maureen's funny about shoving people about when they're out for the count.' She lifted the bandage on Fay's head and peered under it. 'She's got a shocking cut on 'er 'ead, an' all.'

Fay's eyes flickered and she moaned again. The children had silently crept back, pushing grubby faces between the two kneeling over the apparent corpse.

'Sod off,' Linda hissed at a knot of passers-by at the gatepost who had stopped to watch yet another 'real life drama' at the refuge.

'Look here, Teresa, we can't leave her on the bloody floor. Anyway,' she said, heaving Fay's lolling head on to her shoulder and circling her chest with thin arms, 'she's coming round.'

'Oh, all right. If you say so.'

They hoisted her up. Fay emitted such a blood-curdling scream that Teresa dropped her feet and shot backwards, sending another child spinning into the wall.

'Bugger.' Linda lowered Fay to the floor.

'It's my ribs,' she gasped, her face ashen.

'Can you walk if we help you?'

Fay leaned against the wall, taking shallow, painful breaths.

'OK. Sure. Thanks.'

Linda took her arm and Fay struggled to her feet, Teresa watching with an expression of fascinated horror as they lurched into the front room. Lowering herself on to a sagging leatherette settee, Fay closed her eyes, praying for her head to reattach itself to the rest of her body. The room spun. Several more women came in, looking with mild interest at the figure on the sofa. The children grew bored and pushed out between those blocking the doorway.

'Phone Maureen, somebody,' Linda bawled. 'And bring some tea.'

But Fay had already passed out again.

After a few minutes one of the women came back bearing a couple of mugs on a tin tray. She stared grimly at Fay's bruises, already yellowing under the cheekbone. Her cynical glance softened as she handed her a steaming mug which slopped painfully in her lap. Teresa sipped the other.

The tension relaxed and Fay was sufficiently recovered to disguise her shudder as she tasted the cloying brew. She smiled nervously at the tea woman who continued to regard her with intensity, clutching the tin tray to her chest like a breastplate. In an effort to fill the silence, Fay said, 'I fell downstairs.' After a moment of total silence Linda broke into snorts of laughter and the one with the tray doubled up. The rest joined in, nudging each other in the overcrowded room. Fay seemed to have coined some sort of catchphrase.

The front door banged and quick footsteps crossed the bare floorboards of the hall. The door burst open. The laughter subsided.

Fay lifted startled eyes. 'Dr Sutton-Brookes ...' she whispered, her voice almost inaudible.

'You're way out of date, dear girl. Maureen's easier.'

The well-remembered features had thickened and her hair, drawn back in an untidy topknot, was now streaked with grey. But the smile was the same: the big gappy teeth could have been a trademark. The women filling the room melted away, closing the door behind them.

Fay slid her legs off the sofa, anxious not to spill the tea again. She leaned over her aching ribs, feet placed neatly together on the frayed carpet and wondered why, in the past weeks, she had repeatedly found herself in one bizarre situation after another. After years in a quiet backwater leading an uneventful life she had suddenly been pitchforked into – as Hayes would have it – murder, attempted murder, abortion and possibly blackmail. She stared at the faded pattern of the rug and tried to sift the minimum of facts she needed to share with Maureen Patel.

After years of deception, complete candour was difficult to contemplate, dissimilation having become as familiar as an old dressing gown. There were things Robert must never know, things Fay had buried in the grimy corners of memory, things Luke must not find out and things which, even at this desperate pass, need not be mentioned. And if that was not enough for an addled brain to separate, she was now lumbered with Maeve's secrets. The doctor went out.

Fay had roughly assembled her story before the woman re-entered with her medical bag and yet another mug of tea. Maureen Patel was not your average GP. She weighed in at well over twelve stone and was clearly uninterested in frivolities such as any sort of dress code. She wore a thick jersey over a flowing garment which was none too clean. Fay found herself staring at an expanse of bare leg which ballooned over each ankle boot before disappearing under the undulating hem of the voluminous skirt.

Maureen Patel brought up a chair to sit squarely in front of her patient, the medical bag between them. She leaned forward, smiling briefly before removing Fay's dressings. She cast expert eyes over the head wound, touching the stitches with light fingers.

'Nasty. When did this happen?'

'Oh – er – Monday, I think ... Or Tuesday? I'm not sure.'

Maureen Patel sat quietly, saying nothing.

'I fell downstairs,' she blurted out, waiting for the automatic laughter. 'Really! I think I suffered slight concussion. I hurt my ribs, too,' she added.

The doctor frowned. 'Shall we start again? Your name would be a beginning. And you called me by my maiden name. I'd almost forgotten it.'

'I'm an old patient of yours. The Morris Gardens surgery. But we go back much further than that. We knew each other in Israel. The youth volunteers, the Lewis Medical Centre project. A very long time ago ...' she muttered. 'You must have forgotten.'

'Good heavens, that explains it!' She laughed. 'There's a loyal patient for you. It must be a record.' She deftly replaced the grubby bandage.

'It's been difficult tracking you down. If I had known it was Patel it would have been *impossible*.' Fay stifled an awkward smile. 'I'm sorry. I didn't mean to be impertinent.'

'Think nothing of it. I'd not last two minutes in this job if I was that thin-skinned. Go on.'

'I saw your picture in a magazine and was able to trace you here.'

'My memory's terrible. Your name is?'

'Frances Browne. Fay Bassett at the kibbutz but so much has happened since then ...' Her voice trailed off. 'And I came to see you in Morris Gardens – but that was much later, more than ten years ago – I'm getting confused.'

Maureen Patel's gaze was like a laser beam. She leaned forward, taking Fay's hands. 'Slowly now. Slowly. Let's go through the whole thing from the beginning – it's coming back to me. I take it you are not here seeking refuge from a battering husband?'

Fay looked stunned. 'Oh, no. Robert's been accused of enough already without that. I really did fall downstairs.'

'Right. That's settled. Now go on.'

'I need you now, a statement of some kind. Corroboration. You see—'

141

'The beginning,' Maureen persisted. 'Israel. We first met on the Lewis Medical Centre project. I seem to remember the red hair...'

'I was being sent home and begged you to help me.'

'Heatstroke?'

'No. I was pregnant.'

Maureen Patel stiffened.

'We were due to go back on the same flight. I'd only done ten months at the kibbutz but I was too young, too silly to cope. Straight from school, more or less. My parents would be furious. You organised things for me in London and I told my people I'd been sent home because I couldn't stick the pace. You even put me up at your place. Baron's Court, wasn't it?' Fay's colour was returning as the long pent-up narrative spilled out.

'I'll never forget those few weeks. After the abortion you let me stay in your flat when you got that job in Leeds.'

'It's all coming back now.' Maureen grinned. 'You've made too much of it. The best solution all round. No sweat. Here, drink this.' She passed over her mug of lukewarm tea.

'Years later,' Fay continued, 'I heard the name Sutton-Brookes from Maeve, a friend who had seen you at the Penrose Clinic. I knew you were the only person who could possibly help me.'

'You've lost me now.' Maureen Patel surreptitiously glanced at her watch.

'I'd been married for years. Robert was tired of waiting. You see, he'd banked on a family. It went with the house. It should have been quoted on the agents' particulars – "Family house, six bedrooms, large garden, clients to supply own kids."'

Maureen mentally applauded the note of bitterness which had crept in. Healthy. She sank back, waiting for the rest.

'I told you all this when I turned up at the clinic. You don't remember me at all, do you?' Fay accused.

'Tell me again.'

'It sounds so futile, medieval almost. Oh, God, it's impossible to explain in any sensible way.' Fay clasped her hands and plunged in. 'Robert felt cheated, you see. Angry inside. Dreadful rages over trifles and he was staying away all the time, leaving me in that wretched set-up when *he* was the one who insisted we moved out of London, got ourselves what he called a "proper house". He blamed me, of course. And I blamed *myself*. I'd never told him about the abortion. I thought I must have damaged myself permanently. Divine retribution even. I even prayed about it, made bargains with God. All that sort of thing. No earthly use.'

The two confronted each other like earnest raconteurs. Fay started again.

'Robert and I hardly spoke of it, but as time went by I could see he was accusing me as if I had misrepresented myself on my CV. Had cheated in some way. He had it all mapped out, had never failed in anything he'd set out to do, you understand, he'd even got some woman down from London to design a nursery suite, for God's sake. But I made him pay her off. He washed his hands of redecorating the house after that. I suppose it must have been humiliating...'

'I've come across plenty of men like that,' Maureen quietly interposed. 'It's almost an historical dilemma. Why didn't you both take tests?'

'Easy for you to say. You don't know Robert. "What, *me*? Infertile? You've got to be joking!" I mentioned it to him once, not with any real conviction, just a suggestion. But Robert was always so *sure*, Maureen. "It's your fault," he said. And I believed him, dared not let our old doctor dig too deeply in case he found out about the abortion. Robert and I had reached an impasse. I knew without a shadow of a doubt that he would leave if I didn't come up with some sort of miracle. Sounds incredible in this day and age, doesn't it?'

Fay paused, sifting the half-forgotten guilt, deciding after all to empty the whole bag of scorpions on the table. 'The awful thing was,' she whispered, 'I didn't care for babies myself. But I would have used any means to keep him. Still would, to be honest.' She bit her lip and stared unseeing at the carpet between them. 'I don't expect you to understand that.'

Maureen stayed silent and waited.

'I became as obsessive as Robert. Each month's disappointment was a blow of cataclysmic proportions. For him *and* for me, though my fears were entirely selfish. I needed Robert, Robert needed a child. Simple as that. He was beginning to loathe the very sight of me, and making love was turning into some sort of distasteful hurdle. That's when I tracked you down at the Penrose and you suggested I attend the Morris Gardens surgery.'

'Less paperwork,' Maureen muttered. 'A lot of under the table business with Arab women. Mr Pettit was always discreet,' she cryptically added.

'You have no idea how relieved I was to talk to someone sympathetic. After Barons Court I knew I could tell you everything – bottling it up for so long had become insupportable and I had no one I dared confide in. I didn't admit even to Robert that I was attending a fertility clinic – in his own mind the problem was obviously mine, and eventually the tests proving I was apparently OK came as quite a shock to me. I had been brainwashed to accept the blame, if you can call it that, and telling him I had secretly been tested would have seemed pretty murky. Confessing to Robert about the abortion thing was no answer. Saying I had previously conceived another man's child at the drop of a hat would have been like playing an ace, insulting his virility, laughing up my sleeve at all the careful plans he had made. You suggested we adopt before our time ran out entirely. Do you remember?'

Maureen Patel brushed aside Fay's question and motioned her to continue.

'That was equally impossible. Robert wouldn't want just anybody's kid – just his own – a bloodline. I turned it over in my mind and knew that he would never agree to tests *or* adoption. And if he didn't want someone else's child, I wasn't pining. Funny, isn't it, one assumes it's the woman nagging to start a family, not the man?'

'By no means.'

'I remember one particularly bitter January day I had an appointment at Morris Gardens to see you. It was after a rather mawkish Christmas. Robert had got drunk and rambled on and on about stockings and a tree. All that stuff ... Finally, it dawned on me we couldn't go on if I couldn't resolve it, and yet there seemed no answer. I wanted Robert on *any* terms and it was clearly a baby or a divorce. I'm afraid I made rather an idiot of myself in your consulting rooms that day, carried on like a lunatic. Then you suggested artificial insemination.'

'It's all coming back now.' Maureen's smile was sardonic. 'It was that glorious red hair of yours. It occurred to me what a pity it would be not to pass it on. I remember quite well now, it must have been shortly before I temporarily abandoned medicine for a stab at politics.' Her smile abruptly faded. 'My God, I hoped never to set eyes on you again.'

'But I was at my wits' end with it all.'

'That husband of yours had begun to get on my nerves with his macho sensibilities. He wouldn't even consider IVF, you said. I do remember suggesting you got yourself a lover and organized your own baby – simpler all round.'

'I considered it very seriously, you know. Even worked out how I could seduce my husband's partner, but I could never have pulled it off. The donor scheme wouldn't have worked either because I needed Robert's signature on the consent forms and the consultant would have insisted on seeing us together.'

'And that was where my damned interfering nature stepped in,' Maureen wryly admitted. 'No wonder I've been within a whisker of being struck off with women like you around. Unethical.'

'But it was the only solution. Between us we bodged up the forms and, hey presto, nine months later, God's gift of a son.'

'Congratulations,' she said with irony. 'But what's the problem now? It's a bit late for a baby sister, isn't it?'

'Oh yes. There were never any more children, of course. Robert was disappointed but he's pinned everything on Luke.'

'Red hair and all.'

'That was Robert's only regret. He wanted Luke to be dark like him.' They grinned and the tension evaporated.

'But why's it suddenly so urgent that you see *me*? Presumably you have a doctor capable of dealing with broken ribs and concussion?'

'God, this stupid fall makes everything so complicated. I

didn't quit hospital to come all this way for your medical opinion.' She flushed. 'Heavens, that sounds rude. Excuse me. You see, it's about that other business, me forging Robert's signature on the donor insemination papers and fixing the whole thing up without his ever discovering the truth.'

'Surely you're not going to confess it all after all these years? Or did he find out?'

'No, of course not. In fact, he currently believes himself to have fathered his secretary's baby.'

'An optimist, I gather.'

Fay frowned, starting to take up the story again but a thought suddenly struck Dr Patel, who rounded on her.

'You're not trying to say you are parting from this man and want sole custody, are you? It would destroy the boy to find out after all this time, despite any satisfaction you might get.'

'No, no. Please let me explain.'

They were like combatants now, poised defensively in readiness.

'I've never mentioned any of this business to a living soul and I had long ago assumed the ghastly process was safely interred. I destroyed all the documents, of course. I'm not here trying to blackmail you. But –' she hesitated, seeing no way on without complete frankness, '– Robert's personal assistant was killed recently in an accident in my car. She had borrowed it from him, and the police have an engineer's report which suggests the braking system had been deliberately fouled. She was pregnant and Robert had made arrangements for her to have a termination, but she wouldn't go through with it. They may have quarrelled about that. She died in my car shortly after.'

'Convenient.'

'They may even arrest him. But the local police have been temporarily sidetracked by another sudden death and haven't been able to interview him yet. They have this crazy idea he was being threatened by Meg, or by Meg and someone else perhaps. If Robert was not the father of her child and I can prove it, the police will *know* there's another man directly involved who is keeping a suspiciously low profile.'

'You mean you are seriously suggesting I go to the police and

146

admit condoning false signatures on medical documents? I would be struck off! I'm far from popular with the authorities as it is, and the press would have headlines a foot tall over a story like that. I have enough political enemies already with the battered wives campaign, bad publicity querying my professional conduct would just tip the scales enough to close these hostels. I'm in a legal quicksand already because of overcrowding and a lot of support would just melt away if I got myself involved in a murder.'

'I know. I know. Truly, the very last thing I ever wanted was to involve you in all this. God help me, it never crossed my mind there would be any reason for any of this to come out at all after nearly ten years! But in the last resort I must protect Robert because of Luke. Can you imagine the child's reaction to finding his father accused of cold-bloodedly organising the death of his mistress while he was safely abroad? Even the news that Robert was helping the police with their enquiries would be bad enough. Where I live there's no smoke without fire as far as they're concerned, and little boys are not immune from local gossip.'

'What exactly do you want me to do?' Maureen Patel said wearily. 'You know it would be entirely reasonable for me to decide that in order to extract your worthless husband from his own mess, I could jeopardize the hopes of scores of women and children who regard these hostels as their only sanctuary? I would hate to think you were putting pressure on me, a threat to disclose everything if I don't cooperate would seem a cruel reward ... As I've never examined this husband of yours, any medical opinion I might give to the police would carry very little weight in any event. Has it occurred to you that he believed her story, felt trapped, and may, in fact, be guilty of killing this girl by sabotaging the car?'

'Well, nothing's going to bring her back, is it? Luke deserves some sort of future – he didn't ask to be born.'

Maureen Patel drew back, suddenly repelled by the ugly single-mindedness which this spectre from her past was disclosing. Her sympathy waned. 'Having manipulated the boy's existence you seem to think you can manipulate everyone else in order to shield him. You're not God Almighty. It's a very hard bargain.'

'It is precisely because I manipulated his existence for purely selfish reasons that I feel doubly determined Luke must have a decent chance in life. He's always idolized Robert. It's not Luke's fault. What I've come to beg of you – and believe me, Maureen, I'm the last person to threaten anybody – is that if the police look like charging Robert, will you back up my claim he was not Meg's lover?'

'But you think he was.'

'OK. He was. But you and I both know he couldn't have been the only one and this other fellow's keeping his head down, whoever he is.'

'Surely the police could trace this other man?'

'They're not even looking. They know Robert paid for the abortion and they know I had a series of anonymous phone calls. Also, he's known to have a mechanical flair – he tinkers with the cars himself and argues technical points with our printers. The detective in charge seems to think these phone calls to the house were some sort of threat to Robert and me. Anything I say to the police about Robert's innocence is just put aside as a neurotic wife's inability to face up to his infidelity.'

'But giving your son a simple test would prove that your husband couldn't be Luke's father. Why involve me?'

'I'll do anything to keep Luke out of this. He's just a little boy. Why should Luke have tests? Anyway, that wouldn't prove anything about Robert's belief of his paternity of Meg's baby, would it? Can't we put the police off the track without all that?'

'Why not just tell Robert the truth and let him take infertility tests?'

'It need not come out. If I tell him I've lied all these years, foisted a son on him by deception, how do you think we could go on after that? Robert couldn't live with it. Luke's life would fall apart if his father walked out. And who could blame the man?'

'Um, I see what you mean, though for the life of me I fail to understand this chauvinistic attitude. A blood tie doesn't make a father – it's just biology.' She leaned back in her chair, her massive bulk assuming the solemnity of a buddha. At last she agreed. 'All right. I'll promise you one thing. If the inquest turns out badly for him, you can refer the police to me and I'll make a confidential medical report. With luck they'll drop it and start searching for a second man involved with this secretary of his who, I agree with you, must be lurking somewhere. Though I can't see how *he* could tamper with your car, do you?'

'Oh, Meg had the Metro to herself for the whole weekend. It's perfectly feasible she met someone. Nobody seems to know what she was up to.'

'Will you go home now?'

'I can't. You won't believe this, but a man was attacked in my garden. He died a couple of days ago. The police are still in the house.'

Maureen Patel looked aghast. 'Whew! You've got a funny set of priorities, worrying about your husband's sexual self-esteem while a man is murdered on your doorstep. This attack was nothing to do with you?'

'A complete coincidence. Robert runs a business from the house. Someone tried to break in and this man who died, our foreman, had caught him red-handed. Presumably there was a confrontation.'

Maureen looked anxious but after a struggle decided to back her own judgement.

'I'll put you in a private clinic in Hampstead until the air clears on this murder enquiry. I run it with a colleague of mine. Don't look so astonished.' She laughed. 'We have to treat the rich ladies to fund *this* sort of caper. Obviously, you're in need of bed rest and there's no point in travelling back if you've already discharged yourself from hospital. As soon as your husband comes you can go home with him. Is there anyone else who will be worrying about you?'

Fay clapped her hand to her forehead. 'Maeve! She doesn't know where I am.' She frowned. 'I don't really want to tell her my whereabouts at present because Inspector Hayes is bound to winkle the address out of her and pester me before I've had a chance to confer with Robert. Could someone ring his partner?' Fay wrote down a message and a telephone number. 'If you tell Hugo to be discreet he'll know what to do.'

'Fine. As soon as we've got you installed I'll be able to examine you properly. I'm afraid I shall be held up here for a couple of hours and I can't trust you not to pass out again alone in a taxi. Perhaps Linda wouldn't mind going with you to Hampstead. I'll make arrangements.'

Fay solemnly addressed the solid figure standing over her. 'I do appreciate all this, Maureen. I know I'm asking a lot.'

'A bloody lot! I ought to be certified.'

'There's one other thing. Do you remember twin sisters when we were at the kibbutz? Babs and Millie? I recently came across the one we used to call Millie – she still uses her maiden name, Millicent Ambache. To be honest I didn't recognise her at first. She was married to Phil Lewis.'

'Our philanthropic grocer? How could I forget him? Or you, for that matter,' she added.

'Did it ever come out? Did you hear what happened after I went back to England to have the abortion?'

'I did as a matter of fact. Lewis left her, of course. Not immediately, but the gossip was more than he could stomach. Never guess it to see him now, would you? Hardly a man of tender sensibilities these days.'

'I knew the Lewises had split up but I wasn't sure if it was because of me. I was just a stupid kid at the time and everything out there seemed so glamorous and exciting.'

Maureen softened. 'It was. Unfortunately, the consequences sometimes catch up when we least expect it. You haven't seen anything of Phil Lewis since those days?'

'I don't move in his elevated circles. I very much doubt whether he even remembers me.'

'His ex-wife would. I remember Millie Lewis. An ambitious girl. Babs was a softer version of the two but led by the nose by her sister even then.'

Maureen Patel left the room to arbitrate in a wrangle which had all too audibly broken out along the passage.

Fifteen

Finally settled in the Hampstead clinic, Fay slept as if poleaxed, waking briefly and then submerging once more into blessed dreamless insensibility.

Hugo had redirected a basket of fruit from Maeve. Pineapples, grapes and out of season strawberries scented the room, the card bearing only two words in her scrawled handwriting: *Quo Vadis?* Fay smiled. In the limbo of Hampstead, Stamford was becoming less and less real to her. The panic which had driven her to London had seeped away and she shied from reminders of home. So much pain there still...

At three she went downstairs and struck up a spiritless conversation with a girl in a dressing gown. After a dozen banal remarks they drifted apart and Fay took her cup to a quiet corner to observe the other patients. They were mostly women and the general sitting room where they were encouraged to meet had been comfortably furnished in a country house style, generously swagged and with a proliferation of chintz sofas and little tables. There were very few who had bothered to leave their rooms and none were, like herself, sporting bandages. Half a dozen people of various ages lounged about the room, one or two wearing sunglasses for no obvious reason. It occurred to Fay that she was the odd one out. Here, bruises were likely to be the result of cosmetic surgery, and the dour acceptance of tea or coffee gave the impression that drying out was a possible money-spinner for her rediscovered saviour, Maureen Patel, née Sutton-Brookes.

She drifted out on to a terrace, pulling her terry bathrobe to her chest and making a beeline for a sunny spot under the glazed canopy. Several cane chairs stood about as if part of an abandoned film set, and she settled in a corner sheltered from intermittent gusts which blew flurries of dead leaves around her feet. The terrace rose above a square of dank earth where pots of spent marigolds put up a brave show and a mossy bird bath attracted one determined customer, a lone sparrow intent upon sprucing itself up. The one joyful note was struck by a clump of autumn crocus shining like amethysts in the sour soil. It seemed like a victory fanfare.

It started to drizzle. No wonder the other patients preferred to watch TV in their rooms or skulk in the sitting room dreaming of a G&T. Fay breathed deeply, savouring the soft, damp atmosphere – refreshing after the overheated airlessness of the lounge.

Her head seemed like a soap bubble only loosely attached to her body and she guarded its vulnerability to sudden movements and the jarring noises of a building full of hurried footsteps. The smallest efforts of concentration stirred the lake of pain which lay under her scalp. At least it was quiet here. The grey skies absorbed all colour from the earth, leaving only the crocus gleaming with exaggerated brightness. Fay's eyes fixed on them, her thoughts light as the dry leaves which whispered under the garden chairs.

Slowly she realized another person stood behind her. She turned, faintly irritated at the prospect of more inane conversation, and then with a tremor saw Robert. He wore a light raincoat and held a zipped airline bag in one hand. He looked like a man changing trains. They stared at each other with apprehension, so many lies blocking the way. He pulled up one of the rickety cane chairs and sat beside her, the ageing wickerwork cracking with a volley like pistol shots. Taking her hand seemed to trigger a fountain of pent-up rage which burst inside her head like fireworks.

'Robert! Why didn't you come home?'

His face froze to a careful mask. 'I suppose some kind friend told you I flew into London on Monday?'

She nodded, stiff with recrimination. He took time lighting a cigarette, then said, 'I had some business in town. You might as well know. I'd arranged to meet Meg on Monday at a hotel in

Kensington, see how things had gone for her and present a united return next day.'

'No one could criticise your powers of organization.' Her tone was bitter, his careful containment confounding her anticipation of his anxiety for her safety after what, in anyone's book, was an appalling ordeal.

'I phoned Goldsmith from the airport and when I heard the bad news I decided to stick with the hotel booking and give myself a chance to sort everything out before going back to Stamford. Apart from Meg's terrible accident I had some crucial financial problems, and there were meetings with the bank which had to be dealt with urgently.'

'Your priorities never cease to amaze me, Robert.' The irony was ignored and he again smoothly took up his explanation with no hesitation, no embarrassment. He might have been making an official statement. Fay pondered the possibility that he was merely giving his watertight alibi another dunking.

'I hired a car and drove down to the house in the early hours on Tuesday morning – I was too worried to sleep after a day like that. But the house was empty. You had presumably been carted off by then, but I didn't know that. I phoned Hugo but there was no reply so I drove straight back to my hotel. I thought you'd gone away.'

'You thought I'd left you. Because of your involvement with Meg.'

His eyes became steely and they confronted one another on the gusty verandah.

'I wondered how long it would take you to get around to that.' He flicked ash on the wet flagstones.

'Yes, Meg. You made a fool of me, didn't you, Robert?' Fay laughed, a thin ululation which trembled on the edge of hysteria. 'But the joke's on you, my darling.'

He shifted nervously, causing the cane chair to repeat its absurd fusillade. Was there a chink in the man's story?

'What are you getting at, Fay? After I had discovered what had happened to Meg I phoned Hugo and he told me about you falling downstairs, that you were OK but needed rest and quiet. I thought it best if I stayed out of the picture. Especially as this man Hayes was on the rampage. Finding out I'd been at the house the night before would have been tricky – he'd never believe I just drove down to Stamford in the early hours and drove straight back again.'

'Not to mention poor old Bill Goldsmith. You couldn't prove you were miles away from that tragedy too.'

He looked surprised. 'I didn't know you had been told about that.'

Her eyes held a glint of lunacy as his calculated response to all these disasters crystallized. 'Another compartment of your life neatly sealed off, Robert?'

'For God's sake! Out with it, Fay! Are you insinuating I was implicated in my foreman being bludgeoned by a burglar? You don't care a rap about the old man. It's just fuel to your bitterness about Meg. My fling with Meg was over, as it happens. The pregnancy was an unlucky twist in the tale. It was never what one could term a full-blooded affair, though Meg was given to flights of fancy about any sort of romance. Bad timing all round.'

'Bad timing for Meg, certainly.'

'Perhaps not. This DCI Hayes, who seems to be bent on interfering with an investigation quite outside his manor, told me she had cancelled the abortion, so she couldn't have been that distressed by it.' His aplomb was insupportable.

'And I suppose she told you it was yours?' Fay said in a fierce whisper. 'Robert, she lied to you. Fooled you into footing the bill and then threw it all back in your face.'

He paused, choosing his words carefully. 'Obviously one must make allowances for your concussion, Fay. Wrangling like this is bad for you.'

Fay took a deep breath, her anger finally under control. 'Hayes has a police engineer's report which says the brakes were tampered with,' she said evenly, watching the cigarette smoke wreath his head. 'Bearing in mind your well-publicized involvement with your secretary, this clever detective jumped to the conclusion that some anonymous phone calls were in some way linked – a threat, or blackmail, or something of the kind. He has hinted that loosening the brakes was some sort of insurance on your part in case Meg continued to make demands on you. Or perhaps she knew of business secrets which were damaging. Hayes has a strong circumstantial case against you, Robert. At the very least he could turn the firm inside out looking for trouble and cause professional embarrassment which would spell disaster, especially if you are looking for a new backer. Integrity is all. Even Hugo's nervous of your methods these days.'

'Hayes has nothing on me. Not a shred of proof, pure supposition,' Robert calmly replied.

Fay told him about the miniature tool kit that was found in his suit.

'Mrs B was taking it to the cleaners. It was the jacket you were wearing to Maeve's the night someone got into the outhouse and tampered with the Metro.'

'What *are* you talking about?'

'As soon as I saw the little spanners and things it occurred to me that Ottie had not escaped from the garage later. You could have tampered with my car *before* we went out, knowing you would hand it over to Meg after a few miles. The rabbit couldn't have got out otherwise.'

'Then why didn't you hand this tool kit over to the police? With your legal brain, it's tantamount to withholding evidence.'

'Because I can't really believe you guilty. Not that I haven't veered in that direction lately, which only goes to show what a rat's nest of suspicion can grow from a simple coincidence like you having the means, the motive and the opportunity to tamper with the brakes. And all this bound up in a little leather wallet.'

'As you have made up your mind, any protestations on my part seem irrelevant.'

Fay beat the air in total exasperation. 'Robert, what *does* it take to get through to you? Meg's dead. Tell me! Be truthful just this once. I *must* know! Can't you see I've nearly gone crazy trying to shift the blame on to some nebulous manfriend of Meg's and you won't even attempt to defend yourself. I don't know *what* to believe any more.' She tried to calm down and

155

lowered her voice in an effort to make him realize the danger he was in. 'Look, I'm trying to be honest with you, darling, and I'm sadly out of practice. Lately, I've even begun to doubt you myself. God knows what a stranger like Hayes would make of it all.'

'You are so bloody self-righteous, Fay. Decided in your own petty solicitor's brain that I must have done it. Why should I try to justify myself to *you*? Did it ever occur to you *or* Meg what I felt about it? If I'm the one always thinking of himself, as you say, why did I fix up the abortion for her when I was the only poor devil who cared a damn about the child?'

'What child? Meg's? That baby wasn't yours, you idiot.'

Anger froze behind his eyes in a way she had never witnessed before. He half-rose but drew back as she railed on, her pent-up rage spewing out, unstoppable.

'Meg probably guessed the baby wasn't yours. She would have gone through with the abortion if it had been. She was stringing you along. You are sterile, Robert Browne. You are arid as a grain of sand – are now and always have been. Meg's child was some other man's and he's vanished into thin air, leaving you holding the cheque book.'

He struggled to his feet, his cheeks livid.

'I'll never forgive you these poisonous lies, Fay. Never. Being ill is no excuse. You are an evil, malicious woman. I'm going back to my hotel, and when Luke finishes school at the end of term I'm taking him away with me. God knows what perverted lies you have concocted in that diseased brain of yours.'

'Lies!' Her contempt cut the air. 'Luke is not your son. Can't you get it into your head – you *have* no children? If you disbelieve me, ask Dr Patel here. She knows. She's known all along.'

'Are you saying I've brought up someone else's child?'

'If you like. Luke is as much your son as any blood tie could have made him. I've kept this from you until now, Robert, and I never, believe me, intended to tell you. It was your damned self-possession brought all this out. Maureen Patel was going to make a confidential medical report to the police if they cornered you because I begged her to help us. But it's ridiculous that we should all go on shielding you. Her career is at stake. It would be safer all round if you tell Hayes yourself, and then that destroys any possible motive you might have for killing Meg. That's why I've been frantically trying to reach you before Hayes asked you about the pregnancy, to stop you taking the responsibility. Did you admit paternity when they questioned you about Meg?'

'Of course not.' Robert slumped in the chair like a man broken on the rack. 'Is it true, Fay? Say you're lying. For pity's sake, Fay.'

'It's true. Believe me, it's true. Go for tests. Admit it, you know I'm not that cruel, even taking into account my redhead's temper. I was friendly with Maureen Patel years before I met you. Much later she treated me at an infertility clinic prior to Luke's appearance on the scene. I didn't tell you ... never thought I would need to ... It was a cheap trick now I look back on it, I admit that. But I was desperate. If the police question you again you must insist you knew all along that you were infertile and that Meg's pregnancy was nothing to do with you, despite your relationship. There's obviously someone else.'

Robert leaned forward in the garden chair, staring at the mossy paving under his feet. The light was almost gone, mist curling in the dusk around them. She reached across to touch him.

Back in her room Fay splashed her face with cold water and waited for Robert to finish his interview with Maureen Patel. She stared at the face in the bathroom mirror, seeing herself clearly for the first time in days, surprised that the dread was not stamped there, had not turned the red hair white.

It was nearly an hour before he returned, his drawn features bearing the rigidity of shock. He dropped into a chair. Fay made a hesitant step towards him and he looked up.

'She gave it to me straight. Christ knows why you couldn't bring yourself to tell me all this years ago. Hayes is roaring round searching for you, by the way. You'll have to break cover. It's Goldsmith, of course. Even Hayes has lost interest in the bloody Metro's braking system now. Meg's death seems unimportant, and it wasn't really his case in the first place. He's on to a real murder now.'

Fay flinched. Meg seemed to have been swept under the carpet just like poor Barbara Hertz. Was there no end to this trail of blood?

Robert said, 'Hayes is now insinuating I'm involved in hiring someone to knock off that poor old man. Who does he think I am – the Godfather? Goldsmith was working late on the stock list, apparently. The last to leave. That sodding policeman's like a terrier when he gets hold of an idea. For all I know he thinks *I* killed old Goldsmith – for God knows what reason – and then knocked you downstairs.'

'Hayes knows you came back to the house that night?'

'No. But he's such a devious bastard, I'm not sure *what* he knows. Could be up to anything.'

'You may have got hold of the wrong end of the stick. Perhaps he thinks you're covering up for *me*. That I attacked Bill and then tried to commit suicide. He hinted as much at the hospital. He definitely suspects I'm some sort of psycho, and there's something else . . . That woman who died on the railway line. I knew her, Robert.' She stared at him, sick with foreboding.

He shook his head impatiently. 'Please, darling, pull yourself together. You're getting confused. It's the concussion. Everything will be all right if we keep our heads.'

'But Robert, it was my machete that was used on the old man.'

'So what?' He sighed and lit a cigarette, rising to cross to the window. He stared out through the slats of the blind, watching the lights of the rush hour traffic gleaming in the rainy street. 'We had to close the chapel. Police everywhere. In any event it would have been impossible to keep things running without poor old Goldsmith. Hugo's arranged for a removal lorry to take all the stuff back to London.'

'Where?'

'He's rented a small warehouse in Victoria. He'll get the entire stock listed. Got to be done anyhow.' He looked across at her. 'Hugo told you we were splitting the partnership?'

158

Fay nodded, feeling as if the sky itself was falling on their heads.

'The accountants will need Goldsmith's files. I'll probably keep the new place on. I don't much fancy staying on at the house after this, do you?'

'Leave Stamford? But you've worked so hard to get yourself established there. For Luke, you said.'

He turned abruptly, stubbing out the cigarette.

'Your Dr Patel says it's OK if we slip off for a quiet meal round the corner, providing you keep off the booze.'

'Why don't we just go to your hotel?'

He covered the distance between them, playfully tapping her cheek.

'Because, my darling, you look like a punch-drunk, played-out old flyweight and I'm not taking you back into civilized society until those stitches come out.'

They kissed. It seemed for the very first time.

Sixteen

Late the next afternoon, Fay had a visitor. Hugo Suskind entered her room, a bouquet of carnations preceding his quiet entry. Fay held out both arms in welcome. He edged forward, breaking into a smile.

'Dear Hugo, how nice!' she said, hugging him. 'What a darling you are to come.'

He flopped the flowers on the locker and drew up a chair beside hers at the window.

'My dear girl, I couldn't leave you to moulder in Hampstead all alone. Terrible place.'

'Admit it, Hugo. Sick-visiting's not your favourite, is it?'

They laughed.

'But what in heaven's name are you doing here? Last I heard you were tucked up in Stamford, unconscious and likely to be laid up for at least a week.'

'Gross exaggeration. I'd *have* to be unconscious to stay in that place. I know the doctor in charge here. Any news about Bill's attacker?'

'Well, no,' he replied guardedly. 'Mrs B's holding the fort while Hayes rants round. Poor old soul. She was nearly frantic when I phoned through to tell her you were all right. She'd persuaded the police to drag the garden pond for you when you vanished from the hospital. You know, that deep pool by the orchard? Convinced herself you had drowned – had some sort of premonition about it, apparently.'

'Actually, she got *me* going on that one. I worked myself up into a panic thinking it was Maeve who featured in that ghoulish dream of hers; that Maeve had fallen overboard from the boat.'

'Boat? What boat? Are you sure you're not still suffering from that bang on the head, darling?'

'Oh, Hugo, it's a long story. Another time, when we've a long winter evening ahead of us. By the way, thanks for redirecting the basket of fruit she sent. I didn't feel strong enough to cope with another hospital visit from Maeve just yet.'

'That nyphomaniacal friend of yours gets herself in one mess after another,' he retorted, not entirely taken in by her need to lie doggo for the present. 'Come out with it. What's going on? Why did you bolt from Stamford like that? It's to do with Meg, isn't it?'

There was a telling pause before she admitted, 'Well, yes and no.'

'Bill Goldsmith then?' he persisted. 'Come on, Fay, we've known each other too long for this sort of foxtrotting. You don't race round the country with crushed ribs and concussion just for kicks. Don't forget Hayes has been questioning me too.'

'About Meg and Robert?'

'He got nothing from me about that,' Hugo grimly insisted. 'You and I both know Rob had a passing fancy for Meg, but we know equally well Robert would never, in whatever corner he found himself, kill the girl.'

'That's just it, don't you see? Hayes still has to pin it on somebody. Brake fluid doesn't just seep out like that without interference of some sort, and the inquest has already been postponed. I've been desperately trying to throw some light on Meg's love life. A total blank. She was a very private woman, you know. Not even Jessica could give me a lead.'

'Poor Meg didn't stand a chance. Some people are born unlucky. Everyone turned against her in the end. And she wasn't a bad kid.'

'Did she confide in you, Hugo?'

He sat silent for several moments. At last, he began to speak. 'I was probably the last person to talk to her.'

Fay's jaw sagged, numb with the sudden shift of events she had thought immutable.

Hugo said, 'She had mentioned to me that she was pregnant, probably even before she told Robert. All three of us worked

161

closely for years, of course, but Rob was always too wrapped up in his business deals to register much about other people's problems. We had not been hitting it off particularly well for some time and this fling of his with Meg was the last straw. He admitted being responsible for her situation – sorry to be so blunt about all this, Fay, but it's no time for beating about the bush, and you've probably guessed what happened. Robert said he had the matter in hand, could sort it out without me putting my nose in. That poor girl jumped to his tune for years and he spoke about her as if she was guilty of some sort of bungling incompetence. Misfiling or something.' He bit his lip. 'Sorry. Stupid thing to say. But I was caught in the middle, seeing both sides. Eventually, Rob and I had a final bust-up and I said it was time to go our separate ways, like I told you.' He sighed, wrinkling his eyes as if the fading light was a strain.

'At that point,' he went on, 'he accused me of vile things concerning the staff, and once all that poison began to flow between us there was no way to stop it. Robert was planning to shove off on this Texas trip and I dare say hoped I would cool off and forget the whole sordid row while he was away.'

He paused, gazing at the slatted blinds, the sunset, now in its lurid last moments, segmented into horizontal strips. He continued, his face averted, the voice clear and precise. A man slow to rile and relentlessly fair. An implacable combination.

'Late that Wednesday afternoon I had a frantic call from Meg. She was in Stamford, begged me to drive down and meet her in Renham. It was utterly unlike her. We met in the lounge bar of the Prince of Orange.'

Fay breathed a soft sigh, remembering that fateful Wednesday, the night she had been caught up in the death of the woman on the line. They had all three been in Renham then?

'Meg looked dreadful, Fay. In fact,' he said, throwing her a wintry smile, 'almost as knocked up as you do now. She had a black eye. Fell off a ladder stocking shelves she said. Anyway, she had gone home to ask her father if she could go back there for a couple of months next year and have the baby away from London. She had no one else to turn to, you see, if she didn't go ahead with the abortion. Bad luck was, her mother's dead or

162

divorced or something and her father lives alone, probably set in his ways, and definitely not looking to set up shop for a new infant. The moronic man told her to get lost. Can you believe it? In this day and age?'

'Poor Meg.'

'Appalling.' Hugo felt in his cuff for a handkerchief and dabbed the corner of his mouth. 'Trouble was, the bloody hypocrite had known about her affair and seemed to think, silly old sod, Rob should divorce you and marry his daughter. Nice and simple. Just like that!'

'I swear to you, Hugo, Robert's never once mentioned a divorce. There was no suggestion he was seriously involved with *anyone.*'

'Rob goes his own way. Nobody could push him into anything.'

'But Meg knew him so well. Did she ever say Robert had promised to marry her? Had even suggested it? There *was* another man, Hugo,' she insisted. 'Jessica said Meg was hinting about getting married months ago.'

He regarded her sadly. 'That's poppycock, Fay. Meg would have told me. She was in no state of mind to be coy.'

'I know it's true,' she insisted.

'Meg said she wasn't going to the States with Robert as everyone thought. He had arranged for her to go into a clinic during the time she would have been away. I told her not to be hasty. If she could work out how to keep the child I would guarantee a job for her in the new set-up, well away from Stamford. After all, single girls keep babies all the time. I'm sure she wanted to go ahead with it and, come to think of it, intelligent women like Meg rarely get pregnant by mistake.'

'You may be right. But I've been to her flat. It's not the sort of pad to bring up a baby. Much too smart, and probably expensive. By the way, be a dear and return those photographs and postcards to Jessica for me, would you? I'm sure she'll want them back.'

'With pleasure. I shall be glad to be rid of them,' he said primly. 'Incidentally, Fay, I asked round the office if any of the staff knew anything of Meg's men friends and she never mentioned anyone specific. Talk is pretty free among the girls but Meg never seemed to have anything to contribute to office gossip.'

'One thing I learned about her was how astonishingly discreet she was. Secretive, almost.'

Hugo dryly retorted, 'Being in love with the boss is hardly something to chat about over the coffee mugs, dear.'

'Mm.' Fay stared glumly at her open palms, counting the inadequacy of her weapons. Hugo picked up the narrative again.

'Anyway, by the end of that Wednesday evening in Renham, Meg had calmed down. I booked her into a room at the Prince for a couple of nights and she said she'd get a taxi back to Stamford on Friday morning. Rob had assumed she was still staying with her father and, as my name was mud at that time as far as he was concerned, she clearly kept quiet about seeing me in Renham. He thought I was phoning him from town Friday morning.'

'What a complicated life you lead, Hugo!'

'By the way, I didn't tell that suspicious detective any of this, it wouldn't have added anything to his investigation. And I wasn't sure how much he already knew.'

'Presumably, Hayes has had more than Meg to concern himself about since poor Bill Goldsmith was attacked. Doubtless, if the inspector had known you were staying in the area prior to Meg's crash he would have added Suskind to the list of suspects.' Hugo flinched, taken aback by this sudden volte-face. 'After all,' she continued, 'you could have tampered with the brakes of the Metro that Thursday evening while we were at Maeve's. As Robert's partner you had a very good motive to get rid of him and run the whole show yourself. And on your own admission there was no love lost between you, arrangements were already in place to halve the assets. Robert had told you he was swopping cars with me for the run to the airport and Meg had confirmed he was dropping her off at a clinic near Stamford. The brakes worked well for a considerable mileage, but with the way Robert drove – and the distance he would have to cover to get to Heathrow – he must have been the obvious target. Leaving the Metro for Meg's use was a stroke of luck for Robert. If your partner had died you knew I would leave the business entirely in your hands. And come to that, where were you the night Bill Goldsmith was killed? Not at your flat. Robert phoned and got no reply.'

Fay leaned back, a glint of power in her eyes, enjoying Hugo's speechless amazement.

'What a load of rubbish!' he flung out at last.

She patted his arm and pressed home her advantage. 'Exactly. But the case against Robert is just as thin. Circumstantial. The police can draw the most preposterous conclusions from the very flimsiest of evidence. That's why I need all the help I can get.'

'Meg needed a hand, too,' he countered.

'I know. Don't think I'm not haunted by the tragedy. But there's Luke and Robert and the rest of us who still have to go on living. I have a stake in the future, Hugo.'

His head jerked up. 'Funny, you saying that,' he said thickly. 'Those were Meg's last words to me.'

'What do you mean? When she left you in Renham that Friday morning?'

'No, after that. I spoke to her in London that weekend.'

Fay stared, bewildered, seeing the nervous twist of his mouth as the words spilled out.

'Before she left I gave her a spare key to the flat and told her she was welcome to use it if she wanted a few days on her own to think things out. Sharing with Jessica could be pretty wild at weekends by all accounts. Everyone was urging Meg in different directions, you see. I think she had accepted the fact that marriage had passed her by, and having got herself pregnant for God knows what devious reason, she was beginning to look forward to the idea. Despite everything. It might have seemed a fresh start, I suppose, and presumably she was in love.' The room was now almost dark but Hugo's voice flowed on and Fay sat motionless, not daring to interrupt.

'I phoned my flat on the off chance on Saturday from the chapel. She had postponed the abortion but had still not finally made up her mind. Said she would drive on to this hotel Rob had booked for her after the weekend. Take a break. But she had to see a friend in London on Monday, would probably stay over in town and then move on and enjoy Robert's prepaid hospitality at the hotel. She must have left early Monday morning because no one at the office knew she wasn't in Texas at the time. She was an odd girl, Fay, dependent on worthless people to a ridiculous degree, holding on long after anyone else would have let go. She hinted at other relationships in the past, never pretended to be chastely waiting for Mr Right to come along. But once she had had enough she could isolate herself quite coldly. Poor kid was really out on a limb and not a single person to turn to.'

'Except you, Hugo.'

'Oh, me,' he scoffed. 'A broken reed.'

'Perhaps she realized she no longer needed to lean on anyone.'

The silence in the room rippled under a sudden gust which rattled the slats of the blind. Hugo's face stared back at her, suffused with pity.

'When I spoke to her on the phone that last time she was so happy. Bubbling over with fun at the idea of using Robert's hotel booking anyway. It was all paid for she said, she might as well have a little holiday till it was time to re-emerge from her mythical Texan trip. She presumed Rob would get a rebate from the clinic – or he could open an account there, she said.'

Fay grimaced. Ironically, Hugo seemed to have forgotten the identity of his listener in the necessity to unburden himself. They sat quietly, each mentally shuffling the curious circumstances of those portentous few days.

'Fay, I'll do everything I can for Robert. You know that. We've been partners too long for recriminations. But Meg's death, and now Goldsmith's, have scuttled things between us. I can't see us ever forgetting the tragic waste of it all, that wretched girl and a child who had even less of a chance than she did.'

'It was nobody's fault. It's not been proved the brakes were tampered with, it's just the engineer's opinion. A car accident could happen to any of us, any day of the week. Poor old Bill Goldsmith got caught up in another twist of fate: a breaking and entering that went wrong. Pure coincidence. All the local gossip following Meg's death probably alerted someone in the area who thought security would be lax when we had other things to worry about. And there were always wild stories in the village about the value of some of the books we kept in the chapel. Not to mention cash in the safe.'

Hugo's shoulders lifted in a dismissive shrug and he patted her hand. 'On a more cheerful level, my dear, you'll be amazed to hear I've developed a true rapport with that weird cleaning woman of yours.'

'Rose Barton?' Even speaking her name made her smile. 'Did she tell you about her newest psychic adventures? Soul travel, her out of body experiences?'

'Fascinating old bird. While I was sorting out all the problems at the chapel after poor old Bill was killed I was a sitting duck.'

'Did you stay at the house?'

'Not bloody likely. It was crawling with police. I bedded down at the Prince in Renham again. Did you know that Mrs B had been a druid?'

Fay snorted, covering her mouth to smother the laughter.

Hugo nodded. 'Her latest thing is numerology. Number four means death. She warned me that three people had died but the Fates demand a fourth.'

'Three?'

'Meg and Bill presumably. But her counting goes haywire after that.'

Fay sobered. 'She means Barbara Hertz, the woman who fell on the line.' She explained her involvement with the accident at Renham Junction.

Hugo shrugged. 'That must be number three then. Mrs B pinned me down in your kitchen after the police had drawn a blank dragging the pond and insisted there must be a fourth death, "before the bloodline dries up".'

Fay grinned. 'You're not serious? You're making it up, Hugo.'

'Cross my heart. She talks as if you have a virus or something, had set up some sort of circle of death, infecting all within your orbit.'

'Why pick on me?'

He laughed, flinging up both hands in comic incomprehension. 'Search me! I'm only telling you all this to give you a giggle. Honestly, Fay, that cleaner of yours ought to go on the telly. "Mrs Barton's Magic Moments". She'd top the ratings in no time at all. I must go, love, I've got tickets for *Henry IV* tonight. Keep your pecker up.'

He rose and leaned across to kiss her cheek, nodded briefly and left without another word.

Fay sat in the dusk, mulling over the light Hugo had shed on Meg's last few days. There were still several gaps. Who was this friend she had arranged to meet in London the day before she died? And Meg's black eye? After her exposure to the ribald disbelief of the battered women at the hostel, her own credulity regarding 'accidental' bruises was permanently damaged. Did Meg have a boyfriend who lashed out first and asked questions after?

Seventeen

Robert remained in London for the next few days and, occupying the flat over the shop, visited Fay each evening. Hugo stayed in Renham, supervising the warehouse transfer.

The police interviewed Robert Browne several times, leaving him increasingly uneasy after each interrogation. Fortunately, Hayes seemed to have abandoned Fay as a source of information, for the time being at least, but pressed the staff both in London and the country for gossip about Meg's relationship with the two partners and also any loose talk about Mrs Browne herself.

Roger Hayes was baffled. The skein tying everyone together was obvious but the knot remained a mystifying tangle. Nothing new had emerged and he suspected that not only were the chief suspects withholding facts from the police but also from each other.

The period of Fay's recuperation at Hampstead was an invaluable interlude for both the Brownes, making, as it did, no demands on their tentative reappraisals. They licked their wounds in private and spent an hour or two each evening warily approaching each other with nervous gestures of affection, exploring this new strata of their relationship with delicacy, poised for flight. The disclosure of the mesh of lies which underlay an ostensibly ordinary marriage had been forced upon them by a bizarre set of accidents. As a consequence, the unavoidable shift of trust had shaken the pattern of their lives as radically as a kaleidoscope reveals unknown facets of long familiar fragments.

Hayes' investigation, coupled with the truth about Luke's

conception, had left Robert with a vulnerability which seemed oddly piquant to Fay. His own adjustment was more complex, a grudging admiration for her tigerish loyalty, tinged with recrimination. Her deception, coupled with the double-cross Meg had imposed, was even more unpalatable to Robert Browne than the medical confirmation of his sterility. He felt he had been secretly humiliated by the two women. Watching the Glebe House operation being swiftly dismantled was the final straw.

Fay's efforts to establish her husband's innocence were exhausted and she vegetated in the Hampstead clinic, suspended in comfortable torpor, shutting from her mind the indictment which still threatened him. It was as if, having retired from the battlefield, she had paused to watch the remaining conflict from her own no-man's-land.

Hugo's telephone call from Stamford the following Thursday morning jerked her from her spectator's perch and pitched her headlong back into the fray.

'Hello, Fay. How are you on this magnificent October morning?'

'Marvellous, Hugo. I gather you're up to your eyes down there.'

'You should see us all at it, sweetie. Stuff I've never seen before tumbling out of Goldsmith's secret cubby holes. You're well out of it, my dear.'

'I was hoping to get home for the weekend but Robert's insisting I stay on until the middle of next week.'

'Probably all for the best, old girl.'

'What's going on, Hugo?' Fay said sharply. 'You're keeping something from me.' The hearty manner was entirely unlike Hugo's normal style.

He swiftly drew her off on another tack, saying, 'There is one thing I must confess before you get back. We've lost that bloody rabbit again.'

'Not Ottie!' she wailed. 'Not again, Hugo. I don't believe it!'

'Afraid so, darling. That stupid cow, Maeve, let the thing out in the garden to give it a trot round and it was off like a greyhound, of course. That brat of hers was here yesterday,

170

snivelling all over the invoices, begging Carey to search the garden to see if it had found its way back.'

'Poor Flora. She's better off with Rupert.'

'Rupert who?'

'Never mind, Hugo. It would take far too long to explain. Was that the only bad news?'

'I can always get another rabbit for Luke if you're really devastated.'

'Gracious, no thanks! One Ottie in a lifetime's more than enough.'

'There is something else. I rang for a bit of advice.'

'Not Robert being bolshy again?'

'No, not that. Actually, I've not set eyes on Rob since he got back to London. Nothing's been resolved.'

'Take it easy, Hugo. He's changed. You'll be surprised when you see him. This ghastly business has knocked him for six.'

'Maybe. Maybe not. This is something to do with Meg.'

Hugo dropped the name into her smooth existence like a pebble in a pool. She tensed, waiting for him to continue.

'I went over to Meg's flat on Sunday evening to return the bumph you asked me to take back.'

'Bless you, Hugo. Sweet of you to take the trouble but, honestly, the post would have done.'

'Wasn't entirely altruistic, I must confess. Your description of Jessica made me curious and I had a bona fide entrée at my fingertips.'

'Jessica's a plum, isn't she? Admit it, Hugo, you were captivated.'

'Utterly stunned. I telephoned and Jessica asked me to call in about six for a drink. She was going on somewhere later, I gathered. I pressed the bell, clutching my grotty brown paper parcel, and there she stood, framed in the doorway, like Sheba in all her glory. I somehow felt I should be bringing marrons glacés or gardenias at the very least, not some bundle of old pictures.'

'Ah, I know your weak spot now, Hugo: glossy black skin and a Nefertiti profile.'

171

'Shut up for a minute, Fay, and let me tell you. After a couple of gins I decide to escape before I got tangled up with her date.'

'Probably seven foot tall and nasty with it.'

'That had occurred to me. As I'm shuffling towards the door, Jessica lunges at me with this letter in her hand and—'

Fay dissolved into giggles, rolling back on to the bed and pressing the receiver to her ear.

'For Christ's sake, girl, let me finish. I open this billet-doux only to discover it's her bloody telephone bill and in a trice she's rattling on about Meg always dealing with the accounts and so on. I don't mind telling you I was pretty apprehensive about these cryptic financial proposals after only two drinks.'

'Curiosity killed the cat, my friend.'

Hugo blew a raspberry and hurried on with the story. 'Jessica then asks me to look at this horrendous telephone bill of hers and, to give the girl her due, she *had* tried to estimate her own share. She said Meg always totted up all calls made from the flat in a memo pad – careful girl that! – and there were these odd calls to Sao Paulo which Jessica swore were nothing to do with her. Among Meg's jottings she'd listed numbers for her own accounting system. I agreed that Meg sometimes worked from home and the firm covered her expenses, so maybe it was a business call and I would check it out. My God, Fay, the bliss shining in that heavenly countenance would grace an icon!'

'You're a pushover, Hugo Suskind.'

'Anyhow, I hopped off with her telephone bill and Meg's sum book and promptly forgot all about it for a couple of days while I was tangled up down here with poor old Bill Goldsmith's incompetent tribe. Full of contrition, I eventually checked through the damn bill against Meg's notes and, sure enough, these calls to Brazil were placed person-to-person to a customer of ours called Jorge-Maria Cabral. So I comb through the whole lot and extract all the items Meg may have been responsible for and post off a largish cheque to the delectable Jessica. Far from erasing the thing from my mind, it kept nagging away. Cabral was an archaeologist who spent some weeks in London this summer researching a book and planning a dig he hoped to mount in Honduras with some people up at

Cambridge. The man was in and out of the shop for months and it was only when I saw his name in full like that I began to worry about it, God knows why. Then the penny dropped. Do you remember Carey's postcard – the one he pinched from Jessica's collection?'

Fay's confused recollections of that strange weekend at Hugo's flat before her accident gradually crystallized on the memory of Hugo's research assistant in his faded, ragged jeans.

'I think so. A picture of a funny little rain god, wasn't it? Has Jessica missed it?'

'It wasn't Jessica's. It was addressed to Meg and the hand-writing was so execrable we all thought it was from someone called Maria. Don't you remember?' Hugo was becoming irritable. Voices could be heard in the background and the sound of hammering; presumably the dismantling of the ware-house at Stamford was in full swing.

'Vaguely, Hugo. Frankly, I didn't take much notice at the time.'

'Exactly! It wasn't important but I just could not push it out of my mind. Why should Meg call Cabral in Sao Paulo? I checked our account and we had concluded our business with him before he went to the States in August.'

'So?'

'I got on to Carey and extracted that postcard. He was quite sulky about it, the oaf. What do you think, Fay? Shall I check it out myself or do you think I'd better turn it over to the police? In all this time they've not found any sort of lead, no other man in her life. If I hadn't known Meg so well I would have dismissed it from my mind. But she was far too meticulous to mix up personal and trade calls and for the life of me I can't think what was so urgent that a normal invoice couldn't cover. Do you think she was conducting a little private business on the side? Something not going through the books at the shop?'

Fay reclined on the bed, watching a large fly buzz its way around the lampshade and drop, apparently without reason, to struggle feebly on the bedcover for a moment before lying still, apparently dead.

'Are you still listening to me, Fay? What should I do?' His

voice shrilled with barely controlled irritability and, after a pause in which Fay studied the dead fly, he added, 'You don't think I'd be stirring up a lot of muck involving poor old Goldsmith, do you?'

'Don't ask me, Hugo. If you think this Brazilian thing will tempt Hayes off Robert's back for a day or two, try it by all means. After all,' she coldly concluded, 'both Meg and Bill Goldsmith are dead. If they were operating some sort of commercial fiddle between them, they are hardly likely to complain.'

'Thanks for being so enthusiastic,' he dryly retorted.

'Sorry, love. I just can't see Hayes being fobbed off at this late stage with a wisp like that.'

'Honestly, Fay, you astound me. You were the one turning every stone looking for dirt and now you seem to have completely lost interest. I think it's worth a try. The firm's being pulled apart for the accountants anyhow. The inquest on Meg is on Monday and I hate even to consider what sort of mess it's going to be.'

Fay gasped, suddenly filled with anger that Robert had again lied to her.

'Hell,' Hugo muttered, 'I shouldn't have mentioned it. Rob said not to tell you. There's nothing you can do, Fay, you're quite right to stay out of it.'

'Hugo, have you told Hayes about seeing Meg the Friday before the car crash?'

'No. But I think I may have to.'

'It would give the man something else to chew over if nothing else,' she bitterly remarked.

'Oh, Fay, why do I always make such a balls of everything?'

Her anger receded, settling into a knot of misery. 'I'm sorry, Hugo, I'm being unfair. We all added our faggots to Meg's pyre. In fact, you were probably the only real friend she had. But everything's got so confused I'm not sure where the truth even begins any more. Wouldn't it be simpler if we all just told the police exactly what we know and let them sort it out?'

'Perhaps. If I tell Hayes, then I'll have to explain to Robert why I met Meg on the quiet in Renham that Wednesday night and spoke to her again on the phone after he flew to Houston. Poor sod will think we've all being double-crossing him at every turn.'

'Well, I suppose we have.'

'Do you think you could forget about the date of the Heffer inquest? I swear to you, Fay, Stamford's the very last place to be while all this is fermenting. It's not as if your being here could help – quite the reverse. The chapel's in a total shambles with this damned stocktaking, the police are still combing through everything and I'm keeping out of the village as much as possible. A hotbed of gossip, according to Mrs B.'

'Don't worry, Hugo. I won't give the game away about the inquest – or who spilled the beans. But thanks for telling me – this isn't a psychiatric clinic, you know.'

'Probably be more fun if it were,' he quipped. 'Cheerio, darling. I'll ring again if I dig up anything else.'

'Bye, Hugo. God bless. Sorry I'm such a wet blanket.'

She replaced the receiver and rolled over on the bed, both hands pressed against her eyes, trying to shut out rising despair.

The weekend was, predictably a strain. They found themselves drawn back into mutual deception: she refusing to disclose her awareness of the fast-approaching inquest on Meg Heffer and Robert hiding the full extent of police accusations.

They had got into the habit of slipping away to a pub on the other side of the square for an hour at the end of the day. Robert found Fay's room at the clinic claustrophobic and, providing she kept off alcohol, Maureen Patel approved the evening rambles.

In the dingy, smoke-filled bar, Robert lost his tense preoccupation and after a couple of beers was sufficiently relaxed to bring up one of the many issues which confused him.

'I know you hate talking about the wretched business, Rusty, but there is one thing I just can't fathom out.'

'Only one?' She tilted her glass, watching the tomato juice swirl thickly like a bloody whirlpool. Recoiling from any reference to the nightmare of the past fortnight, she slyly avoided any remark he introduced which might lead to a painful rehash of their dilemma.

'The police keep asking me about those anonymous calls to the house, made, apparently, for weeks. Is that true, Fay? They don't believe I knew nothing about it, particularly as Hugo was the one to report the thing in the first place. What's been going on? Why didn't you tell me?'

'There wasn't anything to tell,' she said with careful unconcern. 'Nothing was said. If I'd told you about it you would have pooh-poohed the whole thing and it seemed a bit feeble to make an official complaint.'

'But you evidently discussed it with Hugo. Why not me?'

Fay's head jerked up, instantly on the defensive. 'I did *not* discuss it with Hugo. He was in the house while I was staying with your father and presumably got fed up with all the pointless calls. He thought it was a faulty line. Hugo's a bit of an old woman, you know what he's like, can't ever leave anything alone.'

'And you *swear* nothing was said? Hayes seems to have got it into his head you received threats.'

'Well, Hayes is barking up the wrong tree. I've told him a million times nothing was said. When it was happening I got pretty rattled, I don't mind admitting. I know you think I'm a bag of nerves, Robert, but anybody alone in that great house getting mysterious phone calls night after night would have felt the same. It was a persistent persecution.'

Robert slipped his arm round her tense shoulders and murmured, 'But why didn't you tell me? Am I really such an unfeeling clod?'

'I thought you'd laugh. It seemed ludicrous to me even at the time but that sort of thing builds up. One *knows* it's just some harmless crank, but however sensibly I thought about it next morning, every ring of the telephone after dark filled me with terror.'

He sighed. 'I don't get it. What possible connection could there be between those calls and Meg's death?'

'I think at first Hayes suspected you may have been blackmailed by Meg and the calls were some sort of secret reminder, meant for you, not me at all. As I hadn't told you about them, presumably that theory won't wash – and they continued after you'd gone. Hayes is as baffled as we are. For all I know the police think I lied about falling downstairs and Maeve covered up for me. But Hayes can't prove anything. He's probably still trying to fathom out in his technicolor imagination who it was that beat me up the night Goldsmith was killed. Or maybe he thinks I killed the poor man with my own machete in my own garden and then got drunk from remorse.'

'But the bloody phone calls continued after Meg died.'

'Yes, they did. It puzzled me, too, and then I realized I was only trying to link the calls with Meg because Hayes had put the idea into my head. There wasn't any connection. The calls were meant to frighten *me*, they were nothing to do with you *or* Meg, in fact.'

Robert took a swig of lager and slammed the tankard on the table. 'Fair beats me. I sometimes think I don't undertand the first thing about the whole damned affair.'

'I've been turning it over in my mind since I've been here and I think I may know who was behind those telephone calls.'

'Who, for God's sake?' Robert snapped, at the limit of exasperation. The girl polishing glasses behind the bar eyed them curiously. Having watched their whispered conversations in the same corner all week she had dismissed them as yet another pair of lovebirds meeting in secret. Going to have a tiff over it now, she decided, wondering at the appeal of the pasty-faced redhead.

'Robert, do you mind if we drop this now? My head's splitting. We can talk about it when I get home. It's all over. I'll go and see this person who I think was responsible and let her know I shall go to the police if the nuisance continues.'

'And you won't tell me who this woman is?'

'For God's sake, Robert! Let it rest.'

'Let's go,' he said, stiff with irritation.

They threaded their way between the tables to the exit. Outside, she lingered for a moment, buttoning her coat against the soft drizzle which seemed to condense in the air from a starless sky. The atmosphere between them was electric.

Impulsively, she took his arm, gripping the fabric of his raincoat.

'Let's go home, Robert. We could have the rest of the weekend, together – we've lost so much time already, darling.'

'No.'

He set off abruptly, Fay matching his long strides with her own, miserably aware of her ribs wrenching painfully in her chest. She had started to lie to him again. The business with Millicent Ambache would only drag out all the other old evasions, the secret abortion, her affair with Philip Lewis. All so long ago. Long buried.

Eighteen

F ay drifted round the clinic during the weekend, alternately
bored or filled with apprehension about the impending
Heffer inquest and its possible consequences. The other patients fostered her melancholy being, for the most part, elegantly decaying beauties, the atmosphere only occasionally
lightened by those optimists taking minor cosmetic surgery.

Sunday was like bleeding to death, each minute dripping
inexorably towards Monday. She stayed in her room for most
of the day, pacing from door to window and back again, trying to
decide whether to go or stay. Clearly, Robert wanted to see the
inquest through alone and she felt diminished by the exclusion.

At six thirty she impulsively called Luke's school and asked
to speak to the boy, fully intending to forewarn him of the
possible publicity the Heffer inquest might arouse. She even
didn't know if Luke had heard about poor old Goldsmith being
cut down in their own garden – she should have asked Robert
about it. Fay dreaded the very real possibility that Luke might
glimpse a report in a newspaper about Meg's involvement with
Robert, but the clutching fear remained that Rob would
bitterly blame her if she disclosed the messy details to their
son unnecessarily.

Luke was eventually located in the art room and the sound of
his eager voice shrivelled the words in her throat. After a
moment's initial mumbling she disguised the reason for her
call on the pretext of telling him about her fall downstairs and
quickly rang off, knowing she had funked the truth yet again.

She went to bed and lay in the darkness listening through the
wall to the bland flow from a television programme in the next
room. It was just before dawn before she finally dropped into a

deep slumber, awakening with her mind resolved. She *must* go home.

A girl came in with tea and raised the blinds to reveal a lemon-washed sky. Fay sat up, alert, released from indecision. When the door closed she reached for the telephone, dialled and waited, toying with the teaspoon.

'Hello, Maeve. It's me again.'

'Fay!' She sounded incredulous.

'You'd think I was a voice from the dead.'

'Sorry, love. It's pretty early. I don't really surface till the kids are off to school. You don't want me to pack another suitcase, do you? Your dawn escapes are becoming a bore.'

'I'm coming home. Today.'

Maeve shot up, now fully alert. 'You *are* joking, are you not?' she said without conviction. 'Robert called only last night. He said you weren't due back for several more days.'

'I can't wait about here any longer. I must be home when he gets back from the inquest. Are you going?'

'I thought that was supposed to be privileged information. You're not trying to trap me into giving the game away, are you?'

'Maeve, I've known all along about the inquest being today. Hugo told me. But Robert insists on treating me like an imbecile and toughing it out on his own. God knows if he plans to incarcerate me here till after the Goldsmith inquest too.'

'Stupid macho behaviour, I agree. But then I sometimes think you two hardly communicate at all. Heavens knows how each of you remember which things are currently on the secret list. I'd get hopelessly muddled.'

Fay could well believe it. 'We've had years of experience,' she retorted. 'Could you meet me at Renham Junction if I catch the 11.58? I'm not sure when it gets in – perhaps you could check at your end?'

'Are you sure you're fit? The house isn't prepared or anything. Stay here with us for a few days.'

'No, bless you Maeve, but honestly I need to go home. I feel if I can just get home everything will start being normal again. Are you attending the inquest?'

'No. Ted and Robert are setting off shortly with Stanley Markham.'

'Thank God he's had the sense to get himself a solicitor,' Fay muttered with relief. 'You know how badly things may go for Robert, don't you?'

'Yes,' Maeve replied guardedly. 'But Stanley's very confident. Quite frankly, Fay, I'm glad you've decided to come back. Robert needs you, whatever he says.'

'Is it all right then? You'll meet me from the train?'

'Don't fluster yourself. I'll be there.'

'Maeve, you're an angel from heaven.'

'Never heard that one before. See you later. Must fly now, Dottie's arrived with an early morning cuppa and looking like the wrath of God. The wretched woman has the temperament of a prima donna.'

Fay carefully made up her face, noting the vast improvement. The fading bruises were almost gone and even the bald patch had begun to grow out. She took herself downstairs to persuade a harassed secretary to accept her unscheduled departure and order a cab for eleven thirty.

She flew back to her room to pack her few belongings, scribbled a message for Maureen Patel and placed it, together with some notes for the maid, on the locker. Later, the taxi was waiting to take her to the station and with satisfaction Fay settled in the half-empty carriage. Home. Never before had it seemed more beguiling.

The train arrived at Renham Junction in the afternoon. Maeve came into view as soon as Fay crossed the platform and they hugged warmly, jigging through the barrier.

'It's all over!' Maeve cried, her face breaking into an enormous grin. 'Robert's off the hook.'

'Tell me quick, Maeve. What happened?'

They linked arms and walked to the exit, Maeve grinning and gesticulating in happy abandon, Fay a picture of incredulity.

'Ted phoned before I left – I told him to tell Robert you were on your way home. The whole thing was wrapped up in record time.'

'Adjourned? Open verdict?'

'No, over. Finished. Nothing personal came out about Meg and Robert. He came across as a very caring employer, Ted said – "a business colleague with a kind heart", would you believe? Robert had to speak about leaving her at the clinic, of course, and there was a signed statement from Hugo about Meg deciding to drive on to Wales after a weekend in London. But the main evidence was from a Thames Valley policeman – Amis, was it?'

'Sergeant Ames?'

'Yes, that's the one. And a police vehicle engineer told the court he had examined the car and found that the rubber on the nearside brake cylinder had slightly perished and may have been the cause of the escape of brake fluid.'

'Nothing about a loose nut?'

'Mother of God, Fay, I'm not a mechanic!'

'But that's fantastic, Maeve. Why should Hayes drop the case like that after making all those painstaking enquiries? Too busy with Goldsmith's murder presumably.'

'Divine Providence. But perhaps I haven't got the whole story. They'll be back at teatime, you can ask Robert yourself. Why don't you both stay with us for a few days? It's all been a terrible strain.'

'I still don't understand ... It's like standing blindfold in front of a firing squad and waiting for the gunfire, only to discover they're popping champagne corks.'

'What a super idea. We'll put a couple of bottles on ice as soon as we get in.' She glanced at Fay, now sitting beside her, dazed with relief. 'I presume this new doctor of yours knows you've discharged yourself again?'

'It wasn't a hospital, Maeve. More a cross between a health spa and a drying-out clinic.'

'And extremely expensive, I hope. Robert deserves a ginor-mous bill at the very least. The best thing you two could do would be to take yourselves off for a fantastic holiday when this horrible business is over. Africa. How about that?'

'Mm ... Sounds wonderful, but I'm not sure if Robert can leave just now. There's a partnership row, Hugo's resigning. And there's poor Bill Goldsmith's death still under investigation.'

They reached the car, dropped the case in the boot and Fay got in while Maeve leaned into the back and took up a cardboard box tied loosely with string. She placed it on Fay's lap.

'What's this?'

'An apology,' she said, closing the door and clamping her seat belt. 'But open it carefully. I stopped off at Murray's surgery on the way through. You remember my gorgeous vet? He feels really rotten about your accident. Said it was all his fault.'

'Of course it wasn't. I was plastered.'

'Well, it wouldn't have happened if we hadn't been such lousy sailors.' Maeve laughed. 'He's having a fit of the guilts. When I told him about my losing Ottie as well he sent this as a replacement.'

She blanched. 'Not another rabbit?'

Maeve threw back her head in laughter. 'Just a sec. I'll have to close the windows.'

Fay unknotted the string and lifted the flap. A thin mew wafted out. She opened it fully to reveal a black kitten with eyes like aquamarine.

'He's gorgeous!' Fay carefully extended a forefinger. It spat, arching its thin backbone, and she sharply withdrew her hand. They giggled.

'Satan himself,' Maeve said. 'If Robert objects say it's an Ethiopian Ebony.'

Fay snorted. 'A what?' she gasped, retying the box as Maeve let the car into gear.

'Ethiopian Ebony,' she repeated with precision, manoeuvring the vehicle out of the station yard and on to the main road. 'It's an ordinary moggy, of course, but men are such snobs about pedigrees.'

'You mean it's another "kirtle hound"?'

'That's the ticket. You're learning.'

'And I thought you were sermonizing only this morning about how we should all be honest with each other.'

'Only on unimportant matters. I assure you, you'll save yourself a lot of hassle if you say the wee one is an Ethiopian

Ebony, especially when it starts ripping up the chairs and shitting under his bed.'

'Wonderful! Tell me, what did *you* get?'

'A–ah . . .' The long drawn out sigh spoke volumes. 'And to change the subject, you look remarkably improved since last I saw you in Frau Menkes' Stalag.'

'Heavens, that seems years ago.'

Maeve grimaced, saying nothing, and accelerated into the fast lane.

'Mrs B didn't tell you I'd thrown myself downstairs, by any chance?'

'No, of course not,' Maeve said, surprised. 'But you heard about her making the men drag the garden pool? Poor woman was utterly convinced, even got that hatchet-faced inspector worried. Hugo smoothed it over with the police. Mrs Barton thinks Hugo's a "real gentleman", she told me. It's lovely to hear all the gossipy bits from her. You *are* lucky, Fay. She's so *good*, utterly without malice of any kind. Sometimes Dottie's silent passions get quite creepy. If her current mood doesn't lift soon I shall have to give her the push. All this glowering gets on one's nerves.'

'Mrs B's chatter can get pretty irksome if you're not in the mood. Is she cross with me for sneaking out of the hospital like that, giving everyone a fright?'

'Not a bit. Poor old biddy was so relieved to discover you hadn't drowned yourself she'd forgive anything. She was the only one in the village to visit Meg's father after the accident, you know. The school secretary told me. She knows Mrs B of old, she used to work in the school kitchens apparently. All heart, she said. Ted mentioned on the phone before I left that Heffer wasn't at the inquest, by the way.'

'Extraordinary man.'

Fay touched her arm.

'Maeve, slow down a bit, would you? I've got to stop off on the Barstow road for a few minutes to see someone. You won't mind if I call in, will you? It's a cottage called Cheyney's.'

'I know it. Has a glorious show of climbing roses right up to the roof in June. I didn't know you were pally with the woman

184

there. Ted sold her the house a while back. A bit reclusive he said. Not a fun person at all.'

'I hardly know her to be honest. But her sister was the one who fell on the line. I have to find out if she told the police that I knew Barbara, that I'd lied about her being a total stranger to me.'

Maeve looked worried. 'Surely not now, Fay? Not this afternoon. You could call another time.'

'I can't face Hayes again without knowing. I think Millicent Ambache might be holding it over me. In fact, I think she's the one who's been persecuting me with those silent phone calls I told you about. I must settle it once and for all. You see, I did a terrible wrong to that woman years ago. I had an affair with her husband.'

Maeve's steering swerved wildly. 'You what?'

'Slow down, Maeve!' she shouted. Maeve eased her foot on the brake and Fay continued. 'It got complicated. I had an abortion. The marriage folded because of me and, to be honest, I haven't given her a moment's thought until recently.'

'Who was this Ambache guy?'

'That was her maiden name – the man is a top businessman these days, very rich and hits the headlines in the financial papers from time to time, but not someone you'd call a celebrity. But in her place I'd be pretty bitter to discover the girl who wrecked her life just walked away, only to resurface on her doorstep years later.'

'You recognized her?'

'Not really. The name rang a bell but I'd buried all that sad stuff when I broke off the relationship.'

'He knew about the baby?'

She nodded. 'But I ran out on him and disappeared. Frankly, he was on the spot at the time. Apart from being married he was in hock to the family business and a little bastard on the scene might have blown his chances to take the reins when his father retired. A very traditional lot. Très kosher.'

'Whew! And you've kept this little bombshell to yourself all this time. Does Robert know?'

'God no! I buried it, like I said. Nobody knew except the

185

Ambache sisters, and if my reappearance revived old hostilities I couldn't blame poor Millicent. I need to have it out once and for all.'

Maeve shrugged and turned off at the next fork in the road. 'You know best, love. I'll be outside if you need me.'

Cheyney's was set slightly apart from the other houses and even at this dull end of the season the garden looked immaculate, the lawn swept clear of autumn leaves.

She hurried up the path, half hoping the woman was out. Bearding Millicent Ambache on her own ground was a miserable prospect but Fay knew if she didn't plunge in now with Maeve as a bulwark, she would lose courage and the old wound would fester on.

Millicent opened the door. She seemed unsurprised to find Fay on her doorstep, her reception cool. Maeve watched anxiously from the car but the door closed behind the two women and she settled down to wait. The kitten in the box on the back seat started to mew.

Fay was with Millicent Ambache for nearly twenty minutes and emerged dazed and pale. Maeve hurried to open the gate and pushed her into the passenger seat.

'Jesus, Fay, you look like a ghost. I told you to leave it till later. You're still meant to be convalescing.'

They drove off in a flurry of spinning wheels and, after a while, Fay perked up.

'I was wrong. That woman knew me years ago, like I told you. I thought she was harbouring a serious grudge against me – all those telephone calls and the fact that I was involved in her sister's accident. She wasn't the anonymous caller, Maeve. I can't think now why I thought she was to blame.'

'Are you sure? She'd be bound to deny it.'

'I believe her. I was quite wrong. Those stupid calls were nothing whatsoever to do with Millicent Ambache. We had a long talk about it. I'm going to see her again next week when I have more time.'

'What about the sister? She might have been the crazy caller.'

'They continued after she died.'

Maeve pursed her lips. 'That seems to be that then. Some

harmless phone freak. Kids do it for kicks, I'm told. Pick on any old number in the book and make a party of it. I said you were making too much of it, Fay, letting your imagination get the better of you.'

It started to rain and Fay sat mesmerized by the windscreen wipers, their smooth action calming her nerves after facing up to her supposed persecutor.

Nineteen

They drove on chattering like magpies and pulled into the drive behind Ted's Jaguar.

'Oh, good, they're back already. Wonderful!' Maeve was even more excited than Fay who was still dazed by Millicent Ambache's response and hardly able to believe Maeve's assurance that Robert had been totally exonerated.

'We'll only stop a minute, Maeve. We must get home, start living again.'

'Some tea then, at least. Anyway, they've probably started celebrating already.'

'Shall I bring the Ethiopian Ebony?'

'I think not.' Maeve slammed the car door. 'It'll only pee on the carpet. Leave it on the porch in the box and I'll give it some milk when I make the tea.'

They walked into the hall, Fay light-headed at the prospect of seeing Robert without the awful cloud of dread hanging over them. Thank God I kept it from Luke, she thought as they dumped their coats.

'It's awfully quiet, Maeve. Where *is* everybody?'

'Flora went to Kate Metcalfe's before lunch and she's keeping her overnight. I packed Dottie off home before I left. She was in one of her thunderous moods for some unknown reason – she must be on the change, miserable creature. And the boys stay after school to do their prep on Mondays. Ted brings them home after leaving the office. Grief!' she shrieked, clapping a hand to her head. 'I'd forgotten Ted wouldn't be there. I'll have to dash off for them straight away.' She flew into the drawing room and voices were raised in greeting.

'I'll be back in a jiffy,' she called as she passed Fay still

188

standing in the hall. 'Make some tea. Oh, and don't forget the black beastie.'

Fay drew breath to reply but Maeve was gone, slamming the door behind her.

Ted appeared in the hall, closely followed by Robert who looked utterly drained, bewildered as a man dragged from a plane crash. Ted kissed Fay's cheek and, jaunty with excitement, drew her towards the drawing room. Robert touched her shoulder diffidently and they smiled at each other in dazed relief.

Ted said, 'Isn't this stupendous, Fay? After all that worry! Who would have believed it?'

'It was splendid of you to support Robert the way you have. I've been a rotten coward.'

'Rubbish, darling. Come and say hello to Stanley. He's tickled pink. Never earned a fee with so little effort.'

They entered the lovely room, its smokey blue tones deepening to amethyst in the early dusk. She held out her hand to Robert's solicitor, a small man with slanting dark eyes.

'Shall we open a bottle or wait for Maeve to get back?' Ted said, eager as a schoolboy. 'Maeve will have the boys' supper to deal with as soon as she gets in and she must be exhausted after all that driving.'

'You're right,' Robert cut in. 'How about Fay and I dashing off home now and we can all get together for a celebration dinner tonight?' He turned to Stanley. 'Perhaps Tessa can join us?'

''Fraid not. Another time perhaps. We're booked this evening. Tessa's bridge night with the Robsons.'

'I'll give you a ring and arrange a little get-together another time then. We must keep in touch,' Robert said, already in command, his usual self. 'That suit you, Ted? Tonight I mean. I suppose Maeve can get a sitter at short notice?'

'Dottie doesn't seem to be about today. Perhaps Maeve pushed her off early. But I'm sure she can fix something up. About eight?'

'Fine. I'll try to get a table at The Red House. I could do with a good old-fashioned nosh.'

Stanley Markham drove off, briefly saluting as he circled the drive. Robert fetched his Mercedes from the stable block and opened the door for Fay. She brushed Ted's cheek, squeezing his arm in mute thanks and bent down to gather up the box on the porch. Seating herself, the box on her lap, she blew a kiss as Robert made a characteristic sweeping exit.

'What's that?' he said once they were away, nodding towards the box.

'A surprise present from Maeve. You'll see.'

'I've had enough surprises for one day.'

'What happened, Robert? Maeve seemed to think the whole thing's been wrapped up.'

'Absolutely. I must have a guardian angel or something. Between you and me, Fay, I thought I was for the high jump. The scandal, if not actual charges. But the whole thing went through like a dose of salts. I'd hardly drawn breath and we were all outside again.'

'But why? Was there some new evidence?'

'I sorted out Hayes privately in the car park afterwards. Bloody man's been hounding me for days, I felt I deserved some explanation.'

'What did he say?'

'Pretty tight-lipped about it, still thinks I tampered with those brakes, you know. More or less told me as much. But I gather Hugo discovered a bloke in Sao Paulo and phoned him. Christ knows who gave Hugo the tip-off but it seems this Brazilian admitted having a run round with Meg, but later she found out he was married. She plagued the poor guy to stay in England and, when he went back to his wife, bombarded him with letters and phone calls. This Jorge-Maria Cabral faxed copies to Hugo, sheets of it – all in Meg's handwriting. No question about it. The chap thinks she got herself pregnant on purpose assuming he'd stay with her, but it didn't work. Never does. Anyway, these Catholic fellows are as straight as a dye once they're back on the nest. He thought Meg a sensible English popsie just out for some fun, you see. She did some typing for him, it appears, and he gave her a ring instead of payment and, what with one thing and another, the silly bitch made up her mind to winkle him out of Sao Paulo permanently.'

'And Cabral admitted all this to Hugo?'

'Oh, yes. He was perfectly frank. He seems to know Hugo fairly well and says he had no intention of leaving Meg in the lurch, offered her money and so on. Very fond of her I daresay. But definitely too fly to get himself involved, leaving his family and so on.'

'And you never guessed?'

'Not a breath. I feel pretty sore at Meg over that. I really did think I was the one who put her in the cart and all the time it was this Latin lover of hers. Put me in as long stop, the crafty bitch.'

'And Hugo told *you* all this? I thought you two weren't speaking?' Her incomprehension flapped about like a freshly caught trout.

'Not a bloody word to *me*. He got himself an interview with Hayes' superintendent and passed over all the copies of Meg's love letters to Cabral, who's been very decent about it by the way. Conscience. Promised Hugo to air mail a statement if they pursued their case against me and gave the all-clear to pass his name and address to the authorities if absolutely necessary.'

'Why didn't Hugo tell you all this himself?'

'God knows. Mind you, it probably sounded better coming from a disinterested party. Poor old Hugo probably thought I'd punch him in the eye for interfering. None of his business. Never come across such a nosy bugger.'

'Hugo's saved your worthless hide, Robert Browne! And presumably convinced Hayes' boss? Lucky you and Hugo were known to be splitting up and incommunicado or they may have suspected a conspiracy.'

'I think the big lad in the Thames Valley lot was already fed up with Hayes ferreting away like Sherlock Holmes on an ordinary traffic accident. The superintendent here's got the Goldsmith business still hanging fire without fussing about Meg's car crash. Perhaps Hayes gets up his nose the same as he does everyone else's. The upshot was the Super shuffles through Hayes' reports and calls up another vehicle engineer to go over

191

the Metro again. When he came up with a bit of perished rubber on the brake cylinder, the man made up his mind the whole case was shaky and told Hayes to fold it up nice and tidy. So our poor detective inspector is left spitting and cursing and has to close the file.'

'But that's astonishing, Robert. It's a miracle. You must speak to Hugo as soon as we get home. He's gone back to London now I suppose?'

'Kept out of range the whole time,' he ruefully admitted. 'But you're right. Creepy little berk deserves a pat on the back.'

They turned off into their own lane, the high brick wall of Glebe House flanking the leaf-strewn verge. Even in the darkness the huge letters sprayed on the old brickwork were clearly visible. KILLER.

He braked violently. Fay lurched forward, the safety belt jabbing her mending ribs with a sickening jolt.

'Christ Almighty,' he muttered, stepping into the road. Fay began to weep.

'Get back in the car, Robert. Let's get inside quickly.'

He eased back into the driving seat, staring at the white lettering slashed against the bricks. 'They don't believe it, Fay. They still think I killed that girl . . . Even *you* think I did it, don't you? Bill Goldsmith too? When will it end?'

'Let's go away, darling. Start somewhere else,' she sobbed. They drove through the gates, the blank windows of the house seeming to regard their return with the impassivity of spectators.

The evening celebration with Maeve and Ted limped feebly through, only brightening when the wine-soaked quartet returned to the house for coffee and brandy. It was then that Maeve suggested they all set about repainting the old wall.

'What, all of it?' Fay's voice croaked in astonishment.

'Why not? White all along. Look awfully pretty when it's done and be lots of fun, especially while we're all so tipsy.'

'Like Tom Sawyer's whitewashed fence,' Ted chimed in with enthusiasm. 'Rouse yourself, old lad. Is there any paint in the house?'

'In the warehouse, I think,' he answered doubtfully, leading Ted outside.

'Well, it won't wash off,' said Maeve fatalistically, 'and we can't look at it for ever.'

Fay was beyond tears. 'Dreadfully cruel though, isn't it? How can people be so vile? After all the work Robert has brought into Stamford one way and another?'

'Some twisted little man with a chip on his shoulder about something. Robert's success most likely. The sort who picks up a local issue like the nearest stone.'

They attacked the wall with an assortment of brushes and several half-empty cans of paint. In the darkness the crude graffiti was obliterated but the brickwork looked bizarre under its new white coat and, Fay guessed, would look grotesque in daylight.

But the energy had dispelled the gloom and in the end they all fell, exhausted, into the kitchen while Fay made some coffee and Robert poured more brandy. They sat about, their smart evening clothes liberally spattered with paint, giggling stupidly.

'You'd better stay the night, Ted. You're too boozed to drive home,' Robert said thickly, rocking gently from the combined effects of alcohol and weariness.

'I'll drive,' Maeve insisted. 'The Irish blood soaks up wine like mother's milk.'

'She'll blarney the poor traffic cop if we do get stopped. Come, my gorgeous missus. Home to bed.'

They lurched out into the drive and Robert and Fay leaned against each other under their own porch for the first time in weeks, waving their adieux.

'Home to bed,' echoed Robert, quietly closing the door.

The death of his secretary and his warehouseman had cracked the foundations of Robert Browne's career. The marketing man was in retreat. The chapel store was emptied, the staff dispersed and the house seemed to echo with hollow voices. Mercifully he was kept occupied, checking the stock lists and trying to establish some sort of fair division of assets, but his spirit was broken. It was time to go.

Robert shied away from a full discussion with Hugo and they individually pursued their investigations with a joint accountant who cast himself as an informal go-between. They held brief telephone conferences but both acknowledged the need for a period of readjustment prior to the actual date of severance.

Fay remained unconvinced of the need for a complete break and tended to regard the stocktaking as a gesture. Could Robert really abandon Stamford just like that? But having issued his ultimatum, Hugo was loath to rescind it. He knew that a weakness at this stage would annihilate his last chance to break away from the Brownes and the painful proximity in which the two tragedies had thrown them.

Hayes continued to investigate the attempted break-in which had preceded the attack on Goldsmith, now complicated by a petrol can full of paraffin discovered in the undergrowth. Was he now seeking an arsonist? Or merely scratching the surface of a deep-rooted antagonism to Robert Browne, fanned since the deaths of two locals and aggravated by the abrupt dismissal of the staff? The problem was, no one was sure for how long the petrol can had lain undiscovered. It could have belonged to Goldsmith's assailant or been pitched there at some other time. Perhaps even Browne himself had returned that night to destroy Goldsmith's files and any stock which did not tally with accounts. To fake an accidental fire? Then found Goldsmith's body, dropped the can and scarpered? Or even been discovered by his foreman, challenged, and the poor old guy felled with the machete, which happened to be handy?

Hayes had to smile at the ever-spiralling fantasy this case was leading him to invent. The trouble was, there was nothing to go on. Everyone was tight-lipped, giving nothing away to the police and certainly not to Roger Hayes, an incomer. He suspected that the charmed circle had closed in once before, foiled him in respect of the Heffer killing. He would be more careful this time. Bide his time.

The Goldsmith inquest was adjourned.

Twenty

O ne afternoon in November, Fay reluctantly resumed her attack on the shrubbery which had been, so she thought, only temporarily abandoned. Stumbling unexpectedly upon the clump of Gladwyn iris gave her a nasty turn. The berries still exuded from the slashed pod like an open wound. Obscene. Instantly, she was back to that afternoon when Hayes and Goldsmith had walked towards her across the grass, the afternoon when her suspicions of Robert first floated to the surface, those same flutters of disquiet which, in her infrequent spells of introspection, still mouldered.

Determined to keep busy, she cleared the last twenty yards of tangled undergrowth and straightened to survey the bleak border, saddened by its affirmation of approaching winter. Her ribs had begun their tiresome nagging ache so she threw the fork and gloves into the wheelbarrow and dragged herself back to the house.

Perhaps it would be possible to lift the gloomy atmosphere by immersing herself in the rose catalogue which had been put aside for months. It was the nearest she could bring herself to rejecting Robert's assertion that they would be leaving. Since the dreadful evening when they had joined Maeve's gay conspiracy and painted over the accusation daubing the garden wall, Fay had slowly come to re-accept Stamford, submerging herself in a renewed assault on the garden in a determined effort to ignore the latent hostility that lingered in the village. Now it was Fay who refused to recognize the local antagonism which was driving them out. Out where? Where could they hide?

They had taken to spending their evenings in the study,

Robert working through piles of old order sheets and she making sketches for a walled garden to be constructed from the fallen brickwork beyond the orchard. Entering the study for some notes she remembered having left the previous evening, she stopped short, surprised to find Robert at his desk deep in conversation. He was using a mobile phone she had never seen before, presumably part of the equipment salvaged from the chapel.

'Sorry,' she whispered as he looked up. 'Thought you were out.'

She turned towards the door but he beckoned her, still half attending to his caller. Fay stepped back into the room, silently closing the door. She searched the drawers of a davenport and was about to withdraw as he finished the call.

'I'll do these in the kitchen,' she said, waving a sheaf of catalogues.

'Don't fuss, I've finished. That was Hugo. I'll have to go up to town in the morning, probably stay over till Friday. He wants to go through things with me before the weekend. Why don't we both go? We could fit in a cinema or something?'

Fay was pensive, juggling the options. 'Do you mind if I stay here? I don't much feel like shopping and it's a bit dull for me if you're going to be closeted with Hugo all day. And there's the kitten. In another month or two it'll be no trouble at all, just need feeding, but it's not even reliably house-trained yet.'

'I hope the bloody cat's not another excuse for hiding yourself away here like some sort of bag lady. Once the new business is up and running I was hoping you would start flat hunting. Sell up here. Move into town. I shall need some help now Meg's gone. Aubrey's selling his bookshop in Highgate and has offered me first refusal. I'd like to drive up to see him before the end of the month. Why don't you come?'

'Sounds lovely,' Fay said, brightening.

'No more funny phone calls? I don't like leaving you here while I'm with Hugo if that lark's still on.'

'Oh, that's all finished. I was stupid to let it rattle me.'

'Did you speak to that woman you thought was behind it? Warn her off?'

'I did, as a matter of fact. But I was quite wrong. Too much brooding over old sins.'

'What's that supposed to mean? Glad to hear at least one persecution's ended. But you're no wiser?'

'I think,' Fay said evenly, 'it was Dottie.'

'What d'you mean, "dotty"? Crackers or something?'

'No. Dottie. Maeve's Dottie. I don't know her other name. You know, the housekeeper.'

'Don't be daft, Fay. The woman can't use the phone, she's stone deaf.'

'Of course. But she could have made the calls. She didn't have to speak, and she's far from stupid.'

'Why the hell should *she* do it? And how could she use the phone without somebody seeing her? A deaf mute on the blower would strike even that halfwit Maeve as odd.'

'I can't prove it, of course. But I'm certain I'm right. She lives in a hostel in Stamford. There would certainly be a telephone there and the calls were all made after six o'clock, after work, when everyone would be busy watching TV or having supper or something.'

'But why should Dottie persecute *you*? She's not subnormal is she? People like that can be bloody dangerous, Fay.'

'It was something Maeve told me. Dottie's always disliked me. Then one of the men at the hostel told Dottie some rubbish about seeing me with Ted in the school car park one night and she warned Maeve I was trying to steal him from her.'

'You'd be hard-pressed!' Robert snorted.

'We laughed about it at the time, but you know how devoted to Maeve and the family Dottie is. She looks on Maeve as some sort of Madonna and would simply lay down her life for them all. I suppose Dottie's watched us all assing about together the way we do and concluded I was a femme fatale trying to break up Maeve's home. So she hatched this hare-brained scheme to frighten me off. Heavy breathing – "a mute threat", as they say in court. Worked a treat: I was absolutely terrified. At one stage

I was convinced that the person at the other end of the line was trying to drive me to suicide. Don't laugh, Robert,' she warned, 'you wanted me to be honest and I'm telling you how I felt at the time. There was real hatred in that silence, a sort of hypnosis, as if she was trying to put crazy, evil thoughts into my head.'

'You've only yourself to blame for that sort of reputation, my love. You can bet that overdose you took a couple of years ago went the rounds in the village.'

'That was an accident, Robert. You *know* that!'

'*I* know that, Rusty, but the rest of Stamford prefer to believe the more dramatic version. Probably marked you down as a right nutter needing only the slightest nudge over the edge.'

'What rot!'

'I've lived in this place most of my life, Fay. You can't blame them. A dead-and-alive hole like Stamford seizes on anything that livens things up a bit – just look at all the rubbish they're driven to print in the local paper! Talk about scraping the barrel. Anyway, on a different tack, how's the new car shaping up? Running OK?'

'Smooth as silk.' Fay perched on the corner of the desk. 'It's already ceased to raise interest at the shops. I think it must have been the black and yellow. Distinctive isn't the ladylike word Maeve used to describe it...'

Robert laughed. 'We ought to call it the Tartmobile. Superb little engine, much sportier than the other cars you've had. I didn't fancy another Metro,' he added, his eyes sliding away. 'I'll be off about seven in the morning, I think. Don't get up. I'd like an early start. Hugo and I have a lot to get through. Sure you won't change your mind?'

'Positive. If you're up to it we could always run down to see your father over the weekend when you get back. Pa won't come here for Christmas if you don't bully him. He hates Stamford. Why *is* that? Anyway, you haven't been down for months and—'

'We'll see how I feel,' he cut in. 'It's a hellish long way and that cottage of his fits like a corset after twenty-four hours. Still, I could get in some shooting.' He stood up, brushing ash from his lapel and swung round the desk to pull her close. 'Nice to snuggle up in that skimpy bed of his for a night or two though.'

The following day Fay woke as Robert was leaving, the bedroom stuffy behind closed curtains. After listening to the car scattering gravel with its departure, she roused herself to trail through the empty house to make a breakfast tray and take it back to bed. It was the first time since that sickening fall that Fay had been alone: time things got back to normal.

Felix leapt elegantly on to the bed, purring loudly, snapping his thin black tail and turning sulphur yellow eyes to the jug.

'Evil little creature,' Fay hissed, smiling as she poured milk into a saucer and leaned across the bed to place it on the floor. She ran a shower and was towelling her hair as the telephone jangled.

'Hello, Fay. Maeve here. I'm in a fix.'

'Not another!'

'It's my art class this evening. My model's let me down and I've been promising this life class for ages. The old stagers have accepted the others with reasonable good grace. I felt bound to soften them up with this bribe of a real live model and now the stupid girl's got flu. Do you think you could fill in?'

'What – starkers?'

'Saints preserve us!' Maeve's throaty laugh rang in her ear. 'Just a sitting pose, normal winter woollies, nothing fancy and a break every quarter of an hour, Cross my heart.'

'Oh, all right,' Fay grudgingly agreed.

'You don't sound very keen.'

'Can you blame me? Helping you out last time ended up with cracked ribs and concussion.'

'Ah, well, my love, this time it's absolutely straightforward. Honestly.'

'I've still got my stubbly bald patch. I'm not exactly Mona Lisa, Maeve.'

'I'll bring a hat, a big straw one. The rest of the class can do Hallowe'en masks, something colourful – frighten each other out of their remaining wits.'

'Would you like me to bring my black kitten and a broom-stick and do both?'

'Sarcasm is unladylike, my girl. I forgive you only because you are the answer to my prayer. You won't let me down, will you, Fay?' she added with uncharacteristic anxiety.

'I do believe those students have got you on the run at last.'

She admitted they were a wee bit frosty about having the poor simple souls join the class in the first place and had only just got used to the idea. 'Persuading Tracey to pose was a pledge that standards wouldn't suffer.'

'When do you start?'

'Seven thirty. But I have to be there early to get paraphernalia out, set up the drapes and so on. Shall I pick you up at a quarter to seven?'

'I'll come for you. You haven't seen my Tartmobile yet, have you?'

'The new Italian two-seater? Wow! Ted saw you flaunting it through Renham last week. At least black and yellow matches your eyes.'

'Just one more nasty remark like that and you'll be looking for another model. I'm quite fond of Waspie already. It's the competition you're afraid of, Maeve MacMillan.'

'None of us gets any younger in this wicked world. You'll come for me then. Wear something simple or the poor dar-lings'll be defeated before they even pick up their brushes.'

She rang off. Already the day seemed to stretch less awe-somely ahead. Fay vaguely considered taking up Maeve's open invitation to stay: the prospect of being alone at night had began to pall.

She drove to the MacMillans' just before seven and was mildly surprised to see Maeve open the door before she had stopped the engine. Maeve dropped into the passenger seat, breathless and laughing, and threw a straw sun hat in the back.

'Such punctuality!' Fay enthused.

'I am trying *very* hard. All hell breaks loose if I'm not there before the rector arrives with his gang.'

'How many are there for heaven's sake?'

'Only five or six and utterly sweet, but the old hands tend to bunch up in a corner when they troop in. God knows what they think the poor dears could possibly get up to. They do have their own minder.'

'A nurse?'

'No. Generally a young man called Shamin.'

They arrived at the school and Fay found a space in the car park at the rear. They walked round to the front, in through the lobby and up a wide flight of stairs to the first floor, then along a corridor with classrooms opening off on both sides. People could be glimpsed gathering for the evening session. The school was already beginning to hum with the occasional slam of a door and scraping of chairs. Far off, the plaintive notes of a flute pierced the air, faint as a pipe on a lonely hillside.

They turned off to climb another flight, narrow and steep, culminating in a glazed door. Slightly breathless, Fay paused at the top while Maeve unlocked the studio.

They stepped into a darkness illuminated only by the pale disc of a full moon glimmering through a glass roof which slanted up to meet the ceiling. The lights went on and Fay was struck by the sheer size of the room. Clearly forty feet long, a substantial attic conversion with an expanse of north light, now dark and pierced with stars. Life-size plaster casts stood in nonchalant attitudes between clumps of plants luxuriating in pots placed in groups round the walls. Ignoring the government-issue chairs and easels ranged in a semicircle at one end, one could be in a lush Victorian conservatory.

'What a marvellous studio, Maeve.'

'Super, isn't it? Wasted on school kids. Just think what a fantastic penthouse you could make of it. Tame parrots flying round, a little pool and fountain, soft music. The mind boggles.'

Maeve dragged a carved chair from behind a pedestal desk and draped it in a dark red curtain.

'Looks like a throne.'

'And why not? Tonight you are a queen, an empress, anything at all except Fay Browne. The velvet hides those fiddly armrests. Much too difficult to draw.'

She filled a tray with jam jars and hurried to a door that

opened on to a sink unit set under the sloping roof in a converted cupboard. Fay hovered in the background, unsure of her exact role in Maeve's scheme. A large notice, hand-written in block capitals, was propped against the taps.

PLUMBING REPAIRS. THIS SINK IS *OUT OF ORDER.* USE MAIN KITCHEN ONLY.

'Bugger!' Slamming the tray on the draining board, the jars crashed together and one fell, smashing on to the quarry tiles. She poked under the sink, produced a brush and proceeded to sweep up the splinters of glass.

'Is there a jug or something we could use, Maeve? I presume the kitchens are downstairs.'

Maeve shot the rubbish into a bin.

'There are a couple of empty lemonade bottles under here. It'll have to do. Most of the regulars use oils in any case, but it's going to be maddening to have no water up here to wipe up afterwards.' She glanced at her watch. 'It's nearly half past! I'll run down and fill the bottles and you can be setting out the powder paints and brushes and things on that trestle table over there. Glory be, as soon as I woke this morning I knew it was going to be one of those days!'

Fay grabbed the bottles. 'Wouldn't it be better if I got the water? I don't know where anything is up here or even what's needed.'

'The kitchens are two floors down beyond the refectory. But you don't know the way.'

'I'll soon find them. And if I can't,' she added, making for the door, 'the place is seething with people. I'll ask.'

She flew down the steep stairs, almost tripping in her haste. Careful, she warned herself, the poor head won't stand another whoops-a-daisy.

The building had been constructed on a regular plan, the main structure incorporating a long corridor on each level with staircases at each end. The south wing housed an assembly hall and the north wing the refectory and kitchens. The hump of the swimming pool building rose like a great beached whale on the perimeter of the playing fields. Latterly, the kitchens had been extended to join with the central gymnasium block, thus creating a courtyard which the headmaster called 'the quad'. His finest hour was the interval of the annual alfresco concert when he hosted a buffet supper in the quad followed by a conducted tour of the school gardens. 'Our small Glyndebourne', he was often heard to remark.

The ground plan of the school presented few difficulties and, guided by the familiar odour of steamed puddings, it was easy to locate the kitchens. She dumped the pop bottles in one of the deep metal sinks and filled two large metal jugs she found hanging above the draining board, and carefully stepped around a pile of copper piping stacked by a wooden table which ran down the centre of the room. Dozens of evil-smelling cloths hung stiffly overhead on a drying rack and a notice board by the wall telephone to one side of the sinks bore an accumulation of duty rosters and printed admonitions on Hygiene and Waste. Fay wrinkled her nose. Why were all these establishments so sickeningly alike?

She hurried back up the stairs, along the top corridor and, with heart pumping against her ribs, climbed the last steep flight to the studio, almost colliding with the rector as he opened the door to leave. He stood aside and greeted her.

'Mrs Browne! How delightful to see you up and about again. I'm afraid you had already left hospital when I called in to see you.'

'How kind, Rector,' Fay said, nervously eyeing the studio which had, in her absence, become amazingly crowded. 'Please excuse me.' She held up the jugs. 'They want to start.'

'Of course. Of course.' He buttoned his raincoat. 'I shall be back at the usual time, but would you be so good as to mention to Mrs MacMillan I shall wait in the car park? These stairs,' he added with an apologetic cough, 'are rather exhausting twice in one evening.' He replaced his hat and smiled at Fay still dithering on the threshold. 'I have explained to Shamin. He will escort them down to the minibus at nine thirty.'

Maeve snatched the jugs from her hands and threw a brilliant smile in his direction. 'Bye now,' she lilted, nodding vigorously as the rector turned to wave in the course of his careful negotiation of the stairs.

Fay was thrust on to Maeve's makeshift throne, the straw hat concealing the area of shaved scalp where a delicate golden regrowth barely concealed the scar of her head wound. She froze in the pose and allowed her mind to wander.

Twenty-One

M aeve weaved back to the semicircle round the throne and nodded to Fay.

'Five minutes break for our model, everyone. I'll slip round and check the basic drawing before we take up the pose again.'

Fay stretched and stepped down from the dais and strolled over to Shamin's group. Their efforts were colourful, primitive and lively as cave paintings. Shamin had sketched a delicate spray of leaves from one of the pot plants. She moved along the table. With surprise she recognized another picture: ducks, one behind the other. Maeve closed in and grinned as they both regarded the lively line of wings and flying feet.

'Daisy's ducks. You bought one of her pictures at the show, didn't you?'

The woman carefully colouring webbed feet looked up, enormous slate-grey eyes vacuous as a winter sky.

'Daisy only draws ducks. But aren't they adorable?' Maeve glanced at her watch. 'Come on, girlie, back to it. After the next quarter of an hour we can go down for coffee.'

Fay effortlessly slipped back into the pose and switched off her mind. Nice.

At eight fifteen a buzzer shattered the tranquillity. Chairs scraped and brushes were laid aside. Feet clattered down the narrow stairs. Maeve and Fay followed.

'The coffee's truly abysmal but it's worth it to see my guinea pigs joining in at last. It took a week or two to persuade them to go down to the refectory at all and as the main purpose is for them to mix with the locals, the coffee break's more useful than the painting class by a long chalk. Especially as my toffee-nosed regulars keep strictly apart. It's a try-on really. If my original students don't go on strike and the new lot don't run amok, the county might be persuaded to extend the project. Poor loves need to get out in the evening the same as everyone else.'

'But your six must be hand-picked,' Fay insisted, taking two cups of coffee from the counter and handing one to Maeve.

'Of course they are. I don't pretend they're not the more acceptable ones, but it's not one-sided by any means. Take Daisy's ducks for instance. Bloody ducks week in and week out, nothing shifts her. But they've more animation than anything the rest of us could achieve in a million years. And the little dark man, you know, the one with the poisonous breath, Charlie something, has a colour sense that's inspired.'

They sat at one of the tables in the refectory on the ground floor and Maeve lit a cigarette. Fay glanced round at the close-knit groups, some wearing leotards, overalls or cookery aprons, raised voices augmenting the mounting clatter of cups and saucers.

'Look over there,' Fay said, lifting a hand. 'It's Mrs B. I didn't know she came here.'

'Nor I.' Maeve turned aside to answer an earnest man leaning over to speak to her.

Rose Barton left her friends to push through to their table.

'Fancy seeing you here, Mrs Browne. Do you the world of good to get out of that house. What have you signed up for, duck?'

'Nothing, I'm afraid. But it's worth considering. I had no idea there were so many people.'

'Oh, it's extra tonight because of our whist drive, see.'

She waved towards the noisy group she had just left.

'Them over there. Once a month we have a whist drive here, raise money for the Christmas party and that. There's generally about thirty. I won that rabbit of yours here, you know.' Her heavy cheeks flushed. 'I told Charlie Boakes he could keep his prizes after that. But it makes a nice change. Lovely lot of people. You know, dear, the telly's not much company for them living on their own.'

The buzzer shrilled and, amid renewed scraping of chairs and shuffled feet, the room rapidly emptied. Maeve touched Fay's arm and after a joking exchange with Rose Barton steered her model back along the corridor and up the first staircase. The crush eased as they reached the top flight and Maeve paused by the studio door.

'Can I ask a favour, Fay darling?'

'What now?' Even in her own ears the staccato response was shrill.

'Could you cope with the last half-hour on your own while I slip off for a drink with Murray?'

'I thought you said he was a waste of time. Anyway, I'll be posing!'

'That's all right,' she whispered, her voice running on, low and persuasive. 'No one will notice I've even gone. Shamin will keep an eye on his lot and the others will be beyond help by nine o'clock – the last half-hour's a frantic salvage operation, the less said the better. Just empty the painting water down the sink and the caretaker will clear away the chairs. You remember Heffer, don't you? Miserable toad but useful – your warehouseman used to get him to do deliveries when there was a rush on. I remember being surprised seeing him driving through the village in your van, and wondered if he had decided to give up the school lark after all these years. Go on, be an angel, Fay,' she coaxed. 'The very last time, I promise. Murray's going to wait at the gates. He'll drop me off at home at the right time and you can drive straight back. It'll run like clockwork.'

'Oh, all right,' Fay said with ill-concealed irritation. 'God knows why I fall for your cock-eyed arrangements all the time – I should have my head examined!'

The irony of this final thrust struck them both and they stumbled into the brightly lit studio clutching each other in helpless giggles.

Shortly after the start of the second session, Maeve slipped away and Fay thankfully confirmed that the tempo of the class had steadied, unbroken by any sound but the slop and click of brushes in water. Only Shamin's dark eyes observed Maeve's exit and Fay calculated that one more ten-minute sitting would see her through.

At the end it was difficult to drag them away from their last minute dabs and Shamin darted anxiously back and forth in his polite efforts to assist. They seemed fated to collide in the scurry to clear away and, as Fay withdrew the large wet sheets from the trestle table, Daisy emitted a thin wail of despair. She had been assembling the tins of powder paint and in his haste Shamin's sleeve had brushed across the inevitably wet design of ducks. As he gently mopped the smudged outline, Daisy's skinny forearm flashed across the table to stop him, sending three of the tins spinning on to the floor. A lid flew off and the contents exploded on to the polished floorboards in a cloud of red dust.

Daisy started to cry, gradually expanding into loud gulping sobs as she gazed at the floor. The others crowded round, pushing in to view the disaster. One produced a sodden paint rag, knelt down and energetically began to rub at the soft powder, producing a huge gory stain.

'Stop! Oh, stop!' Fay dropped to her knees to forestall more mess. Shamin's troubled face dipped into view and he raised the enthusiàst to his feet, whisking away the paint rag.

'Come, come,' he murmured, holding the man's hand and drawing him aside.

The life class students had vanished like snowflakes and Fay realized, with rising frustration, that Shamin was to be her only aid. The rest of the studio had been put in order and as Daisy's weeping lapsed into a silent appraisal of the accident, Fay pulled her wits together and smiled broadly with a confidence she was far from feeling. Affectionately squeezing Daisy's shoulder, she propelled her and the rest of the party towards the door where Shamin stood like a man on hot coals.

'Don't worry. It's absolutely no problem. Shamin, you take them down to the car park. The rector will be getting anxious. I'll fetch some water and a cloth from the kitchen and clear this up in no time. It's only powder colour – it'll soon wipe up. Don't say anything at the hostel, Shamin. No need for anyone to think there's been any trouble. Come with me, it will be quicker through the kitchens – they open directly on to the car park.'

Shamin nodded, brimming with gratitude. They noisily trooped down the stairs and Fay led them through the kitchen area and fiddled with the awkward push-bar mechanism of the fire exit. Most of the cars had already gone and in the deserted car park the excited voices of Shamin's party were noisy in the darkness. Waving them off, she hurried back, leaving the door slightly ajar to secure later. She found a bucket under one of the sinks and half filled it with water, snatching up one of the stinking floor cloths.

This is the very last time, Maeve, my girl, she vowed, gritting her teeth as she lurched through the kitchen and back up the long staircase. The school was almost empty but the stutter of closing doors betrayed several more late departures.

Toiling up the last steep flight she set down the pail beside the vivid stain and fetched a dustpan, carefully brushing up the loose power until only the crimson pool remained. She flicked the dust in the bin under the sink in the studio utility cupboard and the door clicked behind her. For a few moments she leaned against the windowsill, lost in the loveliness of the full moon sailing over the town. It reminded her of her strange dream of floating above the roads and houses the night she had been looking after little Flora.

She was roused with a jolt. Heavy footsteps rang out on the bare studio floorboards. She threw open the door. A man in a brown overall stood staring down at the stain. His face was obscured by a peaked cap which cast all but his chin in shadow. He violently started as Fay appeared.

'Oh, thank goodness. It's *you*, Mr Heffer,' she said with relief. 'I expect you're waiting to lock up. Sorry to keep you. I've just got to wash the floor a bit.'

His face stared bleakly back at her and he indicated the darkening puddle with a large industrial torch.

'Another bloody mess of yours, Mrs Browne?'

Fay recoiled at the unexpected venom.

'It's only water paint. One of the students spilt a tin of powder. I'll clear it up in moments.' Thinks he's still dealing with naughty school kids, she thought irritably.

She took a step but his gimlet eyes held her back. Below in the playground, gears clashed as the last cars manoeuvred out of the main gate and the cheerful farewells floated up like sounds from another planet. Fay resolutely took another step and bent for the floor cloth as he coldly spoke again.

'Another bloody mess, I said.'

She squeezed out the cloth and mentally castigated Maeve as she began to wipe up the spillage. She wrung it out, the water sliding in red rivulets between her fingers. The man seemed mesmerized by her hands as they plunged first into the dirty water, squeezed the rag and then moved back to the floor. She seemed to be making no progress, merely adding to the slop. Her increasingly panicky movements in the silent studio claimed his entire attention, while her own thoughts went racing ahead. She stood up, holding the dripping cloth as they both surveyed the pool at their feet.

'You can't wipe it away, can you?' he said.

His gaze shifted to the sanguine stream which ran through her fingers, staining her skirt and dripping on to her shoes.

In that instant she recognized him.

'You!' she gasped. '*You* were the man who tried to stop me in the street that night. In Renham. I thought you were asking for money.'

'Money! I only wanted to speak to you, woman. I'd waited bloody hours in all that rain. Your lot's all the same – no time to listen to the likes of me. Turned me off like I was a beggar.'

'You followed me to the station, didn't you?'

'I only wanted a word. To ask you to give my girl her chance.' His voice began to rise. 'I lost my temper. I should have bashed *you* not my poor Maggie.'

Light dawned, her words becoming almost inaudible. 'You gave Meg a black eye – you hit her! She ran off and phoned Hugo to come and help her. That Wednesday – we were all in Renham together that night but didn't know ... You tried to push me under the train.' Full realization hit her between the eyes and her voice echoed in the empty studio. 'You shoved that other poor woman by mistake.'

He came on, his face a mask, and she fell back, knocking over the pail. The water streamed across the floor and his shout rang out as she ran to the door, flinging it shut in his face as he reached out to grab her.

She clattered down the stairs, her feet hardly touching the treads as she stumbled to wrench open the door leading on to the corridor. Every classroom was dark and only one light glimmered at the head of the stairs. She ran, electrified by fear, and gained the second staircase. He pounded behind her, grunting like an animal in pain.

In the headlong descent her mind riveted on the possible closure of the front entrance and she made for the one familiar path through the school – via the kitchens.

Beyond the second staircase the building lay in darkness, silent as a tomb. Close behind she heard the scuffle and spark of boot nails on the stone steps, gaining in pursuit.

As she reached the kitchens Heffer was only twenty yards behind. She swung round the door, grasping the roller towel, and forced herself to stand still, stifling her panting breath, hoping she had given him the slip. She listened as he slowly paced the refectory like a predator circling its prey. Her fingers clung to the dirty towel as if to a holy relic, pressing the soiled linen to her mouth to smother a latent scream. Hardly daring to breathe, she stood behind the door, shaking with fear. Presently, the measured tread on the parquet on the other side of the door ceased.

He began to mutter, at first inaudible phrases interspersed with sighs. But gradually she detected a thread of meaning.

'Blood ... more blood ... Why my Maggie? Should have been her. Would have been *her*.' An ugly sob caught in his throat and Fay's resolution wavered. She hesitated, wondering if she could make a dash for the back door which led on to the car park. The moment passed in indecision. With mounting horror she heard him shuffle towards her hiding place. Her eyes had adjusted to the dark. Moonlight streamed through the big windows casting an eerie clarity on the metal draining boards and the disposition of aluminium steamers and kitchen utensils. She froze behind the half-open door, rigid with fear.

'She's in there,' he muttered. 'I can smell it.'

Her heart thudded in manic accompaniment to the man's laboured breath.

'Fancy scent,' he slyly whispered against the wooden panels. 'Maggie got some too from that man of hers. Same man. Same smell.'

As he lurched through the doorway Fay let go of the roller towel and swung the door into his body with all her strength. It drove like a rockfall against his face. He cried out in anger and pain as Fay slithered across the greasy floor towards the dim outline of the metal sinks.

In the grey dark, the long shadow of the central table lay between them and Fay stepped back, feeling for the cold rim of the sink, not taking her eyes off the man now only ten feet away. Her breath came in quivering gasps and in the silence, as Heffer regained his balance, he regarded her across the table with undisguised menace. The only sound was the tattoo of a tap dripping with banal regularity into one of the sinks.

She forced herself to rerun her careless glances around the kitchen when she had filled the jugs and the bucket. A telephone. Yes, there was a wall telephone. Near the sink, beside the notice board. If she could reach it there might be time to ring for help ... The proximity of Heffer only the width of a table away annihilated this wild hope almost before her mind shaped it.

He snapped on the powerful torch beam. She stood immobile, dazzled, like a rabbit caught in headlights. The dripping tap remorselessly continued, and it seemed the only possible escape was in delay, keep him talking, try to calm him down. She found her voice and croaked, 'The phone calls. *You* made them. It was you, here in this kitchen. Night after night. I remember the dripping tap.'

In the murk, the peak of his cap cut a sharp silhouette and she was reminded, as she had been on that night in Renham, of a bird of prey. The huskiness of his reply floated from the shadows.

'The phone calls were a warning. You knew what you had to do. He was *her* man. Browne wanted to marry my Maggie, asked her over and over again. She told me his wife wouldn't let him go. You should have listened. If you'd gone away then, left my girl to take her rightful place, none of it would have happened.'

'Her man?' Fay's voice cracked with incredulity. 'Robert wasn't her man. You made a mistake. There was *another* man. Abroad. Didn't she tell you?'

'Don't you lie to me!' His response came like a hammer blow. 'You women are all the same. All tarred with the same brush. You. Doreen. Even Maggie. Liars, the lot of you. Think you can take what you like and never pay for it.'

He was rambling, getting confused. It was no use. But if she could just keep the dialogue going ... Fay edged sideways towards the back door, keeping her voice even. 'I wasn't keeping Robert from Meg. She wanted someone else. You should have waited, Mr Heffer, it would have come right ...' She sidled along the line of sink units, her hands slithering along the icy rims like a swimmer reluctant to give herself up to the water.

'I saw you with that estate agent bloke, him with the big car, cuddling away, you was, and my poor girl hardly cold. Not only him neither. Maggie told me about that man in the firm staying at your 'ouse all the time. Couldn't get himself there quick enough once Maggie and her bloke went to America.'

'Hugo? You're mad. Hugo works from the chapel warehouse sometimes, of course he does. Naturally he's often at the house.'

'More lies! You fornicating bitch.'

He raised his arm in the darkness, his unbuttoned overall flapping, the torch beam flashing across the cracked ceiling as he gesticulated. 'Him too. Browne let her down in the end. Thought he could shovel his rubbish on to me. You and him both laughing your 'eads off. After Maggie died *I* knew what to do. Fire the bleeding books. Destroy that chapel of wickedness.'

'The chapel? You? Were you the man trying to break in?' Fay's voice faltered on the inescapable conclusion. 'Bill Goldsmith saw you in the garden?' she whispered.

'Aye. No quarrel with him. He saw me before. That other

time near the outhouse. Was waiting to catch me 'anging round again, he said. To warn me off. Give me another chance, he said. What bleedin' chance have *I* ever had?'

The torch weaved a searchlight, seeking her out. The voice dully continued, remorseless yet pitiable.

Fay ceased to listen, gradually easing herself along, sliding one foot to the other in a crab-like glide, never taking her eyes from Heffer half hidden in the shadows, muttering his seamless complaints. She reached the edge of the last sink and poised for a rush to the door. It rattled on the catch and blew inwards for a tantalising inch before settling back.

Heffer had moved too, continuing his threatening monologue while shuffling along the other side of the table, parallel with Fay but so submerged in vilification that he was unaware of the escape within reach.

A scuffle rippled across her shoe. She screamed, terror surging into a howl of misery. Heffer instantly broke from his trance and leapt round the table, seizing Fay's arms and pinning her against the wail.

'A mouse!' He laughed, his breath hot on her cheek. Fear rose like nausea as he clamped her arms, flattening her against the clammy tiles.

'Afraid of mice, are we? You do surprise me, my fine lady. And you with rats the size of cats running out of that rotting shed you call a garage.'

'Rats?' In a flash of horrified recognition it became clear. 'It was a rabbit,' she stuttered, breathless under the weight of Heffer's body pressed against her. 'You let it out. It ran off when you were tampering with the Metro.'

He released her a fraction and, unprepared for the shift, she buckled at the knees. He pushed her upright.

She fought for breath. 'Why did you do it? I thought you loved Meg. Why did you loosen the brakes on her? My God, you killed your own daughter!'

He shook her violently, smashing her head against the wall.

'I didn't do it for her, you fool. It was for *you*!' he screamed. 'You wouldn't take no notice of the phone calls. I warned you! You wouldn't even listen to me in Renham, hear me out. The

Metro was *your* car. I knew that. My girl was going to America with him. If you was dead when they got back there would be no more hindrance. It was *your* fault, you grasping bitch.'

He shook her again, sending a circuit of pain from her temples to her straining eyes and back again. 'You switched the car, you calculating whore. *You* killed my Maggie.' He spat with deliberation in her face.

Fay retched, feeling the bile rise at the very moment his arm rose above her. The torch smashed down on her head. She felt her scalp split like torn calico and pain filled her skull, drowning his voice in a miasma of fire. In wonder she watched the arm arc, slamming the torch against her cheek with a massive thud. As she sank forward he held her shoulder and swung the weapon again.

Fay collapsed a split second before the blow fell, dimly aware of the tinkle of broken glass briefly preceding the mind-shattering peal of the fire bell. Then darkness came down. Within the velvet blackness she faintly heard the diminishing reverberation of the alarm and, in that moment before unconsciousness, believed herself to be again at the bottom of her own stairwell with the sour taste of blood filtering between her lips.

As the cacophony of the fire bell struck Heffer's clouded brain, he leaned over the body huddled at his feet and shone the torch over the broken box on the wall. The continuous ear-splitting noise seemed to immobilise him and he stood focussing the beam on the emergency apparatus with incredulity. Only the rush of footsteps in the car park released him. He lumbered off through the refectory and back into the empty building.

Rose Barton reached the rear door of the kitchens only moments after Heffer had left and heard the clatter of his boots as he retreated into his own familiar territory, the warren of unlit corridors and empty classrooms. She ran inside, immediately stumbling across Fay's inert form.

'Oh, my God! Dear God, please not . . .' she gasped, fumbling amid the broken glass to discover Fay's sticky matted hair. She knelt beside her, smoothing the oozing mess above the temple, murmuring wordless endearments, weeping uncontrollably.

Fay stirred and the old woman rose to her feet, pushing aside the rows of plates on their drying racks to reach the tumblers behind. With shaking hands she filled a glass with water and bent to lift Fay's head.

'Here, my duck. Just a little sip. Please, my little love.'

Rose Barton's moon-like face swung and wavered within Fay's flickering focus and she moved her lips in silent response. The familiar voice ran on, fading and returning, the words incomprehensible, warm as milk.

'I saw that new yellow car of yours still here when I left and I couldn't get it out of my mind. It was so late. I even got on the bus. Got off again at the next stop to come back and see if it was still out there in the playground. I had this terrible feeling – the taste of blood in my mouth. I knew something was up. Then I heard a scream and the fire bell, and when I saw Syd Heffer's torch shining round in here it struck me like lightning what he must have done.'

The fire alarm continued its infernal racket, rendering her words inaudible. 'Mrs B. Missus B Missus ... Missus ...' Fay moaned as if repeating an incantation. She slipped back into the void.

The old woman assured herself of the soft breathing, laid Fay's head on the floor and scrambled up. 'I've got to get to him quick, my love. Someone will be here any minute now to help you. I'll put on the light. But I must save that poor man.'

She ran with surprising agility across the kitchen and into the school. In her headlong flight she located the switches as she ran and the arriving firemen and police officers followed her progress in the wake of lighted windows, suspecting an arsonist. She flitted like a substantial ghost from room to room calling Heffer's name.

Her pleading voice died as she entered the swimming pool building. Her screams brought two policemen racing up, stumbling inside, making it echo with their shouts and the scuffle of boots on the tiled floor.

'What the hell are you up to, woman?' one of the constables yelled, grabbing Rose Barton as the other found the switches.

The lights blazed, the intense blue of the water seeming to strike their eyes.

Her screams filled the air, a gathering tumult under the high dome of the roof. Face down, Heffer lay spread out at the bottom of the pool, the brown overall billowing around his body in the gentle current of the filter's flow.

Pushing her roughly aside, one man plunged in, shouting and splashing as he brought the unconscious man to the poolside. They dragged him out and applied emergency aid, the woman leaning over, weeping softly. At last Heffer spewed out a final stream of water and opened his eyes.

Two firemen ran in and lifted Heffer up. Another led Rose Barton away.

'I seen it, I tell you!' she cried. 'I seen it all before as clear as we seen it then! But I thought it was *her*,' she babbled. 'It was that brown overall of his. I said it was a brown coat! I thought it was the lady what died.'

Twenty-Two

S uperintendent Waller pulled Hayes into his office and grimly invited him to take a seat. Hayes eyed him with barely concealed curiosity, the sight of the big man in joggers and a striped rugger shirt a first for his number two, and unlikely to be repeated.

It was three in the morning and Waller had already spent a considerable time at the crime scene, followed by a lengthy wait for statements from Heffer and Rose Barton. Dragging Maeve Macmillan into the investigation took some explaining, but the news of the brutal attack soon brought her round. It occurred to Hayes that explaining away her own early departure from the art class would need some fancy footwork in the marital home but, from his experience of these people, damping down scandal was no different from political spin. He'd bet his boots Maeve Macmillan would survive the storm.

'A drink, Hayes?'

'Thank you, sir.' Roger Hayes hardly looked the part either, having been summoned to the school from a concert in Oxford, his formal gear substituted by denims and cowboy boots. But Waller, eyeing him obliquely over his bifocals, felt in no position to carp.

'Any news about Mrs Browne, Hayes? Bad do. Lucky if she survives, I reckon.'

'I checked with the hospital – she's going to pull through, they say. But another hour would have been too late.'

'Really? Well, that's a relief. Bloody miracle that caretaker bloke was saved as well,' he said, passing a generous tot of whisky to his surprisingly subdued officer. 'Two dead bodies on one night wouldn't have gone down well with the commissioner.'

'Only thanks to that woman, the Browne's cleaner. If she hadn't run off to follow the guy he would have drowned – and Mrs Browne would certainly have died.'

'How do you think the fire alarm went off? Odd that.' Waller looked pensive, wondering if Hayes had tied up all the loose ends.

'An unlucky twist of fate according to his statement. Otherwise he might have got away with it.'

'And we'd still be no wiser about the Goldsmith killing. Blimey, Hayes, three deaths, all down to one crazy nutter.'

'Two were accidental. Heffer never intended to push the Hertz woman on the railway line and the poor devil lived in torment after his daughter died in the car intended for Fay Browne.'

'But Goldsmith? He admits killing Goldsmith?'

'Yes. Coughed the lot. Heffer's made a full statement, got nothing to live for now his girl's gone. He says he regrets killing the old bloke with the machete, it was never planned. But there's no remorse about bludgeoning Fay Browne and he's made no effort to deny it.'

'Poor cow didn't deserve it though. Ran herself ragged trying to get her husband off the hook for that secretary's accident. The medical evidence from his consultant confirming his infertility's on the file I take it?'

'Two separate opinions, sir.' Hayes sipped his whisky, growing thoughtful. 'But that didn't prove anything without Heffer's confession, did it? Browne could have *thought* he'd fathered the girl's baby at the time – we've only got his word for it that he knew all along he was not the father; there's no previous medical evidence that he was aware of his shortcomings in the sperm department. So putting her out of the frame by fixing the brakes would still have carried weight if we were investigating her death. Unfortunately, it wasn't really our case.'

'You believed him guilty all along, didn't you?'

'I reckoned he'd got away with it,' Hayes ruefully admitted. 'I was wrong. But it seems a harsh conclusion that Fay Browne had to be attacked by the real killer before I was convinced.' He smiled grimly and finished his drink, rising stiffly to his feet.

Waller sat on, deep in thought. 'Perhaps you're not such a hotshot detective after all, Hayes,' he ventured with a grin. 'It came bloody near to a complete cock-up, only saved by Heffer's confession. Maybe after this we can take a closer look at the complicated lives of even the folk in a quiet backwater like Renham.'

Hayes drove home with an overwhelming feeling of relief. Getting a full confession from Heffer had probably saved him years of wondering where he'd gone wrong with the case. If the old woman, Rose Barton, had not come back, or Heffer had just walked away, the chances are that finding Fay Browne's body would have remained a mystery. There was, after all, nothing to implicate Heffer. The fire exit was open, anyone could have slipped in, thinking the school was empty. Arson attacks by kids were not exactly unknown . . . Heffer could have shot back to his caretaker's flat, disposed of the torch – and any bloodstained clothing – and appeared on the scene claiming he had been alerted by the fire alarm. Hayes felt the sweat break out.

If Heffer had just walked away, and the Browne woman had died, would he *ever* have known why three people had been murdered?